SECOND
CHANCE

By the same author

EXTENUATING CIRCUMSTANCES

FIRE LAKE

LIFE'S WORK

NATURAL CAUSES

DAY OF WRATH

DEAD LETTER

FINAL NOTICE

THE LIME PIT

SECOND CHANCE

Jonathan Valin

Delacorte
Press

Published by
Delacorte Press
Bantam Doubleday Dell Publishing Group, Inc.
666 Fifth Avenue
New York, New York 10103

Library of Congress Cataloging in Publication Data

Valin, Jonathan.
    Second chance : a Harry Stoner mystery / Jonathan Valin.
        p.   cm.
    ISBN 0-385-29912-5
    I. Title.
PS3572.A4125S44   1991
813'.54—dc20   90-23259
                                                                    CIP

Manufactured in the United States of America

Published simultaneously in Canada

May 1991

10 9 8 7 6 5 4 3 2 1
BVG

*To Katherine, as always,
and to Dominick, at last*

1

▌▌

Two roads diverged in a wood, and I . . . I took the one to the right, which put me back on Camargo Pike, heading south.

I'd been driving through Indian Hill for better than ten minutes, trying to find a little side street called Woodbine Lane. The woman who'd phoned me early that snowy Sunday morning had said to watch for an antiques shop on the left-hand side of Camargo. An antiques shop—like a gas station in the sticks. With the snow blowing and the tires skating along the frozen blacktop I'd had trouble staying on the road, much less finding her antiques shop.

It would have helped if the side streets had been clearly marked, but the only signs in that rich, Byzantine neighborhood were planted along the main drag. Everything else was private property—unnamed access roads that ran screaming off into the woods the moment they spotted you, tar drives that turned their backs behind gateposts or rested their elbows on hedgerows and glared through the brambles as you drove by. Nothing as mundane as a name on a mailbox. Not that I could have seen a mailbox in the snow. It had started falling as soon as I left the office. By the time I got to Indian Hill, it was as thick as smoke from a grease fire.

After emerging from the woods onto Camargo for the third time, I swallowed my pride and went looking for an open gas station or convenience store with a phone booth— and got absurdly lucky. Six miles down the pike, almost at the corporation limit, I spotted a gabled building that looked like a converted residence. If there was a sign saying

"Antiques" in one of its windows, the snow had covered it up. But there was a parking lot in front and an access road to its left.

I took a chance and turned left onto the unmarked road. A half-mile farther on an estate house squatted in a grove of pine trees—English-style country home, all mullioned windows and snow-dappled slate, big-eyed and brindled as a cow. I pulled up in a drive to the right of the house, parked the rusty Pinto beside a new Mercedes with a physician's plate, and sat there for a moment, listening to the wind howl and wondering whether I had the right address or whether the folks inside were already on the phone to the Indian Hill cops. The lady who'd called that morning had said her name was Pearson, Louise Pearson. She hadn't mentioned that she or her husband was a doctor.

As I sat there brooding, a tall woman in a dark blue Icelandic sweater and khaki slacks stepped out the front door of the house. She peered at me for a moment through the blowing snow, hugging her arms to her breasts against the cold. I got out of the car and waved at her.

"Mrs. Pearson?" I shouted.

She said something that was swallowed by the wind, but I could tell from her expression that I'd lucked on to the right spot. I hustled across the snowy yard, through the door, and inside.

The woman smiled knowingly as she closed the door behind me. "You had trouble finding us, didn't you?"

"A little trouble."

"You don't have to be polite about it," she said with an abrupt laugh that made me smile too. "Everyone has trouble finding us. In this weather it must have been murder." She held out her hand. "I'm Louise Pearson."

"Harry Stoner," I said, shaking with her.

I had realized that she was tall, but up close Louise Pearson's size and build were startling. She was a statuesque woman in her late thirties—big-breasted, big-hipped, with short curly brown hair and a tan, sportive, square-jawed face, a little wrinkled by the sun around the eyes and at the corners of the mouth but strikingly attractive in a no-nonsense way.

"Come into the living room and warm up, Mr. Stoner."

I followed her down a hall into a large, fussy living room. The walls were covered in pale grey watered silk, the moldings painted a deeper grey. The furniture was cozy English —chintz couches, Queen Anne tables and sideboards. On the far wall a wingback chair sat in front of an open fireplace. Louise Pearson patted the back of the chair as if she'd put it there especially for me.

"Sit," she said.

I sat.

"Can I get you something to drink? Coffee or brandy maybe?"

"Coffee would be good."

There was a silver service set on a sideboard behind her. She walked over to it and poured coffee into a blue china cup. "I'm really sorry to call you out on a miserable day like this," she said over her shoulder, "but we've got this . . . situation. At least Phil thinks it's a situation." She turned back to me, the steaming coffee cup in her hand. "Maybe he's right."

She said it dubiously, as if that wasn't often the case.

"Phil is?"

"My husband," she said, handing me the cup. "He should be back any minute—he had an emergency at his office."

"He's a physician?"

"A psychiatrist."

Louise Pearson walked over to the fireplace and leaned up against the mantel. Behind her in a far corner of the room a large tinseled Christmas tree flickered like a loose bulb.

"Drink," Louise Pearson said in her peremptory way.

I drank.

The woman was altogether too ripe and sturdy for lace and chintz. I wondered if she'd inherited the house from someone else, if she'd stepped into that cozy room from a more robust kind of life—a life among men. That was the way she talked, as if she was used to handling men, parrying them, fending them off. It amused me to speculate about her in that way—it was a sure sign that I found her attractive.

Between the fire and the coffee I slowly warmed up. I started to smell things again: the fresh cut pine of the Christmas tree, the cedar logs on the fire, the coffee. And something else. Something sweet and sensual that I didn't place until the woman came closer to me, and I realized it was her scent.

"I don't mean to sound cynical about Phil," Louise Pearson said, drawing a chair up across from mine. "It's just that most psychiatrists tend to read portents into normal behavior, even their own behavior. Believe me, it can be grueling to have your inner life constantly analyzed and second-guessed like a parlor game. I know Kirsten, my stepdaughter, feels that way." She turned her head to look at the fire, and her hair caught the light and turned reddish gold. "Kirsten's the reason we called you."

"She has a problem?"

The woman smiled sadly. "The world is Kirsten's problem," she said. And then, as if she didn't like the melodramatic sound of that, she added: "She was badly wounded by life with her mother—her real mother, Phil's first wife. Those childhood years left Kirsty . . . well, they've made her an emotional cripple. She and her brother, alike. Phil's tried his best to make it up to both of the kids—to give them a fresh chance. So have I. But even loving parents can't erase the past or control the future. I'm not at all sure it's a good idea to try—or to hire someone else to."

I said, "You don't think I'm needed, do you?"

The woman shrugged noncommittally. "I don't know if you are or not, Mr. Stoner. I don't know if Kirsty can use anyone's help. Without trying to minimize her neuroses, which can be pretty damn disabling, I tend to think that the more time she spends on her own the better. I'm sure Phil will have a different view of it, but that's the way I feel."

As if on cue, a tall handsome man with black hair and beard stepped into the room. There was half-melted snow in his hair and on the shoulders of his overcoat.

"*Is* that the way you feel?" he said to the woman.

Louise Pearson stiffened in the chair. "You could have announced yourself, Phil."

"And spoiled your spiel?" He laughed, brushing the snow out of his hair and beard as he walked over to the fireplace. "I love to hear you talk psychology, Lou. You know that. It turns me on."

Smiling expansively, he came up and extended a hand. I shook with him. Like his wife, Pearson made a tall, imposing figure, although he looked older than she did up close, and worse for wear. His tan skin was heavily lined and deeply grooved at the cheeks. His eyes were a brilliant blue, nervously, almost shockingly alert. For a second I found it difficult to hold his stare. It was as if he was looking for something I didn't have.

"Phil Pearson," he said.

"Harry Stoner."

"Good," he said, dropping my hand. He clapped his own hands together loudly and said, "Good," again.

"I guess you'll want to take over now, Phil," Louise Pearson said, rising from the chair. "That's the way it usually works, isn't it?"

For a split second the man looked crestfallen, as if he was losing his audience in the middle of a speech. "You don't have to leave, Lou."

"Oh, I think I do."

She smiled at me warmly. "It was a pleasure meeting you, Mr. Stoner. I'm sure we'll talk again."

She walked out of the room, leaving her husband staring blankly after her. The woman's exit effected an immediate change in Pearson's manner. He stopped smiling. He stopped talking, too. In fact he didn't say another word until he'd unbuttoned his topcoat, draped it on the sideboard, and poured himself a cup of coffee from the silver server.

"Not everyone shares my sense of humor," he said in a subdued voice. "I can be abrasive at times."

I didn't say anything. I didn't feel like coddling a grown man. He looked chastened by my silence, as if I'd boxed his ear. Then he looked resentful. I started to get the feeling that this wasn't a grown man, after all.

Pearson sat down across from me and took a sip of coffee while he collected himself. "Living with a psychiatrist can be tough," he said after a time. "My wife's had her fill of me recently. Of me and my kids. You know what they say about psychiatrists' kids, don't you? Like ministers' kids." He smiled pastily. "Has Lou told you about Kirsten?"

"She said that you were having a problem with her. She didn't tell me what that problem was."

"Of course, she wouldn't," he said quickly. "The kids are *my* responsibility, after all. I think we can agree on that."

He glanced quickly at the door, as if he was hoping Louise was listening in as he had been listening to her. In spite of the friction between them, the man seemed lost without his wife.

"Has Kirsten run away, Dr. Pearson?" I said, trying to put him back on course.

He sighed. "Not exactly. I'm really not sure what's happened to her, if anything."

"Then why call me?"

"Why call you?" he echoed. "I'm worried, that's why. My daughter has serious emotional problems, as Lou may have told you. They were severe enough to put Kirsten in a hospital this past summer. She returned to school this fall, to the University of Chicago. But I'm not sure she was ready to be on her own again."

"You have reason to think she's not doing well?"

"There have been signs," he said vaguely.

"What kind of signs?"

The man shifted uneasily in his chair. "At the moment, I'm concerned that she hasn't come home for the holidays."

"Concerned enough to hire a detective?"

"Yes."

"Couldn't Kirsten have gone to visit a friend over the break, Dr. Pearson? Kids often do that."

"I talked to her myself on Wednesday of last week, and she said she was planning to fly home Thursday afternoon. Since then I've been in touch with her roommate, her therapist, the airlines, and several university officials—not one of them knows where she's gone. Not one."

"Your daughter's problems," I said delicately, "are they . . . are you worried that she may have become depressed?"

He nodded. "Yes."

"Have you contacted the police in Chicago?"

"I haven't been able to bring myself to . . ." His voice dropped to a whisper. "No, I haven't called the police."

A peal of feminine laughter rang out somewhere in the house. It made Phil Pearson start in his chair. He glanced toward the hall almost desperately, as if he longed to be near his wife again—to make it up with her.

"I may be overreacting," he said, looking quickly back at me, looking to see if I'd caught his mind wandering. "Still I'd feel better if you could find Kirsten."

"I can try," I told him.

"Good," he said, rubbing his hands together nervously. "Good."

2

After finishing with the Pearsons I went to my apartment on Ohio Avenue, packed an overnight bag, called the airport, and booked a seat on Delta for two p.m. I would gain an hour on the flight, so I figured on arriving at O'Hare about the same time that I'd left Cincinnati. Pearson had promised to call Kirsten's roommate, a girl named Marnee Thompson, to let her know I'd be coming. He said he'd contact the university too, although I didn't expect him to find anyone home on a Sunday afternoon during Christmas break. Before I left his house, he gave me duplicate keys to Kirsten's apartment in case the roommate was out.

In spite of the Brent Spence traffic and the inevitable slowdown at the cut of the Ft. Mitchell hill, I managed to get to the Delta terminal by one-thirty. The snow had stopped falling by then, and the temperature had risen enough to turn the roadside ice to slush. I'd been worried that the bad weather might delay the flight, but the attendant at the Delta booth said the only delay would be on the Chicago end—at O'Hare.

With a half hour to kill I walked down to one of the boarding area bars and ordered up the usual round of artillery. It was a short flight, so I settled on two double Scotches, straight up. If they didn't kill the preflight jitters, I promised myself a third shot on the plane.

"You said *two* doubles?" the bartender asked.

"I don't like airplanes," I told him. "I don't understand them. And I don't want to discuss it."

He served up the booze and left me alone.

Pearson had given me a photograph of his daughter, a

high school snap. I dug it out of my coat pocket and took a look at it between swallows of Scotch. Kirsten was a studious-looking, half-pretty girl with dark brown hair and her father's blue piercing eyes. If I'd known more about her, if Pearson had been more forthcoming about her "problems," past and present, I might have been able to make something specific of the vaguely hostile, vaguely damaged look of those eyes. But Phil Pearson had kept his daughter's history to himself—at least enough of it to make it next to impossible for me to personalize her. The girl in the photo could have been anyone's troubled daughter. Given the fact that I hadn't liked the man, I decided it was better that way.

The flight to Chicago was mercifully short. We arrived at O'Hare about forty minutes after we took off and were backed up on the ground for another forty minutes. I didn't understand the guy sitting next to me, who kept complaining about the long wait on the runway.

"We're on the ground!" I finally said to him. "What the hell's the matter with you?"

It was two-thirty central time when I got out of the terminal and caught a cab to Hyde Park. It had been snowing heavily in Chicago, and the traffic on the Eisenhower was bumper-to-bumper all the way to the Dan Ryan. By the time we got to the 51st Street exit it was a quarter of four.

I said to the cabbie, "It took longer to get from O'Hare to the south side than it did to fly from Cincinnati to Chicago."

"What are you going to do," he said philosophically. "It's Christmas, and this ain't Cincinnati."

Kirsten Pearson's apartment was on 54th Street near Blackstone. The building was a three-story brownstone tenement, the third in a dismal block of brownstones. The stained facades of the tenements, the dirty snow, the bare bent maples planted in the sidewalk boxes, reflected the raw grey of the winter sky. A few months of that kind of weather would have left me feeling just as raw.

The outer door of the Pearson girl's apartment house opened onto a tiled vestibule. The framed-glass inner door was locked, but I could see through it into a wainscoted lobby with a dark wood staircase leading to the upper floors. The vestibule smelled like dust and heat and cat piss. I could have used one of the keys that Pearson had given me, but I didn't want to startle anyone. So I pressed an intercom button on the side wall.

A girl answered in a sharp, distracted voice. "Yes? Who is it?"

"My name's Harry Stoner. I'm working for Phil Pearson, Kirsten Pearson's father."

"I know who you are," the girl said ominously.

A moment went by then a buzzer went off, unlocking the door. I stepped into the dark foyer. A red-haired girl with a pale, starved, willfully unhappy-looking face appeared at the head of the stairs. She held a book in one hand and a pair of tortoiseshell glasses in the other. It was obvious that she was annoyed by the interruption.

"Marnee Thompson?" I said to her.

She nodded. "You're the detective?"

"I'm the detective."

Marnee Thompson studied me for a moment, bouncing the glasses in her hand. "Kirsten isn't here, you know. I told Phil that last week."

"Have any idea where she's gone?"

"No. I'm not in charge of her."

"No one said you were."

"Tell it to Phil," the girl said bitterly. "You realize this is

ridiculous, don't you? And borderline illegal? Kirsty's almost twenty years old. I mean, why do they have to send
detectives after her? It's humiliating."

"Her father's worried."

"Her father's an asshole. Everyone else knows it. Now
you do, too."

"Miss Thompson, I'm just trying to do a job. If you'll let
me come up and look around, I can be out of your hair in a
few minutes."

The girl glanced behind her, toward an open door at the
top of the staircase. "All right," she said, turning back to me.
"But make it quick."

I started up the stairs.

The apartment was spare, functional, serious as all
hell. Board-and-brick bookshelves stuffed with books and
weighted down on top with more books, an easel-desk with
a gooseneck lamp clamped to it, a stool in front of the desk,
a Camus poster on one wall, a Vermeer print on another, a
Goodwill chair with claw legs and a silk throw over it, a gas
hearth with a droopy asparagus fern in the fireplace, a tatty
rug. No other furnishings. Through an archway I could see a
bedroom, with a mattress lying on the floor and a mirror full
of grey winter sky propped against the inner wall.

The bare utility of the place was like an advertisement for
Marnee Thompson, for her own seriousness and respectable student poverty. But Kirsten Pearson had lived there,
too. And I couldn't help wondering where she had fit in.
There was no second desk in the front room, and when I
thumbed through several of the books on top of the book-
shelf they all had Marnee Thompson's bookplate in them.

"Her room was at the end of the hall," the girl said, as if
she'd read my mind. "She preferred it that way."

"Preferred what?" I said, putting down a green-and-black paperback copy of *Dubliners*.

"The privacy."

Marnee Thompson walked over to the armchair and sat down. The girl had a style of her own—that early in life—a blunt self-assertiveness that was snotty but impressive, too. If Kirsten Pearson had identity problems, I figured this one'd probably been good for her.

"How long have you and Kirsten lived here?"

"Since September." She put on her tortoiseshell glasses, tilted her head, and studied me with pale blue eyes. "She could have lived anywhere, you know. Phil has plenty of money."

She said it like a boast, as if she were telling me that, instead of Phil's money, Kirsten had chosen her.

"Where did you two meet?" I said, sitting down on the desk stool across from her.

"We were in several classes together, last year. We hit it off so well we decided to set up this place during the summer, but . . . Kirsty couldn't move in until the fall."

"Kirsten had some trouble last year, didn't she?"

The girl didn't say anything.

"She had to leave school?"

"She was taken out of school, yes," Marnee Thompson said.

"By her father?"

She nodded.

I studied her grave young face, softly shaded by the fading window light. Her pale hollow cheeks, her high brow, her blue lashless eyes, reminded me of the Vermeer on the living room wall—a woman counting pearls. "If Kirsten's having trouble again, I might be able to help."

"How? By taking her away again?"

"I've been hired to find her, Marnee. *Not* to bring her home."

The girl gave me a wary look.

"Think about it." I got up from the stool and walked down the hall to Kirsten's bedroom.

3

The door at the end of the hall was closed but unlocked. Kirsten, or someone who had lived there before her, had tacked a little handwritten warning to it: NO SECOND CHANCES. I went in anyway.

It was life on a different block in Kirsten's room. Dirty clothes hung from the open drawers of an oak dresser and dribbled out the door of a closet. Books, stacked like old newspapers, climbed in crazy towers four feet up each wall. Typed papers, dozens of them, were scattered thickly across the top of a desk, on the desk chair, and the floor. A portable TV with a brassiere dangling from its antenna sat on a stool across from an unmade bed. An ashtray full of cigarette butts, Winstons, was lying on the pillow of the bed. A *Soap Opera Digest* nestled in the blankets at its feet. A urinous smell of mildewed paper, cigarette smoke, and unwashed flesh hung heavily in the air.

After the strict order of Marnee Thompson's life, the rank clutter of Kirsten Pearson's bedroom startled me. I knew it was just a messy college kid's messy room, but it still startled me—the way a crime scene can get to you. I had the unmistakable feeling that violence had occurred there.

I did my job anyway, going through the closet first, sifting the soiled clothes on the floor, searching the pockets of the blouses and jeans left on the hangers. I didn't find anything but loose change and wadded-up tissues.

I tried the top drawer of the desk next and found an address book in the rubble of pencil stubs, coins, paper clips, and linty ballpoint pens. None of the names meant anything to me, except for Phil Pearson's. I found what

looked like a manuscript in the side drawer, boxed and
sealed with tape. Someone had written "We have to talk
about this!" on top of the box and underlined the words
twice to show he meant it. I put the box aside with the
address book.

There were some postcards under the manuscript—a
dozen of them from a dozen different midwestern towns.
Yellow Springs. Madison. Antioch. Columbus. College
towns. The postcards were the sort of things that motels
give away, along with letterhead stationery and embossed
pencils. Each one pictured a mundane motel facade with
the words "Greetings From" printed in a corner. Each one
was signed "Ethan." Whoever Ethan was, he had moved
around over the past year. The oldest card, from The Green
Gables Motel in Forest Park, Missouri, was postmarked November 16, 1988. The latest, November 5, 1989, from The
Bluegrass Motel in Ft. Thomas, Kentucky.

I put the postcards with the manuscript and the address
book and moved on to the dresser. A vanity mirror and a
glass dish were sitting on top of it. The dish had held
makeup judging from the traces of face powder on the
glass, but I couldn't find a makeup kit in the drawer. I did
come across an empty birth control pill dispenser, however,
stashed among some underwear.

I also found an old photograph of Papa Pearson,
facedown in the panties. Or half a photo. The picture had
been torn lengthwise, indicating that someone else had
been photographed along with Pearson—someone Kirsten
apparently hadn't liked.

I left the photo where I'd found it and took the postcards,
address book, and manuscript with me back into the living
room. Marnee Thompson was still sitting silently in the
Goodwill chair. When she saw the booty I was carrying, she
looked dismayed.

"You can't have that," she said, leaping to her feet. "That's Kirsty's."

"I don't want to take it, Marnee. I want to talk about it."

I put the stuff on Marnee's desk and sat on the stool. The girl sat back down slowly on the chair. It was almost dark outside, and the gooseneck lamp, lighting the desktop and Kirsten's belongings, was the main light in the room. Marnee Thompson stared forlornly at the little pile of spot-lighted things—her friend's things.

"When's the last time you saw Kirsten, Marnee?"

"Thursday morning. She was packing the car, getting ready to leave. I had a conference to go to. When I got back that afternoon, the car was gone. I assumed she went to the airport."

"What kind of car does she drive?"

"A yellow VW Bug. I don't know what year it is, but it's pretty beat up."

"Did Kirsten plan to see anyone before leaving for home?"

"She might have mentioned stopping at a friend's."

"What friend?"

The girl balked. "Look, I don't know what to say. I don't want anything bad to happen to Kirsty. But I don't want to feed her dad's obsessions, either. If you knew what he's done to her, what he's put her through . . ."

"Why don't you tell me about it?"

Marnee Thompson bit her lower lip so hard it turned white. She'd started to look younger, less cocksure of herself. More like a nineteen-year-old girl who was worried about a friend and didn't know what to do about it.

I smiled reassuringly. "I just want to find Kirsty, Marnee. If she's okay, I go home and make my report to her dad."

"And if she isn't okay?"

"Then we can talk about what to do—you and me and Kirsten."

"You're not going to . . . de-program her or something?"

I laughed. "Somebody'd have to re-program me, first."

The girl half smiled. I had the feeling that that was all she ever permitted herself—half a smile—like it was a kind of dieting.

"We could get some coffee, maybe," Marnee Thompson allowed.

"Okay," I told her.

The coffee shop was on 54th Street and Lake, a little storefront with an icy awning over its window. It was a student hangout, warm, trendy, and virtually empty on a Sunday night. We sat at a wooden table with a big bowl of unshelled peanuts in its center. The hardwood floors were covered with peanut shells that crackled underfoot. Peanuts seemed to be the theme.

I said, "I wouldn't want the job of sweeping up in here."

Marnee Thompson gave me her Weight Watchers grin. "They don't sweep up. They harvest."

I laughed. "Are you from Chicago?"

She shook her head, no. "Cleveland, Ohio. I came here because I didn't want to go east."

The way she said it, "east" sounded like the place where the rich snobs congregated.

"Chicago's a serious school," she said, unbuttoning her topcoat. "And, believe me, I'm serious about my education."

I believed her.

"What's your major?"

"English Lit," she said. She stored her mittens carefully

in the pockets of her coat. "Kirsty's an English major, too, but she's a writer not a scholar."

"What does she write?"

"Poetry. Several of her pieces have been published in small magazines. *TriQuarterly. Antioch Review.* Last spring, one of her poems was almost accepted by *The New Yorker.* Kirsty's very talented—the most talented person I know."

I was surprised and impressed by Kirsten Pearson's achievements. I was also impressed by the pleasure that Marnee Thompson took in her friend's success. In my day students weren't quite so gracious about each other's accomplishments. "The manuscript I found in Kirsten's room," I said, "is poetry?"

Marnee shook her head, no. "Kirsty's been working on a novel. She completed the first draft right before the break. I haven't seen it yet."

"Someone must have read it. It had a message written on it in big letters."

"That's from Dr. Heldman," the girl said. "He's Kirsty's adviser."

"Maybe I should talk to him?"

"It couldn't hurt. He lives in Hyde Park. His address is in Kirsty's book."

Marnee Thompson toyed with the bowl of peanuts, while I sipped coffee.

"If I talk to you about her," she said, without looking up, "it's because I'm worried. I don't want to do Phil any favors. And I don't want to get Kirsty in trouble. But I *am* worried."

"Why?"

Marnee Thompson cracked open a peanut between her thumb and forefinger. "I think she started to see Jay again a few weeks ago."

"Is Jay the friend she said she was going to visit before leaving on Thursday?"

Marnee nodded. "He's the one who caused all the trouble last year. Jay Stein. He's an adjunct instructor in the department. He and Kirsty . . . they had an affair last spring." She dropped the cracked peanut shell back in the bowl and looked up at me nervously. "Nobody's supposed to know that. I don't even think Phil knows it. If he did, he'd probably kill the son of a bitch."

"This guy, Stein, teaches at the university?"

"Creative writing," Marnee said with a forced laugh. "He's just a thirty-year-old swinging dick—one of those perpetual grad fellows who hang out in English departments instead of singles' bars. If Kirsty hadn't been so damn naive, it wouldn't have happened. Jay hits on everybody in the world, but Kirsty didn't understand that. She thought he was someone special, and he took advantage of her. Christ, she didn't know anything about sex."

She knew now, judging from what I'd found in her bureau drawer.

"What happened this spring?" I asked.

"What always happens with a guy like Jay," Marnee said sarcastically. "She got attached to him and he dropped her. He stopped seeing her. He wouldn't take her calls. Kirsty was so emotionally vulnerable anyway . . . Jay just pushed her over the edge."

"She had a breakdown?"

"That's what Phil called it. She did get pretty violent for a while, but I think she would have been all right if he'd given her a chance to recover on her own. She was under medication and seeing a therapist at the university clinic. But that wasn't good enough for Phil. He came storming up here like God Almighty and just . . . took her away. She didn't have a choice. He just did it to her."

Marnee Thompson gave me an incredulous, accusatory look, as if that was what men always did to women.

"If she was suicidal . . ."

"You don't understand," Marnee said angrily. "It goes way beyond paternalism with him or concern for her health. It's sick the way he spies on her and interrogates her and runs her life. He acts like he owns her soul."

Some kid at a nearby table laughed loudly, and Marnee scowled at him as if she thought he was laughing at her.

"Drink some coffee," I said to the girl.

"Don't patronize me!" she snapped.

"Don't drink, then," I said. "You're a hard person to be nice to, Marnee."

"I don't want to be made nice to. Christ, you're just doing a job." She dropped her head. "And I'm helping."

"You're helping Kirsty."

"I hope so," she whispered.

4

||||||||||||||||||||||||||||||||||||||||||||||||||||||||||||||||

Marnee Thompson didn't have anything more to say to me at the restaurant. She was feeling guilty, and she wasn't trying to disguise it. But then she loved Kirsten and despised Papa Phil. Her hatred of the man was so intense that it made me wonder if she'd told the whole truth about the past summer. It was possible that Marnee had taken it upon herself to phone Phil Pearson when Kirsten became distraught over her failed love affair. It would have been the natural thing to do under the circumstances. If so, she'd unwittingly put her friend in a mental ward—and that would have made anyone vengeful. Her anger toward Pearson had that kind of feel to it—the feel of betrayal.

It occurred to me that, even if I was only half right, Marnee Thompson had to be more worried about Kirsty than she'd let on or she wouldn't have said anything at all.

I didn't force the issue. As it was, she'd given me enough to get started. More than enough.

So we finished our coffee in silence, then walked in silence through the bitter cold to the apartment house. Upstairs, I found Kirsten's address book and looked up Jay Stein and Professor Heldman. Stein lived at 8550 Kenwood, apartment 917. Arthur Heldman lived on 56th and Blackstone.

While I was waiting for a cab, I thumbed through the postcards I'd found in Kirsty's desk. There were no messages on any of them—just the name Ethan. Marnee Thompson watched me from the living room chair.

"They're from her brother," she said, breaking the long silence between us.

"He seems to travel around a good deal."

"I think that's all he does. He's sort of a Gypsy. Kirsty's the only person in the family he talks to. In fact he called the other night to talk. Kirsty says he's got a terrible grudge against Phil."

"How come?"

"I don't know. Maybe Phil put him in a mental ward, too."

"It's an odd family," I said, putting the stack of cards back down on the desk.

"It's a tragic family," she said solemnly.

"Fathers get panicky and do stupid things, Marnee. It happens."

"That's not what I meant." She shook her head, instead of completing the thought.

A car honked outside, making the girl jump.

"That's the cab," I said.

As I put on my coat and hat, Marnee stood up and came over to me.

"I haven't been much help, have I?" she said, biting her lip.

"Enough."

"If she isn't with Jay . . ."

"I'll find her, Marnee."

It was past six when the cab dropped me in front of Jay Stein's apartment building on Kenwood. It was a modern high rise set on pylons sunk into a concrete plaza. The ground floor was all glassed-in lobby, with a bank of brass mailboxes and elevators in its center. A border of potted ferns and chrome-and-plastic benches ran around the edges like selvage.

The outer door was unlocked, but the inner door leading

to the lobby had an intercom system. I found Stein's name and pressed the button. Through the plate-glass window I could see the cab heading down the icy block. If Stein wasn't home I was in for a long walk back to Kirsty's apartment.

But I was lucky because Jay Stein buzzed me through. He must have been expecting someone because he didn't bother to ask who I was. If I was really lucky, he might have been expecting Kirsten Pearson.

I asked myself what I was going to do if the girl was there —or showed up—and decided to see how she reacted to me before doing anything. I had no legal right to interfere in her life, although, after what Marnee told me, I knew that I wasn't going to like Stein.

A tall, spindly man with a drooping moustache and lank brown hair was waiting for me in the ninth-floor hall, just outside the elevator door. His face was pale and horsey, with a sad-eyed look of suffering to it that might have impressed the young girls. He wasn't that old himself. Maybe twenty-eight or -nine. He was dressed even younger than that in torn jeans, cowboy boots, and a faded lumberjack shirt.

"Are you Jay Stein?" I asked.

"Why don't you tell me who you are first?" the man said nervously. He'd been smiling when the elevator door opened, but the smile went away as soon as he saw me.

"My name is Stoner. I work for Phil Pearson, Kirsten Pearson's father."

The man's right hand shot to his shirt pocket as if he'd felt a chest pain. He pulled out a pack of Winstons and shook a cigarette into his palm. His hand was trembling so much that three extra cigarettes fell onto the floor. Making a disgusted face, he reached down and scooped them up.

"I don't think I want to talk to you," he said, stowing the extra cigarettes back in the box.

"You're Jay Stein, aren't you?"

The man lit a cigarette and took a puff.

"C'mon, Jay. You don't have to think about that."

"I'm *Professor* Stein," he said indignantly. "And I've got nothing to say to you—or Phil Pearson. Now get out of here before I call security."

"And what are you going to tell security? That you're screwing one of your students?"

The man's eyes got very large. "That's an outrageous lie!"

There was an open door down the hallway on the left—probably the door to his apartment. Stein started to move in that direction, and I stepped in front of him.

"This is ridiculous," he said, backing up. "I don't know where you're getting your information, but there is nothing between Kirsty Pearson and me." He tapped the cigarette, scattering ashes down his shirt and onto the floor. "We're friends. No more than that."

"You haven't seen your 'friend' in the last couple of days, have you?"

He shook his head, no.

"If you're not seeing her, then I guess you won't mind if I look in your apartment."

"Of course I'd mind. I don't know who you are or why you're asking me these questions. Maybe if you told me what this was about . . ."

"Kirsty's been missing since last Thursday. Her father hired me to find her. I'm told that she's been seeing you."

"Told? By whom, told?"

I didn't say anything.

Stein got an ugly look on his face. "It was that roommate of hers, wasn't it? She put you up to this. Christ, what a joke!" He laughed bitterly.

"I don't think it's funny," I said.

"That's because you don't know what's going on." He laughed again, a smoother laugh, full of confidence. "It's okay. I see what it's about now. I think I can clear this up."

He tried to edge past me, toward his apartment door. But I didn't budge.

"I'm not going to run away," he said calmly. "Let's go down to my apartment, have a beer, and talk this over like civilized people."

Stein's front room was a couple of steps up from Marnee Thompson's Spartan digs. But just a couple. The bookshelves were varnished pine, instead of brick-and-board. The chairs and sofa were cheap Naugahyde copies of top-grain Italian originals. There were a few more ferns, hanging in baskets. Classier artwork on the walls. But it still had the feel of respectable poverty—the assistant professorial kind.

Two archways opened off the living room. One to a lighted matchbox of a kitchen, the other to a dark bedroom. I glanced at the kitchen as I came through the door. The plastic drainer sitting by the sink had one plate in it, one cup, and one saucer. There were no dishes on the counter. No food or drinks, either.

The living room was just as tidy and unpromising. An open book, *Snap* by Abby Frucht, sat on an ottoman in front of an armchair, a stack of papers on the floor beside it. The rest of the furniture looked unlived in, as if it had just been delivered the day before. The only item in the room that smacked of Kirsten Pearson was the overflowing ashtray on the windowsill. And that was just as much Stein as it was Kirsten. He'd already lit another by the time he shut the door.

"Have a seat," he said, walking into the kitchen. "You want a beer?"

"No, thanks."

"I thought guys like you always drank beer," he called out.

He came back with a can of Bud in his hand and the cigarette drooping from his lip.

"You're a detective, aren't you? A private cop?"

"Let's talk about you, instead."

Stein laughed—a real laugh this time. Popping the tab on the beer can, he plopped down on the couch and slung his leg over the armrest. He was obviously feeling a lot safer inside his own apartment, and whatever edge I'd had in the hall was just as obviously gone.

"Tell me the truth," he said. "It was Kirsty's roommate who gave you my name, wasn't it?"

"No."

He grinned. "It had to be her."

"And why is that?"

"Because she's insanely jealous of anyone who comes near Kirsty. The whole world knows Marnee's gay. Except Kirsty, maybe." He took a sip of beer. "Kirsty doesn't think like that. She sees people in terms of her own needs. But she doesn't see *their* needs." He took another sip of beer and scattered cigarette ashes on the couch. "I wouldn't get seriously involved with a kid like her. I couldn't if I wanted to. Sex scares the hell out of her. Men scare the hell out of her."

"You're telling me you two didn't have an affair."

"That's what I'm telling you."

"Then why'd she have a breakdown last spring?"

He shrugged. "Kirsty's crazy, Stoner."

"Crazy enough to fake a relationship with you?"

"Crazier than that. Look, I did take her out a few times,

after class. But there was no great romance between us. That was just her fantasy—or her roommate's. Kirsty didn't really want romance."

"What did she want?"

"A daddy. Someone to look after her, someone with a little more spine than her old man. I mean that kid's need for affection is tremendous."

I said, "Empathy doesn't seem to be one of your strong points either, Stein."

His face flushed angrily. "Kirsty has a long history of emotional trouble dating back to her childhood. There was nothing I could do about her past except encourage her to write about it. And that's exactly what I did."

"What about her childhood?"

"Her father didn't tell you?" he said, looking surprised. "Kirsty's mother was schizophrenic. In and out of mental wards all her life. When Kirsty was six, the mother killed herself. Violently." The man ducked his head as if he was embarrassed by his own avid gossip. "When you're carrying around that kind of genetic baggage, there isn't a whole lot anyone can do to help. I've tried to be a friend to her, but that's not always an easy thing. Kids can . . . misinterpret."

"Try somebody other than a kid."

He didn't say anything.

"When's the last time you saw Kirsten?" I asked.

"Last week. Thursday morning. She came over here to talk." He gave me a pointed look. "*Just* to talk."

"About what?"

Stein sat back in the sofa, clasping his hands behind his head. He was tired of me and the conversation. "Her brother, Ethan, came to town. He wanted to see Kirsty, but she wasn't sure she should go."

"Why would she have a problem seeing her brother?"

"Because he's crazier than she is. He drags her back to the past, and that's a place Kirsty doesn't need to visit, especially now."

"You've talked to the brother?"

"Once. When he came through Chicago last year. I don't think I've ever met anyone that intense. But then writers aren't exactly a relaxed bunch."

"Ethan's a writer, too?"

"Journalist. At least that's what he calls himself. He looks like he's a step above homelessness to me. I think his wife is the only thing that keeps him grounded. That and his weird obsession with his mother. That's really all he and Kirsty share—the mother. Neither one of them has been able to come to terms with her suicide. If you ask me, they never will."

There was a knock at the door. Looking relieved, Stein stood up.

"If you don't mind, I've got some company."

I stood up, too. "What did you tell Kirsty to do about Ethan?"

"I told her not to see him. To go home to Cincinnati. Apparently she didn't take my advice."

"Did she tell you where her brother was staying?"

"Somewhere in town, I guess."

"Can't you do better than that?"

"I've answered enough questions," he said sharply.

Stein went over to the door and opened it. A pretty girl was standing outside with a bottle of Chianti in her hand. She couldn't have been more than nineteen or twenty.

"C'mon in, Lucy. Mr. Stoner's just leaving."

The girl smiled at me winningly as she came into the room.

I walked over to the door. "Stein, if you're lying to me

about Kirsty Pearson, I'm going to get your ass fired. That's a promise."

The girl gasped, as if she couldn't believe anyone would speak to a professor like that.

"Don't threaten me," Stein said, reddening furiously. "If you come here again, I'll call the police."

He slammed the door in my face.

5

The trouble with a dramatic exit is that you can't go back and ask to use the phone.

I had to walk two blocks south on Kenwood to find a booth. By then I was so cold that I figured it would be worse to wait for a cab than to keep walking. So I pushed down the icy, gaslit sidewalks, head ducked against the wind, until I got to 56th Street.

Arthur Heldman's house was on the corner of 56th and Blackstone—a Prairie-style bungalow, L-shaped, parasol-roofed, with dark, glistening curls of frozen ivy climbing its board-and-stone walls. The front door was off to the side, down a driveway. The windows were lighted on that side of the house, as was the lamp above the door.

I knocked hard on the door and could barely feel my fist through the glove, I was that cold.

A tall, heavyset man of about fifty with ruddy cheeks and silvery hair and beard answered my knock. He was wearing wire-rim glasses, a black turtleneck sweater, and checked wool slacks that made him look, rather winningly, like a spiffy St. Nick.

"Can I help you?" he said in a friendly voice.

"You can if you're Professor Heldman."

"I'm Art Heldman. And you are . . . ?"

"My name is Stoner, Professor Heldman. I'm searching for a student of yours, Kirsten Pearson."

"She's lost?" the man said with alarm.

"She's been missing for four days. I've been hired by her father to find her."

"Poor kid," he said, shaking his head. "Please come in."

Heldman ushered me down a hall to an oak-paneled study. The room was furnished with Georgian pieces—a stately armoire, a desk like a three-tiered ship of the line, two mahogany armchairs with embroidered backs, and several bookshelves with mullioned fronts and leaded glass panes. A facsimile of Dr. Johnson's dictionary sat on a stand in one corner, spotlit like a shrine.

Heldman was clearly proud of the room. On his salary, a lot of scrimping and saving must have gone into fitting it out. He let the knickknacks work on me for a moment, then went over to the armoire, took out a bottle of Dewar's, and poured two fingers of Scotch into a tumbler.

"Here." He handed the drink to me. "You look frozen."

"Close to superconductivity."

Heldman laughed hoarsely.

I swallowed half of the drink, and my eyes clouded up. Another couple of swallows, and I started to feel my body again, as if I were putting it on piece by piece like a suit of clothes.

Heldman seated himself on a chair beside a small cherry wood table. There was a second chair across from him. I sat down on it.

"You say Kirsty's missing?" he said.

"For four days."

"You've tried her apartment, of course?" he said, leaning forward with the air of a friendly neighbor.

"That was the first place I looked. She wasn't there. Her roommate suggested that she might be with a man named Stein."

"Jay?" Heldman drew back slightly, as if the neighborhood had changed.

"I was told that Kirsty had been seeing him on a regular basis. He claims that she hasn't been."

The man nodded slowly. He'd started to look less like St.

Nick and more like St. Sebastian, as if the mere mention of Stein caused him physical pain. I figured it was because I was talking about a colleague, but it was also possible that he knew the truth about Stein and Kirsten and wasn't happy about it.

"You've spoken to Jay?"

"About twenty minutes ago. He hasn't seen Kirsty since Thursday morning. Apparently she stopped at his apartment before leaving town. Stein says to discuss her brother."

"She stopped here too. The same morning. And she *did* mention her brother."

He said it like he was trying to back Stein up. But it was clear from his tone that Ethan Pearson hadn't been the only topic of conversation.

"She was thinking about going to see Ethan while he was in town," Heldman went on.

"Did she say where he was staying?"

"No, just that he was eager to talk to her."

"Do you know what about?"

He shook his head. "Kirsty's always been a little vague when it comes to Ethan. At least, she has with me. I don't think he's a healthy influence on her—if that's what you want to know. At least, he doesn't seem to be from what I've read of her novel."

"Which novel is that?"

Heldman spread his hands as if he were opening a book in front of me. "Kirsty's been working on an autobiographical piece for the past couple of months. A kind of therapeutic exercise to help her put her life in order after this past summer. She calls it *Second Chance.*"

"Why *Second Chance*?"

I thought of the sign on Kirsty's door.

"Because she doesn't believe in them," he said wryly. "At least, not for her."

"Is Stein in this book?"

Heldman sighed. "Yes. She hasn't finished the last chapter yet, but he'll be a large part of it—and so will her father and her brother, Ethan. You see, Kirsty believes in living out what she writes—or writing what she lives. Sometimes it's hard to tell which."

"Did she mention Stein when you talked on Thursday?"

"Yes." The man stood up, walked over to the armoire, and poured himself a stiff drink. "You already know that she became involved with Jay last year."

"He had an affair with her?"

"I don't know," he said, turning back to me with the bottle in his hand. He splashed a little more Scotch in my glass. "She was pretty damn attached to him—I know that. I'm afraid she still is. She told me on Thursday that she was seeing him again."

"Seeing him meaning sleeping with him?"

"I think so."

The man pursed his lips as if he'd bitten into something rotten. Or maybe he just caught a whiff of what I was thinking about Stein.

"Look, I care for that girl deeply," he said. "And I'll do anything I can to help you find her. But Jay isn't the reason she's disappeared. There isn't one reason."

"Stein blamed it on genes."

Heldman blushed. "I realize he can be an obnoxious ass. But you've got to understand that he stepped into a situation he wasn't equipped to deal with—a situation very few people could deal with. Kirsty's life has a pattern to it that predates Jay—a pattern that has slowly solidified into something like a fate. Events have conspired to make her believe that no matter what she does, she is bound to end as her mother did—crazy or a suicide. Her brother has apparently done a lot to reinforce that belief by constantly obsessing about the mother's death. And of course, so has her father, whose overprotectiveness kept Kirsty a child in many ways. But the point is—so has Kirsty herself.

"For years now, consciously or unconsciously, she has been making choices that will lead her in the direction of suicide. The Stein thing is just one more instance. The fact that she's infatuated with Jay is beside the point. In a way, Kirsty understands that herself. Deep down she's chosen Jay Stein precisely because she knows he will reject her."

"It's a theory," I said.

The man gave me a rueful look. "You don't believe me?"

"I believe the girl is deeply troubled, but I think it's a bit too damn enlightened to blame Kirsten for Jay Stein's callousness. Or to dismiss a need for affection as a death wish."

Heldman blushed. For a second I thought he was going to get pissy, but he surprised me. "I didn't mean for it to sound that way. All I meant to say is that Kirsty honestly believes we are trapped by our pasts. Our childhood pasts. And *no one* gets a second chance at childhood."

He wanted it to sound profoundly sad. It only sounded sadly adolescent to me. But most literature professors I'd known developed that same lump in their throats when they spoke of life's inequities—kind of like narrators in PBS documentaries.

"Was she depressed when you saw her on Thursday morning?" I asked him.

"Not depressed so much as agitated, excited."

"About Stein?"

"Yes, and about seeing her brother, Ethan. It was almost as if she felt she had to choose between the two of them, if for no other reason than to find an ending for her book."

"What does the book have to do with seeing Stein or Ethan?" I asked.

"As I told you, she is living out what she writes. Stein and Ethan represent different paths to her—present and past, roughly. Frankly I'm afraid they lead in the same direction."

"Suicide?"

He nodded. "She thinks it's her destiny."

"I don't believe in destinies," I said, getting to my feet. "Could I use your phone? I need to make a couple of calls."

The man pointed to a phone on the desk. "I'll leave you alone," he said, standing up and walking to the door. "If there's anything I can do . . ."

"I'll let you know," I told him.

I had only one contact in the Chicago area—an ex-FBI agent named Brandt Scheuster, who had opened his own P.I. agency in Skokie. I found his number in my address book and phoned him. All I got that late on a Sunday night was an answering machine. I left my name, Kirsten's number, and told him I'd be back in touch. I tried calling Marnee Thompson at the apartment, but there was no answer there either. Marnee obviously hadn't been forthcoming with me about Kirsten and her brother. But then, I was working for Papa Phil, and Kirsty was her friend.

I thought about phoning Pearson himself, and decided to wait. Judging by how much of his children's pasts—and his own—he'd already concealed, I didn't think I'd get him to talk openly without some leverage. Or a body.

After a time Heldman came back into the room. He had a beautiful little girl of about ten with him.

"This is my daughter, Katie. Katie, Mr. Stoner."

Katie curtsied as if I were royalty.

"Go on, toots," he said, giving her a smack on the rear.

She gave her father an indignant look and marched off up the hall.

"She thinks she's too old to be given a potch on the tuckus."

"She's very pretty."

Heldman smiled proudly. "I think so. Did you finish your calls?"

"All except for a cab to take me back to Kirsty's apartment."

"I could drive you."

"That's all right, Professor. I need you to run another errand."

"Anything," he said.

"How close are you to Jay Stein?"

"He's a colleague," the professor said with a stilted air of professional courtesy. "He came here this past year as an instructor, fresh out of the Iowa workshops. I very much doubt he will be renewed this coming year—if that's what you're getting at."

It wasn't what I was getting at, but I was glad to hear it anyway. Glad to know that forbearance had its limits, even among professors of literature.

"I'm sure that Stein has told me a few self-protective lies," I said. "But there is probably a certain amount of truth mixed in with them. It's important for me to know what Kirsty and he actually talked about on Thursday morning— if she did in fact tell him she was going to see her brother or someone else. Do you think you could . . . ?"

"What?" Heldman said uneasily. "Pump him?"

"I was thinking of something a little more hardball than that. It wouldn't be a lie if you said that you'd just talked to me and that I'd raised some disturbing questions about his conduct, would it?"

"You want me to threaten him?" Heldman said with horror.

"I want you to find out where Kirsten went. Otherwise, she may well be destined for calamity."

Heldman thought it over for a moment. "I'll do what I can" was all he said.

6

I called for a cab and, before leaving, told Heldman to phone me at Kirsten's apartment after he'd talked to Stein. He wasn't comfortable with the idea of blackmailing the man—that was obvious. But I had the gut feeling that he'd get the information I wanted, because he really did care for Kirsten, as I myself was beginning to care for her in spite of my initial misgivings about the case.

On the cab ride back to the apartment I wondered why Phil Pearson had waited for the girl to go missing before calling for help. He had talked vaguely about "disturbing signs" in Kirsten's behavior—he'd talked vaguely about everything having to do with his daughter, as if her past was a personal embarrassment to him. But the signs of Kirsten's disintegration were quite clear to everyone who knew her. They had to be just as clear to her father, who was a trained psychiatrist. Perhaps Pearson couldn't bring himself to intervene in his daughter's life again after his disastrous rescue attempt of the previous summer. Perhaps he thought that another such intervention would drive her over the edge. I didn't know. But there was an inconsistency about his behavior, about everyone's behavior toward Kirsty, that almost amounted to ambivalence. It was as if her friends had decided to let her life run its course, even if it meant her death.

I'm sure they felt they were respecting her wishes, showing her the courtesy of treating her as an adult. But it seemed heartless to me when she was so obviously *not* fully an adult. Even Professor Heldman seemed irresponsible, knowing as he did that Kirsten was close to suicide and still letting her walk off to her self-pronounced doom. Maybe that was the way enlightened people treated each other in academia.

It was past nine when the cabbie dropped me off at the brownstone on 54th. No light was on in the second-floor apartment windows, and no one answered the entry buzzer. I fished through my pocket, found the keys that Pearson had given me, and let myself into the front hall. The hallway was dark, and the cat piss smell was over-whelming. I fumbled up the staircase to the apartment, unlocked the door, and went in.

A sliver of moonlit sky hung in the darkness like a halluci-nation. It took me a second to realize that it was being reflected off the mirror in Marnee Thompson's bedroom. I found the desk light and clicked it on.

The boxed manuscript was the first thing I saw. The box had been opened and the manuscript removed. At first I thought that Marnee Thompson must have taken it out to read. But on further thought I couldn't see Marnee tamper-ing with Kirsten's things—not with her fierce sense of pro-priety. Which meant one of two things. Either someone else had broken in and stolen the manuscript. Or Kirsty Pearson herself had come back for it. I liked the idea of Kirsty taking it, for several reasons.

One, the apartment lock hadn't been tampered with, so whoever had removed it had had a key to the room. Two, Kirsty hadn't finished the book yet. According to Art Heldman she was waiting for real life to supply her with an ending. Maybe she'd found that ending over the past four days.

There was a third reason why I liked the idea. If Kirsty had taken the manuscript, it meant she was still alive. And I wanted her to stay alive until I could find her.

I went down the hall to Kirsty's bedroom, flipped on the

light, and went through the trashy room again—carefully this time—looking for any other sign that Kirsty might have returned to the apartment. But nothing else had been moved or taken—the clothes were still disarrayed, the books made their tipsy towers, the birth control pills were hidden in the underwear drawer, the picture of Phil Pearson lay facedown in the panties.

I hadn't examined the loose papers scattered on her desk the first time I'd searched the room. This time I read each one through. They were fragments of prose, mostly. Journal entries that made little sense to me and one that made too much sense, a scrap cut from *The New York Times Magazine* and pasted to a blank page:

> Suicide was a crime—ironically, a capital crime—in most Western nations well into the nineteenth century. In England, failed suicides were frequently nursed back to health in order to be hanged.

There was a fragment of a prose poem, copied out several times. Presumably one of her own:

> *Closing windows at dawn*
> *Against the heat of the day,*
> *He is suddenly lost among bulky*
> *Colorless furnishings*
>
> *The windows stick*
> *in swollen tracks,*
> *the blinds will not close*
>
> *under thin sheets*
> *his feet search out her legs*
> *his hands . . .*

And that was all, as if she'd stopped those hands with her own. I put the paper down and thought about Jay Stein—about paying him another visit—when the phone in the living room rang. I went back down the hall and picked it up. It was Brandt Scheuster, returning my call.

"I've got a missing person, Brandt," I told him. "A Cincinnati girl, going to school up here, who dropped out of sight about four days ago. She's unstable, possibly suicidal. I need you to check with the cops—see if she's been picked up or if they've got her in a morgue. You could canvass hospital emergency rooms and psych wards, too."

I gave him Kirsty's name and physical description.

"I'll see what I can do," Brandt said. "Does she have a car?"

"A yellow VW Bug. I don't know the plates yet, but if you could run her name through Illinois BMV, I'd appreciate it. I'll check in Ohio myself to see if she registered the car down there."

"You want this to go out as an APB, Harry? You want to make it official police business?"

I didn't even have to think about it. "Yeah. I want the kid found."

"If we do locate her . . . ?"

"Call me. I'll be checking into a hotel later tonight. When I have a new number I'll let you know. Until then you can get me here at the girl's apartment."

After finishing with Brandt I called Al Foster at the Cincinnati Police Department and asked him to run Kirsten's name through the Ohio BMV computer. I told him it was urgent.

I'd just hung up when the phone rang again. This time it was Art Heldman.

"I've talked to Jay," he said in a guilty-sounding voice.

"What did he have to say?"

"He repeated the story that he told you—about Ethan, Kirsty's brother." He cleared his throat dramatically. "However, when I . . . pressured him, he admitted that Ethan hadn't been the only focus of the conversation. He and Kirsty did talk about their own relationship as well. Apparently Kirsty wanted to start seeing Jay again—romantically."

"What did Stein say to that?"

"He claims he didn't commit himself either way. He told her that he cared for her and that they would talk again after the holidays. He's fully aware that Kirsten is still in love with him, and he's determined to ease her out of the infatuation slowly and gently."

"Like he did last year?" I said acidly.

"Jays knows he behaved badly last spring. He simply panicked. Kirsten can be demanding. Her needs are so great."

"That's the way it is with nineteen-year-old women, Professor, especially when you abandon them."

Heldman didn't say anything.

"Did Stein give you any sense of how Kirsten reacted to his spiel?"

"He thought he'd talked her into putting everything on hold—the renewed romance *and* the visit to Ethan. He thought she was going back to Cincinnati, as she originally planned to do. I thought she was, too, Stoner. That was definitely the impression I got."

I sighed. "Well, something must have changed her mind."

"I did learn one more thing that may be of interest. Jay didn't tell you because he didn't trust you—possibly because you're working for Kirsten's father, and Kirsty has made it clear to any number of people that her dad *isn't* to be told anything about her life here in Chicago. Dr. Pearson may be a well-meaning man, but he can also be an overbearing one. At times of crisis he seems to overreact. It's almost as if he's afraid that Kirsty's emotional problems will reflect badly on him."

"I have that feeling too," I admitted.

"That's why Jay left out part of the conversation."

"Which part?"

"The part about where Kirsty's brother, Ethan, is staying."

"Stein had an address?"

"Not an address—a name. Kirsty mentioned a motel in Evanston. The University Inn. I looked up the address myself. It's on Lake Shore, south of the campus. According to the desk clerk, Ethan Pearson is still registered there."

"Good work. I'll get a cab immediately."

"I'd like to come along," Heldman said. "I mean I have a car. And I know Kirsty. If she is in a bad way, perhaps I can help."

"All right," I said. "Let's do it."

7

Heldman picked me up outside the brownstone a little before ten.

It took us about thirty minutes to drive up to Evanston, and another fifteen to find The University Inn on the south side of town—a run-down, fifties-style motor court with a small office building in front and Quonset-like motel rooms stretching in parallel rows behind it. The ice-shagged neon sign on the highway berm said "Vacancies." And always would.

Heldman pulled up by the office. Through the steamy picture window I could see a night clerk, resting his elbows on a countertop.

"You want to go in?" Heldman asked. "Or should I?"

"I'll handle it, Professor."

"We're not going to do anything rash, are we? I mean we're not going to use force, right?"

He laughed nervously, but his eyes were dead serious. He was beginning to have second thoughts about intervening in Kirsten's life—second thoughts about me.

I said, "Let's see if Kirsten is here before we decide what we're going to do."

Heldman didn't look reassured. "I don't know. I don't know about this."

I got out of the car and walked into the motel office. A middle-aged clerk in a striped shirt and black gaberdine pants was reading a comic book spread out on the counter. He looked up at me balefully, as if his instincts told him I wasn't a paying customer.

"Can I do for you?" he said, flapping the comic book shut.

He had a slight cast in his left eye that gave him a queasy, distracting stare.

I tried to smile at him pleasantly. "You can tell me what room Ethan Pearson is in. I'm supposed to meet him here around eleven, but I forgot the damn room number."

"That'd be fourteen. Down there on your right."

"Great." I turned toward the door, then looked back at him. "You don't know if Kirsten's here yet, do you? Dark-haired girl, blue eyes, about nineteen?"

"Ain't seen nobody but his wife and kid," he said, flipping the comic book open and bending over it again.

I went back outside and got into Heldman's Audi.

"Room fourteen," I said to him. "On the right."

The professor wheeled the car slowly around the office and down a driveway that ran between the two rows of motel buildings. There were numbered parking slots on either side of the drive—most of them filled with frozen slush. But the one in front of room 14 had a car in it, a yellow VW Bug.

"Christ, I think that's Kirsty's car," Heldman said excitedly.

"It *is* her car. Pull over on the other side of the drive."

Heldman parked the Audi on the right hand berm, flipped off the lights, and turned in his seat to look back through the rear window at number 14. For a moment we both sat there, looking over our shoulders at the lighted motel room window.

"What do we do now?" Heldman asked.

"Talk to her, if she's willing."

"And if she isn't?"

I didn't answer him. What I had to say wasn't what he wanted to hear.

As I started to get out of the car, Heldman grabbed my

coat sleeve. Without thinking, I jerked away—hard. The professor looked shocked, then frightened.

"I won't be a party to coercion," he said, trying to make his voice resolute.

"I'm going to do my job," I said, feeling sorry that he'd come along. "If that bothers you, stay in the car."

"No, I'm coming with you," he said, as if I'd challenged him.

I got out of the car and Heldman got out too. Side by side we walked across the icy driveway to number 14. I stopped by the VW for a moment—to take a quick look. The doors were locked and the windows were solid ice. There was thick ice on the hood and roof, as well. Clearly the car hadn't been used all day—perhaps not for several days.

A short cement walk led from the parking area up to the motel door. I automatically slowed my pace as I neared the door, and Heldman almost ran up my back.

"Sorry," he whispered, and dropped a step behind me.

The curtain in the window was too thick to see through, but I could hear a television going inside the room.

I gave Heldman a glance—to make sure he was out of the way—raised my fist, and knocked.

The television went off abruptly, as if a hand had been clapped to its mouth. There was a moment of dead silence, in which I had the sure feeling that someone inside the room was straining to listen. Then the door opened slowly, and a stocky young woman with a badly bruised face peered out the crack.

Even in the dim porch light I could tell that the bruises had come from a recent beating. She'd tried to hide the black eyes with makeup, but there was nothing she could do about the swollen nose or the fat, twisted bottom lip. She touched at the lip involuntarily, when she saw that my eyes were drawn to it. Then she covered her whole mouth with her right hand, as if that would divert me.

"Yes?" she said behind her hand. Her voice sounded hoarse and weak, as if she'd used it up earlier that day—screaming. "What is it?"

"My name is Stoner. I'm looking for Kirsten Pearson."

"She's not here," the woman said. "She's gone. They're both gone."

The woman dropped her head like a prisoner being sentenced. "They've gone and left us here alone."

A young boy with the solemn, big-eyed face of a refugee was sitting on one of the double beds inside the motel room. He couldn't have been more than three or four, dressed in pajamas and furry slippers. He hopped up and ran over to the woman as we came through the door, hiding his face in her robe. She hugged him to her and sank down on the bed.

"Maybe we should call an ambulance?" Heldman said, staring aghast at the woman's battered face.

She looked up quickly. "No. There's no need. I'm all right." Her voice was queerly placid.

"You don't look all right," Heldman said.

"Nevertheless, I am." She wiped her eyes with the back of her hands. "Who did you say you were?"

"My name is Harry Stoner. This is Professor Arthur Heldman. We're looking for Kirsten Pearson. She's been missing for several days."

The woman nodded as if she already knew that Kirsten was missing. "She's been here with Ethan. Since Thursday, I think. They left this afternoon. Left me here with David."

"You're Ethan's wife?"

The woman nodded again. "Hedda Pearson." She laughed suddenly. "I guess I'm still his wife."

"He did this to you?" I asked.

Hedda Pearson didn't answer me. She sat on the edge of the bed and stared at her frightened son. "Are you police?"

"No. I'm a private investigator. I was hired by Kirsten's father—Ethan's father—to find Kirsty."

"I've never met Ethan's father," the woman said matter-of-factly. "Ethan's told me about him, but we've never met."

The woman stopped talking for a moment. I took that moment to look quickly around the room. There was a lamp table to the right of the door, with a manila folder on it. The folder was open, and I could see a pile of newspaper clippings inside. There were more loose clippings on a bureau across from the beds. And a handful of bloody Kleenex.

"What am I going to do?" Hedda Pearson asked, calmly stroking the boy's head. "Ethan took all our money, the credit cards, the car."

"I can get you money," I told her.

The woman reacted angrily. "I couldn't leave here if I wanted to. I can't go anywhere. Where would I go?"

"Don't you have relatives? Parents?"

"We don't talk since I married."

From where I was sitting I could see why. But the woman obviously didn't.

"I'll simply wait here until he comes back."

"From where?"

"From where he went of course. From the searching . . . from the hunting." The woman shook her head suddenly, violently. Her voice rose to a near-hysterical pitch: "Madness!"

The little boy began to moan softly, as if he'd been infected by his mother's hysteria. The woman glanced down at him guiltily, and her face slowly resumed its queer look of resignation.

I glanced at Heldman, who was standing just inside the door. "Maybe you could get some coffee?"

He nodded. "Of course."

"Do you want some coffee, something to eat?" I said to the woman.

"Some milk for David, please," she said softly. "He hasn't had anything since this morning."

I had the feeling that neither one of them had eaten in hours.

"I'll get the food," Heldman said, and turned to the door eagerly, as if he were only too glad to escape the scene in the bedroom.

He went out, leaving me alone with the woman and her son. The boy, David, stopped crying and crawled up on the bed beside his mother. Frightened or not, he was sleepy and his eyelids kept drooping down over his solemn brown eyes. He didn't look as if he'd been hurt, but I couldn't be sure.

"Is the boy all right?"

"Of course he's all right!" the woman said with outrage. "Ethan would never hurt David."

"What caused the fight?"

"The same thing that always causes our fights," Hedda Pearson said wearily. "He'll read something in the paper. See some anonymous two-inch column, and it starts up again."

"What starts up?"

But Hedda Pearson didn't hear me. "I didn't know about it when I first met him. If I had, I'm not sure what I would have done. Probably the same things. Just like he does." She stared sadly at the sleeping boy. "Only this time . . . I'm frightened for him. I'm frightened he won't come back."

"Why are you afraid for him, Mrs. Pearson? Where have Ethan and Kirsty gone?"

"To look for him—the man in the newspaper." Her eyes got very large, as if she'd suddenly remembered something terrifying. "You've got to find them!"

"Why?"

"Because they're dangerous. They make each other dangerous. And Ethan . . ." Her head dropped to her chest and she began to cry. "Ethan has a gun!"

8

∎∎∎

Ten minutes passed before Heldman returned with food and coffee. By then the woman had stopped crying and settled back into her strange waiting state. She woke the boy and fed him a hamburger and some milk. She didn't eat anything herself at first, but after a while she began to eat, just chewing and swallowing automatically.

Heldman hovered over her, trying to help with the boy—trying to help. While he busied himself with Hedda Pearson and her son, I scanned the newspaper clippings on the bureau, looking for the one that had apparently set Ethan Pearson off. As far as I could see, it might have been any of them, for they were all the same. Two-inch columns cut from the back pages of newspapers, the pages with the court news—each column detailing the arraignment, conviction, or release of a murderer. The name of the paper and the date of the article was written in pen at the bottom of each clipping.

> Willie Johnson, 42, is to be released this afternoon from Joliet penitentiary, after serving seven years of a 10–20 year term for homicide in the death of his common-law wife . . .
> *Chicago Sun-Times 8/26/83*

> Arthur Braddock, 35, of 4609 Winton Terrace has been arraigned on the

charge of felony homicide in the
death of Leona Smith . . .
>   *Cincinnati Enquirer 11/18/76*

Stanford Isaiah Lewis, 45, convicted
slayer of Moira Hamill, has been
granted probation after serving ten
years of a life sentence in Lima State
Penitentiary . . .
>   *Dayton Daily News 3/7/86*

Calvin "Beebee" Jackson, 34, of 8567
Prospect has been convicted of ag-
gravated homicide in the death of
LaQuicha Morgan, also of 8567 Prospect . . .
>   *Cleveland Plain-Dealer 12/2/76*

There were twenty of them on the bureau. Twenty homi-
cides, twenty murderers. I couldn't be certain on the basis
of their names alone, but I had the feeling that they were all
black men. They were all about forty-seven or forty-eight
years old, all from the Midwest, and all of them had killed a
woman.

It took me a while longer to spot it, but the criminals had
something else in common. Judging by their dates of release and dates of conviction, it appeared that each of them
had committed a murder in the latter part of 1976. I didn't
know what that meant, but it clearly had some significance
for Ethan Pearson.

As I was sorting through the last of the clippings I noticed
that Hedda Pearson had begun to watch me. I could see her
face in the bureau mirror. She looked more curious than

concerned, as if she wanted to compare notes about her
husband's odd collection of killers.

"He started cutting them out after his mother died,"
Hedda Pearson said into the mirror.

I turned to face her. "Would that have been in 1976?"

"Yes. You're sharp, Mr. Stoner. Estelle died in September
of 1976." The woman pointed to the manila folder on the
lamp table by the door. "It's all in there, all the details. At
least the ones that the reporters could dig up. They missed
the real story, though."

"And what is the real story?" I asked.

"What happened afterward. How it changed the family.
Ethan most of all. Kirsty was deeply affected by Estelle's
death, too. But she was closer to her father. And, of course,
Phil was there to look after her. Ethan wasn't close to Phil.
He blamed his father for Estelle's breakdowns. He still
does. He had no one to lean on once Estelle was gone. No
one to console him, to help him channel the anger and
frustration from such an enormous tragedy. His mind
couldn't handle it. Gradually he went . . . a little crazy.
You saw for yourself. All those men in the newspapers. All
those men."

"What does he do with the clippings?" I asked the
woman.

"He keeps track," she said. "Keeps looking, hunting,
searching for the reason Estelle died, for a reason that
makes sense to him. His logic is simplicity itself: my mother
couldn't have committed suicide and still have loved me,
therefore she didn't commit suicide, she was murdered. By
one of them—one of the faceless men in the newspaper
clippings."

"Was he this . . . obsessed when you married him?"
Heldman asked.

The woman smiled. "You mean, *why* did I marry him if he was so crazy?"

She was a smart woman, when she had her wits about her.

"Yes," Heldman said with a blush. "I guess that's what I did mean."

"I didn't care that he was crazy," Hedda Pearson said simply. "I didn't see him that way. He was only nineteen—a sophomore at Oberlin. And I was just eighteen."

Hedda Pearson lightly touched her bruised lip, her swollen eye, down her cheek, as if the bruises didn't matter, as if they weren't there. Then her face changed.

"If I hadn't gotten pregnant, it might have worked. But I did get pregnant. Ethan wasn't ready for fatherhood, for a job and a family. That's when this craziness started in earnest—at least, that's when it started to have an effect, that's when we started to move from city to city."

"Has he ever gone after one of these men before?" I asked.

Hedda Pearson smiled. "No. He never wanted to confront any of them—he wanted to get away from them. He said it was because none of them was the right man—that he had to keep moving until fate delivered the right one to him. But I always told myself that that wasn't the real reason. The real reason was that he didn't ever want it to end. He wanted to keep looking forever, to keep Estelle alive forever. At least that's what I thought until last week."

The woman shuddered, slopping a little coffee on her robe.

"What happened last week?" I asked.

"We were in Ft. Thomas, Kentucky. I'd been working there at NKSU for a couple of months. Ethan was writing an article on the campus. But he started having trouble with the piece. Then he got a rejection on one of his poems. I knew the signs by then, so I could see what was coming. And sure enough on Wednesday morning he marched into the department office and pulled me away from the desk. In front of everyone, he pulled me away.

"He took me out to the car. David was already in the backseat. Our bags in the backseat. He took off, driving straight through to Chicago. To this godforsaken place."

"He came to see Kirsten?"

She nodded. "He had this clipping from a Kentucky paper. A small photograph. He thought she would look at it and remember."

"Did she recognize the man in the photo?"

The woman laughed derisively. "Of course not. There's nothing to remember. There never has been. That isn't the point. Kirsten didn't have to recognize the man. All she had to do was come here and talk to Ethan. Just talk." Hedda Pearson got an ugly look on her face. "She does weird things to him. She always makes him worse, and he makes her worse. It's horrible to see. Like they're having some kind of vicious sex."

"Kirsten came here on Thursday morning?"

"I think it was Thursday. I know they spent the weekend here. The two of them in this room with David and me . . . telling tales about the past, talking baby talk, crying about Estelle as if she'd just died a day or two ago. They just kept getting crazier and crazier, until they were ready to . . ." The woman dropped her head.

"When did they leave?" I asked.

"Late this afternoon." She touched her bruised face.

"You tried to stop him?"

"He had a gun," she said with horror. "They went and bought one yesterday. When I tried to take it away from Ethan, he . . ."

"He beat you up." I said it for her.

She nodded.

"Where was the boy?" Heldman said, looking sick. "Where was David when this happened?"

The woman waved her hand around the tiny room. "Where do you think?"

"He saw?"

"Kirsty held her hands over David's eyes."

"She didn't try to stop it?" Heldman asked.

"She watched," Hedda Pearson said coldly.

9

||||||||||||||||||||||||||||||||||||||||||||||||||||||||||||||||||

I tried to get the woman to describe the man in the Kentucky newspaper—the man that Ethan claimed had killed his mother. But Hedda said she'd never actually seen the newspaper photo—Ethan had only told her about it. If the picture was something more than Ethan's fantasy, he'd taken it with him when he and Kirsten had left that afternoon in the grey Plymouth Volare, heading south to finish their lives in an act of murder.

"There is another picture," the woman said, almost as an afterthought.

"Of this man?"

"Of the man Ethan says killed his mother. He drew it right after Estelle's death. He even tried to show it to the police, but of course no one believed him. Not even Ethan's father. It's one of the things that Ethan has always held against Phil." She pointed to the lamp table by the door. "The drawing's over there, in the manila folder on the table. The folder with the clippings about Estelle."

I went over to the table and picked up the folder. Heldman crowded beside me, eager to take a look.

I didn't bother with the clippings. The picture was in the back. It was a surprisingly skillful pencil drawing of a black man in his mid-to-late thirties with lumpy skin, peppery hair, and a thin, mean, frightening-looking face—all sharp bony points from brow to cheekbone to chin. The boy had drawn what I took to be a pointed goatee at the V of the chin, which only added to the man's devilish appearance.

I had the feeling that the drawing was more metaphor than anything else—the portrait of the bogeyman who had

robbed a ten-year-old child of his mother. And yet, metaphor or not, the search for the bogeyman had become quite
real. Ethan and Kirsten were out there looking for him—
looking to kill him. And they had a seven-hour head start on
me.

The woman wouldn't take charity, so I ended making a
trade. Two hundred dollars for the manila envelope with
the clippings and Ethan's drawing of Estelle Pearson's murderer. And another fifty for four chapbooks of Ethan Pearson's poetry.

The woman had a suitcase full of the damn things, like a
brush salesman.

As I walked across the deserted motel lot to Heldman's
car, holding that pile of yellowed clippings and Ethan's
chapbooks in my hands, I had the disturbing feeling that
none of what had occurred was real.

Art Heldman had the same feeling. "It's so damn weird,"
he said in a bewildered voice. "What are we going to do?"

I told him the truth. "I don't know."

Snow began to fall again on the way back to Hyde Park—
a needle spray of snow, fierce and fine as icy rain. Through
the driver side window I could see it falling on the lake,
windblown above the dark water. The only sound in the car
was the whisper of the snow beneath the tires.

"I owe you an apology, Stoner," Heldman said after a
time. He thought I was still angry from the scene in the
parking lot. I wasn't—I wasn't thinking about him.

"You were right. Something has to be done. I guess it
should have been done long before this." Heldman glanced
over at me quickly. "If you still need my help . . ."

"Thanks. I'll let you know."

"Will you go back to Cincinnati?"

"It seems like the place to start."

"Perhaps the police should be . . . informed."

"They already have been—in Chicago. I'll take care of the rest of them tonight."

"You have somewhere to stay?"

"Just drop me at Kirsty's apartment. I'll see if I can get an early flight in the morning."

"I am sorry," the man said again. "Sorriest of all for Kirsty."

"Her life isn't over yet, Professor. We still have a shot to change things."

I said it, but I wasn't sure I believed it. And neither was he.

Heldman dropped me at Kirsten's apartment at half past twelve. The freshly fallen snow along 54th caught the streetlight, turning the dismal brownstones the pale, low-wattage yellow of gaslamps. I watched Heldman's car disappear down Blackstone, then looked up through the falling snow at Kirsten's second-floor apartment. There was a light in the front room, which might have meant that Marnee Thompson was back. That is, if I hadn't left the light on myself when I'd stopped there earlier that night. I went into the foyer and pressed the intercom on the side wall, thinking I'd use the keys if no one answered. But Marnee Thompson buzzed me through.

As I climbed the stairs to the second-floor landing, the apartment door opened and the girl came out. Although she was wearing a terry robe over men's-cut pajamas, she didn't look as if she'd been sleeping. On the contrary, her face was wide-awake and frightened-looking. For a second I was afraid she was going to tell me that Kirsten Pearson was dead.

"What happened?" I asked.

"An hour or two after you left, Kirsty came to the apartment," the girl said breathlessly. "Mr. Stoner, she was . . . crazy."

Marnee Thompson wrung her hands, as if she'd been infected with some of the same craziness. "I didn't know what to do. After she left I just waited here. I didn't know what else to do."

I put a hand on her shoulder. "Calm down. This could be important."

Marnee Thompson shrugged my hand off. "I know it's important! Don't you think I know that? I wanted to tell you, but I didn't know where you were. Couldn't you have called?"

"I did call. You weren't here."

"I was with Kirsty," she cried. "That's why I wasn't here. I was with Kirsty!"

The girl was almost shouting and very close to tears.

I edged her out of the hall and into the apartment, closing the door behind us. "Easy, Marnee. I'm a friend, remember?"

She gave me a wet-eyed look of frustration. "It's just that I spent a couple of hours, driving around with her in this beat-up car, trying to talk her into staying with me. But she wouldn't listen! I'm so afraid . . . I'm afraid she's going to die."

Marnee Thompson stamped her foot and started to cry. She ran into the living room, curled up in the armchair, and cried—with her hand over her eyes and her knees tucked against her chest.

I went into the tiny kitchen, found a kettle in the cabinet, and started boiling water for coffee. It wasn't just for the girl. I was afraid that if I didn't wake myself up, I'd miss something important—or lose my concentration completely. And then I was pissed off at my bad luck. If I'd stuck around the apartment, I would have found Kirsty in time to stop her and Ethan. Instead, she'd slipped away. For a moment I felt as if fate really was conspiring toward her death, just as Kirsten herself believed.

There was a can of instant on top of the refrigerator. When the kettle started to shriek, I mixed two cups and took them back into the living room.

The girl was still sitting in the chair, stiffly now, her feet planted on the floor as if they were weighted with chains. I handed her a cup and sat down across from her on the desk stool.

"Let's start again," I said. "Kirsty came back here around . . . ?"

"Eight, I think," Marnee said in a dull, cried-out voice. "Maybe a little after."

"She wanted the manuscript?"

"Not just the manuscript. She wanted to say good-bye to me. To tell me . . ." Her voice started to tremble again, but she caught herself before she broke down, crossing her arms and squeezing tightly as if she were physically holding herself together. "To tell me she loved me and to say good-bye."

"Did she tell you where she was going?"

"All she said was that she was going away. That she'd made a decision. The right decision, she called it."

"What was this decision?"

"To kill herself, I think," the girl said with a hopeless look.

I didn't want to give her the chance to brood about it, so I raised my voice a little, startling her. "Was Ethan with Kirsty?"

"Yes. He didn't come into the apartment. But when I went out to the car with Kirsty, he was sitting in the backseat. Kirsty dropped him off at The Eagle while we drove around and talked. I guess she must have picked him up later."

"What did she talk about in the car?"

"Jay, her dad, her mom, her breakdown—everything. She said she'd been confused for so long about her past and that she was just now beginning to see what it meant her to do. She talked like that—like her past was this guiding light. She said she thought, at first, that Jay was her destiny. But now she knew that was wrong. Her destiny was with her family. The way she talked about her mom . . . it scared me."

"What did she say about Estelle?"

"She said she was just like her."

"You mean, suicidal?"

"More than that, I think. She said that for years she'd hated her mother and never understood why. She used to feel terribly guilty about it, as if she had driven her mother crazy. She'd punished herself for that. She talked as if Jay and the breakdown were somehow part of the punishment. But this summer, when she was in therapy, her shrink gave her Pentothal and she remembered something about her mom. She wouldn't tell me what it was, just that it had terrified her at first. But now she said it didn't scare her anymore. Now she understood that she'd been punishing the wrong person."

"Who was the right person?"

Marnee Thompson shook her head. "I don't know."

We sat in the living room for a while, drinking coffee. Marnee slowly calmed down, and once she got her bearings back she started asking *me* questions.

"How did you know that Ethan was with Kirsty?"

"Stein said Kirsty planned to see him this weekend." I gave Marnee a monitory look. "You knew that, didn't you?"

She ducked her head. "I knew a lot of things," she said in

a whisper. "I just couldn't . . . I was afraid to tell you. Except for Jay, I mean."

The girl looked up guiltily. "Did you talk to him? To Jay?"

"We had some words."

"What did he say about me? Something ugly?"

She flushed as if she already knew what Stein had said, as if he'd said it before and it had come back to her.

"Don't worry about him, Marnee. Guys like Stein aren't worth the time."

"I'd like to believe that." She stared at me for a long moment. "Are you going to stay here tonight?"

"I'll probably get a motel room by the airport. I have to fly back to Cincinnati tomorrow, early."

"You could stay," the girl said shyly. "I want you to stay. I could use the company."

"I can't, Marnee. I'd like to, but I can't."

She ducked her head. "Okay," she whispered. "I understand."

But she didn't understand. She thought I was rejecting her because of what Stein told me, and there was no way short of spending the night to prove that I wasn't.

It was a sad way to end it. But she had the resources to survive. Her friend didn't.

As I went out the door I told her that I'd call her, when I had some news about Kirsty.

10

███

I caught a cab to O'Hare and checked in at the airport Hilton. If the bars had been open, I might not have bothered with the room. But the lounges were shut, and I needed a place to sit and think. I also needed a phone.

The room was clean and featureless, with a view of the snowy runways, still busy with mail and parcel traffic even at that hour of the night. I took a hot shower, ordered some coffee up from room service, then phoned Delta reservations and booked a seat on their first flight to Cincinnati at seven in the morning. After the busboy arrived with the coffee, I called Phil Pearson.

Pearson must have been used to late-night calls. Either that or he was expecting trouble, because he sounded fully alert when he answered the phone. There was no easy way to break the news, so I just told him outright—at least as much of it as I understood. He didn't say a word as I went through his kids' bizarre history—his own history. When I finished, the silence at the other end was so profound that I thought he'd gone off the line.

"Pearson?" I said. "Are you still there?"

"I'm here," the man said in an awful voice.

"Look, I know this is a terrible shock. But there are some things that have to be done immediately if we're going to prevent a tragedy."

"I'm listening."

"Ethan and Kirsten were still in Chicago as of early last night. I'm not completely sure where they've headed, but it's possible that they're going to Cincinnati."

"To find this man, this convict?"

I said, "Yes. They've had at least four or five hours on the road, which would put them south of Indianapolis, almost to the Ohio line. If we alert the Ohio State Patrol and the Cincinnati police, we might be able to stop them before they get in trouble."

"Stop them, how?" the man said in the same deadened voice. "With guns?"

"Of course not. We could arrange to have them detained as missing persons."

"You said my son had a pistol, didn't you? What makes you think he'll stop for anyone?"

He had a point, but he'd also made one. "Someone will have to stop him," I said.

"I don't want the police!" Pearson said, his voice rising. "My children aren't criminals. *I'm* not a criminal."

It was an odd thing to say under the circumstances. But he was badly upset, and it was already clear that he felt personally responsible for his children's problems. And more than a little embarrassed by them.

"I don't want Kirsten or Ethan hurt," he said in a cooler voice. "I don't want anyone hurt."

"Then let me notify the police."

"What exactly would you say?"

"Standard missing persons reports. I don't have to go into detail."

It was precisely what he wanted to hear.

"Do it, then," he said resignedly. "But don't volunteer anything more than necessary. If Kirsty and Ethan are going to survive this—if the family is going to survive this—it's essential that they know I still love them."

He said it with great feeling. But he was saying it to the wrong person. At least that's the way it sounded to me—like a plea for approval.

* * *

After finishing with Pearson, I made the necessary calls to a friend I knew with the State Police and to Al Foster at the CPD. I phoned Brandt Scheuster, too, leaving a message on his machine. By then, it was almost three.

I lay down on the bed and tried to sleep, but the coffee had kicked in. Anyway I knew I was going to have to get up again in a few hours. Clicking on the reading light above the bed I picked Ethan Pearson's manila folder up from the nightstand. The clippings fell out on the bedclothes. A dozen of them, yellowed with age.

I gathered them together, sorted them by date, and read through them one by one. The first clipping was from the September 5, 1976, edition of the *Enquirer*. It was a short article, two paragraphs long, detailing Estelle Pearson's disappearance.

INDIAN HILL WOMAN REPORTED
MISSING

Estelle Pearson, of 3 Woodbine Lane, Indian Hill, has been reported missing by her husband, Dr. Philip Pearson. Mrs. Pearson disappeared on the afternoon of September 3, after failing to show up for a doctor's appointment in Clifton.

Mrs. Pearson has been ill for some time, and it is feared that she may have overmedicated herself or is in some way incapacitated by her illness . . .

A brief description of the woman followed, along with a number to call if Estelle Pearson was found.

The next article appeared two days later. It was considerably more detailed and its tone was grim.

INDIAN HILL WOMAN FEARED
DEAD

Indian Hill police have launched an extensive search for Estelle Pearson, wife of Dr. Philip Pearson. Mrs. Pearson, 34, was reported missing by her husband on September 3, when she failed to return home after missing an appointment with Dr. Sheldon Sacks, a Clifton psychiatrist.

Mrs. Pearson has a long history of emotional problems and has been recently hospitalized for depression. It is feared that she may have taken her own life . . .

There was a small photo of the woman with the article. It was difficult to tell much from the newspaper halftone, but she looked like a pretty woman with bee-stung lips and a thin, angular, careworn face.

There were several more paragraphs over the next week, reporting the lack of progress in the Pearson case. And then the big one—the front-page story—on September 14.

INDIAN HILL WOMAN FOUND DEAD
ESTELLE PEARSON, APPARENT SUICIDE

The body of Estelle Pearson, of 3 Woodbine Lane, Indian Hill, was discovered late last night in the Great Miami River by two fishermen, Claude Carter of Delhi and Sam Livingston of Terrace Park. Mrs. Pearson, wife of Indian Hill psychiatrist Dr. Philip Pearson, has been missing since September 3.

The fishermen found Mrs. Pearson's body floating in an estuary of the Miami River, east of Miamitown. She had been in the water for at least ten days, according to Hamilton County Assistant Coroner Dr. Jeffrey Hillman. Pending an inquest, the Cincinnati Police Department is reserving comment on the cause of death. Foul play is not suspected.

Mrs. Pearson was first reported missing on September 3, after she failed to show up for an appointment with her psychiatrist, Dr. Sheldon Sacks of Clifton. There was concern at the time that she might have taken her own life. Dr. Sacks has indicated that Mrs. Pearson was hospitalized for de-

pression in June and on several other
occasions over the past ten years.

Mrs. Pearson, née Estelle Frieberg,
was 34 years old, a Cincinnati native,
and a graduate of Miami University
and the University of Cincinnati
Medical School. She is survived by
her husband, Dr. Philip Pearson, a
psychiatrist, and her two children,
Ethan, 10, and Kirsten, 6.

There was a death notice the following day, an obit with a
large picture of Estelle, taken when she was younger and
less troubled. And about a week later one final paragraph
detailing the findings of the coroner's inquest. Not surprisingly the coroner had ruled Estelle Pearson's death a suicide by drowning. There was no hint that she might have
been murdered.

Ethan's drawing was the last item in the folder. After I'd
read the brief history of his mother's life and death, the line
sketch looked less like an anonymous bogeyman to me and
more like a picture of how the kid himself must have felt
following the suicide—jagged, frightened, full of rage.

Skimming through his chapbooks only confirmed that
feeling. I didn't read all four of them—the poems were
mostly of a piece, anyway. Sentimental elegies for his
mother and his lost childhood. Angry jeremiads about social
ills, full of violent adolescent gripes and not so veiled refer-
ences to his father and other father figures—men who said
they knew best but constantly let Ethan down. There was a
love poem dedicated to his wife, and one very odd poem
called "The Anniversary."

When we meet again, as we will
We'll talk about that last fall day
And the smell of burning leaves
The sunlight on the lawn
The sound of the wind in the trees
Where I met you.

Seeing is a meeting, after all
Even from a high window
Myself a child of ten taking leave
Of her in the smell of burning leaves
The sunlight on the lawn
The sound of the wind in the dark trees
Where you waited

We'll meet again where you waited
In the trees, in the burning,
in the darkness, in the sound of the wind
And the child will be there too
In the darkness where you waited
A knife blade in the darkness where he's waited
To commemorate this anniversary.

I wouldn't have bet money on it, but I had the feeling that the poem was addressed to Estelle Pearson's murderer. Even if it wasn't, it had a nightmarish resonance to it. Just the thing to drowse over.

11

I didn't get much sleep, maybe three hours. Enough to leave me logy on the flight back to Cincinnati. In a way it was a blessing to be that tired. I didn't have enough energy to get scared about the plane ride.

We landed at Cincinnati International around nine, having lost an hour on the way back. After a cup of coffee at the airport cafeteria I picked up the car in short-term parking and drove to town.

It was a mild, blue December morning. A bit of snow from the previous day's storm still laced the hillsides along the expressway, in the crannies that the sun hadn't yet touched. It would melt within the hour. The day was that warm, like false spring.

I stopped at the office first—to phone the State Patrol and Al Foster at CPD. The grey Volare hadn't been spotted, although Al had managed to get a Kentucky plate number and registration. The car was registered to Hedda Pearson. The address she'd given was 1245 Hidden Fork Road, in Ft. Thomas, Kentucky. There was a phone number on the registration.

I dialed the number and got the manager at The Bluegrass Motel and Motor Court. The name Bluegrass Motel rang a bell, but it wasn't until after we'd begun talking that I remembered that the last of Ethan's postcards was addressed from the place.

The manager, a man named Wilson, was officiously polite in the bow-and-scrape tradition of southern hospitality. I asked him if Ethan Pearson had checked in or out, and he said neither. The Pearsons had left town, but their room was paid up through the end of the month and he expected them back soon. I told him who I was, gave him my phone number, and asked him to call immediately if Ethan did come back. I made it sound important, so Wilson would feel important. He said he would surely call.

I called the Pearsons next—to see if they'd heard from their wandering children. Louise Pearson answered the phone.

"We haven't heard a word, Mr. Stoner." She sounded exhausted, but then she and her husband had had a rough night. "Phil's worked himself into quite a state. This business about the police . . . it would help if you could come out and talk to him. Give him a sense that he's participating in the process and not just sitting back and letting it happen around him. It's the feeling of helplessness that's getting to him—getting to all of us. It . . . well, it stirs up bad memories."

I'd read about those memories the night before. Up to that moment it hadn't hit me that Pearson had been down this road before—waiting for the police to discover what had happened to someone he loved, someone self-destructively crazy. The woman didn't make the connection explicit, but the change in her tone of voice—the change from the backbiting bitterness of the previous day to genuine concern for her husband—was itself telling.

"All right," I told her. "I can make it out there in about an hour."

"Bless you," she said.

There were several Mercedeses parked in the Pearson driveway, when I pulled up around ten-thirty. Two of them had physician's plates. The other one had a bag from Saks in the backseat. I walked around to the front of the house and knocked on the door.

A smart-looking woman with snow-white hair answered. She was in her sixties, immaculately dressed in a Chanel suit and pearls.

"Yes? What can I do for you?" she said coolly.

"My name is Stoner. I'm here to see Dr. Pearson."

Her blue eyes lost their "No Vendors" look. "You're the detective, aren't you?"

"Yes."

"I'm Cora Pearson," she said, holding out her hand and withdrawing it before I could shake with her. "I'm Philip's mother. Please come in."

I followed her down the hall to the grey sitting room. The woman walked as if she were balancing a book on her head, which was probably the way she'd been taught.

Louise Pearson was sitting in one of the red armchairs by the fireplace. She smiled familiarly when she saw me come in.

"It was so good of you to do this, Mr. Stoner," she said, smiling gratefully.

"I wish I had something good to report."

She made a gesture with her hands, as if she were shushing a heckler. "Believe me, just talking to Phil will help."

She glanced at the mother, who was standing by the sideboard, taking the conversation in over her shoulder. The older woman nodded as if she agreed with Louise.

"You've met my mother-in-law, Cora Pearson?"

"Yes."

Louise Pearson stood up a little shakily and started across the room to the door. The mother-in-law touched Louise's left hand sympathetically as she passed, and Louise smiled at her.

"It'll be all right," Cora Pearson whispered.

"I'm going to go see about Phil," Louise said. "He's in with Shelley right now. They should be done soon."

"Shelley?" I asked.

"Sheldon Sacks. He's Phil's best friend. Sort of a family counselor. He's been seeing Kirsty, too. I mean—he saw her over the summer."

She didn't say it, but he'd also been Estelle Pearson's psychiatrist. I'd seen his name in the newspaper clippings.

"It might help if I could talk to Sacks about Kirsten," I said.

The woman bit her lip. "They don't usually talk about their cases. It would breach their code of ethics."

There was a hint of sarcasm in the way she said "code of ethics." But it was slight compared to the way she'd spoken about her husband's profession the day before. Everything about her had changed slightly from the day before, even her looks. She hadn't made up her eyes or mouth, and she was dressed down in jeans and a white blouse. The sunlight pouring through the undraped window washed her complexion out even further, making her seem younger and more vulnerable. In any light she was strikingly good-looking.

Louise left the room. The elder Mrs. Pearson stared after her with concern.

"She doesn't deserve this," she said in a bitter voice. "She's been such a rock." The woman looked down at the silver tea service as if it were all that remained of the family fortune. "None of us deserve this."

I wasn't sure she was talking to me, so I didn't reply.

Mrs. Pearson poured coffee and, as an afterthought, asked me if I'd like a cup.

"Yes," I said. "I've been living on the stuff for the last thirty hours."

She didn't look impressed.

"There is something you should know," she said, handing me the cup.

"Yes?"

"My son has a heart condition. He doesn't like to dwell on it. He resents illness of any kind, as most doctors do. But the fact is he was hospitalized once already, this past summer when Kirsten acted up. If this current tumult doesn't end soon, the children may succeed in killing him."

She said it as if that was their intention.

"I'm doing what I can to end this, Mrs. Pearson," I said. "But unless we can find them . . ."

She threw a hand at me. "They'll be found. They want to be found. And if no one comes to look for them, they'll make their presences known. Attention is all they want. It's all they've ever wanted. I know whereof I speak. After Estelle's death I had the two of them on my hands for almost a year, until Louise relieved me of the burden. They were spoiled then, and they're spoiled now. No one's life goes smoothly. Do you think my life has gone smoothly? No one made that promise. One picks up and continues."

She sounded like she was reading from that book she was carrying on her head. I could imagine what life had been like at Grandma's.

"Self-indulgence is a sin. Harboring resentment against your father is a sin. My son has sacrificed his life for other people. First when his own father died. And then when Estelle killed herself. He's owed a little peace, a little simple gratitude."

Her face flushed and she turned away. I thought she was overcome with anger until I realized that someone else had entered the room. A paunchy, balding man in a rumpled business suit was standing in the doorway, looking vaguely embarrassed.

"Are you Stoner?" he asked.

I nodded.

"I'm Shelley Sacks." He came in and shook with me.

"Louise'll be along in a minute. She's still talking to Phil."
He glanced at Cora Pearson. "Are you all right, Cora?"

"Fine," the woman said without turning toward him.

The man arched an eyebrow skeptically. He had a round face, round mouth, snub nose, round blue eyes, a round bald spot on the back of his head—like a kid's drawing of Dad. His roly-poly paunchiness made him look younger than he probably was, judging by the grey in his hair.

"Has there been any news?" he asked me.

"None."

"I guess I don't have to tell you that this isn't a good situation," he said grimly.

"Do you have any suggestions?"

"I'm not a detective. But from what I've been told I think it would be a good idea to find this man Ethan has fixated on —as quickly as possible."

"That's what I intended to do."

"I think you might keep a watch on this house. Perhaps on Stelle's grave. On places Ethan associates with her."

"Like your office?"

The man looked surprised—unpleasantly so, as if he didn't like surprises.

"What do you mean?"

"You were Estelle's psychiatrist, weren't you?"

He nodded slowly. "How did you know that?"

I told him about Ethan's clippings.

"That's very sad," he said thoughtfully, as if he found it more interesting than sad. "Obsessions are always sad. They trail the past endlessly, like beggar children."

"Obsessions aren't always this dangerous, are they?"

"No. Usually they only damage the one who has them. Ethan's case is special."

"This may be a stupid question, but is it possible he really *did* see someone on the day his mother died?"

"Quite possible. Someone on the street. In a car, in a newspaper photo. It isn't the seeing that's at issue. It's the connection he made to his mother's suicide."

"No question it was suicide?"

He shook his head, no. "Estelle was a deeply disturbed woman. I believe she was fated to end her own life."

I winced at the words—at the echo of Kirsten's words—wondering if Sacks was where she first heard them. It was certainly a convenient way to rationalize your failures.

"I didn't mean to sound cynical," he said, as if he had read my mind. "But there *is* a fatality to mental life, to certain disorders in particular. We can ameliorate schizophrenia, palliate. But we can't cure. In all too many cases, we can't even help."

"In Kirsten's case . . . ?" I asked.

"I don't know," he said. "Obviously it depends on the next few days. She has a fresh insight into her problems. She's regressed at the moment. But if she can channel what she's learned . . ."

The man was being vague, and he knew it.

"It's difficult for me to talk about this," he said apologetically. "You do know that Kirsten is my patient?"

I nodded.

"Let me just say that I'm not without hope."

"That's swell, Doctor, but hope's not going to help me find her."

He smiled. "It may help her find herself."

Louise Pearson came back into the room. All three of us turned toward her, and she flushed prettily, as if she was embarrassed by the attention.

"Phil would like to speak with you now, Mr. Stoner," she said.

"All right."

"We'll talk again," Sacks said, as if my hour was up.

I walked out into the hall. Louise led me to a closed door at the end of the corridor. She paused outside.

"Phil's suffering from certain health problems," she said. "Your mother-in-law told me."

"She shouldn't have," Louise said. But I had the feeling that she was relieved that I knew.

She knocked at the door, and Pearson said, "Come in."

The woman patted me on the shoulder. "I'd like to speak with you again before you leave."

I nodded and went into the room.

It was a study lined with bookshelves and mullioned windows. Pearson was sitting on a leather wingback chair in the center of the room, behind a glass desk with brass-sawhorse legs. Even at a distance I could tell that he was in bad shape. His face was drained of color, except for the dark circles beneath his eyes. His hand trembled when he waved me toward a chair in front of him.

"I'm glad you're here," he said.

"I'm afraid I don't have anything to report yet."

He nodded stupidly. His blue eyes had lost their piercing intensity. His speech was dulled too, as if he were heavily tranquilized.

"The police . . . ?"

"I reported Ethan and Kirsten as missing persons. That's all the police know."

I thought that would please him, but it didn't.

"I've given you the wrong impression," he said, looking pained. "I do that sometimes."

He tried to draw himself up in his chair, grimaced, and slumped back again.

"I want you to find my children. I don't care what it costs or what it takes. I was wrong to react the way I did last night. I was thinking of myself, of my own feelings. You know now that my first wife, Estelle, committed suicide.

The thought of having that tragedy dredged up again and publicized . . . it unnerved me."

"You don't have to apologize."

"I feel that I do. I feel that I owe you an explanation of why I withheld certain facts about Kirsten and Ethan. It was not because I don't love them. On the contrary, I'm afraid that I've loved them too much." The man blushed furiously, as if his love for his children was shameful. "When you lose someone you hold dear, when you lose that person to irrational violence, you hold even more tightly to those who are left behind. I have done that to my children. In trying to protect them I have smothered them. Now I'm afraid that it's my fate to lose them too—to lose all that I love."

Pearson's lips trembled violently.

"It is my failure as a father that I was trying to conceal from you," he said with effort. "It was my failure as a husband that made me a coward."

I shouldn't have said anything at all. But I did. "I think you may be shouldering too much blame."

He shook his head. "You don't know. The children do."

This time I didn't answer him.

"You have a plan of some kind?" Pearson asked.

"To try to find the man from the newspaper before Ethan and Kirsty do. The police will be looking for their car. We'll notify local hotels, hospices, and hospitals. Someone should spot them soon."

"Good. I've canceled my appointments for the week. I'll be here if they decide to come home."

"Do they have any special friends in town?"

"I don't think so," Pearson said. "At least I don't think Kirsty does—she's always been so shy. I haven't seen Ethan in some years."

Pearson stared forlornly at his desk, as if he was struck by the pathos of what he'd just said.

"Find them, Mr. Stoner," he said heavily. "Bring them back. Give me the chance to make amends."

"I'll do all I can," I told him.

After finishing with Pearson I went back down the hall to the living room. Sacks and Cora Pearson had left, and Louise Pearson was sitting alone by the fire. She stood up as I came through the door.

"Thank you again, Mr. Stoner," she said warmly. "For everything."

"I'm working for you. No thanks are necessary."

"Thanks anyway for sticking with us, especially after the mixed signals I gave you yesterday. I was very wrong about Kirsty. I thought she was recovering. Maybe she would have if Ethan hadn't shown up. He's always had a powerful effect on her, although he's never managed to talk her into doing anything this stupid before."

From the disgust in her voice, it was obvious that she had had her fill of her stepson long before Sunday night.

"Ethan's given you trouble in the past?"

"He's been nothing but trouble," Louise Pearson said wearily. "He's never forgiven Phil for Estelle's death. And he never will, in spite of Phil's efforts to bribe him back into the family."

"Your husband gives Ethan money?"

"Since he was a kid. It's all that's left between them—the blood money that Phil gives him every month."

"Why do you call it blood money?" I asked.

She smiled. "I meant the term loosely, though in some way I suppose Phil is compensating Ethan for Estelle's death. And keeping this stupid obsession alive."

"Has Ethan ever been in trouble with the police before now?"

"He hasn't the guts for that," Louise Pearson said with crude satisfaction. "Ethan's not much of a doer, but he's a ferocious, bullying talker. Witness how he twisted Kirsty around his finger."

"I don't think it was Ethan alone that led Kirsten to this," I said. "She's had a rotten year. And last week an important relationship went awry."

"What kind of relationship?"

"A romantic one."

The woman looked surprised. "She was having an affair?"

"She was trying to. There's some question about whether she succeeded. The man . . . he's an older man. A teacher at the university."

"You didn't tell Phil that, did you?" Louise Pearson said with alarm.

"No. I didn't tell him much of anything. He didn't look as if he could take it."

"He can't," Louise Pearson said flatly. "Especially that."

The woman took a step closer to me and I caught her sweet, powerful scent again.

"Mr. Stoner, if things should go wrong, please call me. I mean, before you talk to Phil. He'll need careful handling if Kirsten and Ethan land in real trouble."

She handed me a piece of stationery with a phone number on it.

"That's my private number here at the house. I've got a fairly busy social schedule. If I should be out, an answering service will know where to find me."

I told her I'd call when I had some news.

Leaning forward hesitantly the woman kissed me lightly on the cheek. It wasn't meant to be provocative, but it had that effect on me. It must not have felt right to Louise Pearson either, for she pulled away at once.

"I'm sorry," she said, reddening. "I'm feeling a little frail at the moment. And then I'm a physical sort of person, anyway."

"It's all right," I said. "I liked it."

She laughed feebly.

"Go," she said, waving her hand down the hall to the front door. "Before I make a fool out of myself."

12

From the Pearson house I drove downtown to the main branch of the Public Library on Vine Street.

The first-floor periodical room was relatively empty that early on a Monday morning—a couple of earnest-looking college students, a few old-age pensioners, and two or three bums, who'd come in out of the cold and fallen asleep on scattered benches, their shopping bags of belongings rolled up for pillows. I skirted the snoozing bums and got a brief workout running down a fleet-footed librarian, who kept turning corners in front of me as I tracked her through the stacks. Once I ran the woman to ground I asked her for advice on where to begin looking for Ethan Pearson's photograph.

"If the article you're interested in was from a paper purchased in the Ft. Thomas area, you should begin with the *Kentucky Post*," she said. "It has the largest circulation in that part of northern Kentucky. You should also try the *Louisville Courier-Journal* and the *Cincinnati Enquirer*, of course. Many northern Kentuckians read the *Enquirer*."

"Do you keep back issues in circulation?" I asked.

"For seven days, then they're recorded on microfiche."

She pointed me to the newspaper stacks and told me to come back if I needed to use a microfiche machine.

I found the Wednesday, December 16, edition of the *Kentucky Post* and read through it slowly. The court news was in the local section, but there were no photos or paragraphs on released felons. I tried the *Courier-Journal* next, without any luck. Then the *Enquirer*. Ethan's mystery man wasn't there—or if he was I wasn't seeing him.

I was very tired, and concentrating on the newsprint was maddeningly difficult. I was worried that the fatigue would cause me to overlook something—and even more worried that Ethan's photo didn't exist. If that was the case I'd have nothing to go on, save the chance that the Volare would be spotted by the cops. That is, if the Pearson kids had come back to Cincinnati, which was no ironclad cinch.

I sat, brooding, at the library table for a full minute, before it dawned on me that the photo didn't have to be in Wednesday's papers. Ethan could have spotted the picture in an older newspaper—a paper from the day before or the day before that. Or it could have been that he'd gone down to the library like I had, and combed through months of back issues. Years of them.

That way lay madness.

I dragged myself to my feet and returned to the stacks. The Tuesday the 15th and Monday the 14th editions of the *Post* were the last two papers on the shelves. Anything before them meant sitting in front of a microfiche machine for hours.

I tried the Tuesday paper first and found nothing.

Then I tried the Monday paper—and got lucky. On the fourth page of the Monday the 14th *Post,* the court news page, there was a tiny mugshot of a middle-aged black man. According to the paragraph beneath the photo his name was Herbert Talmadge, and he'd been released from Lexington the week before on parole, after serving thirteen years of a twenty-to-life sentence for the rape and murder of a Kentucky nurse. The killing had occurred in Newport in December, 1976, and it must have been particularly brutal or they wouldn't have printed Talmadge's picture.

Talmadge was clearly a bad character, and that bothered me. But the newspaper picture itself, the tiny mugshot, was just as unsettling. I sat there and stared at it dumbly for a full minute, wondering whether my lack of sleep and the general weirdness of the Pearson case were combining to unhinge me. Simply put, Herbert Talmadge had the same face as the man in Ethan Pearson's drawing—the same V-shaped goatee, the same pointed chin, the same peppery hair and slanted, menacing eyes.

Even allowing for the crudity of a ten-year-old's drawing skills, the resemblance was close enough to give *me* a feeling of déjà vu. It must have scared hell out of Ethan Pearson. What I couldn't imagine was where a ten-year-old kid had run across the likes of Herbert Talmadge. He *had* to have seen him somewhere, because the likeness he'd drawn was just too damn close to be coincidental.

I made a dozen copies of the article on a Xerox machine. Then I found a phone in the lobby and called Al Foster at CPD.

"I need another favor, Al," I said. "Get me a last known address on an ex-con named Herbert Talmadge. He just did thirteen years in Lexington for rape and murder."

"This have something to do with your missing persons?" he asked.

"It might."

"I'll see what I can turn up."

"One more thing?"

"We're here to serve and protect you, Harry."

"Can you dig up a file on Estelle Pearson?" I spelled the name for him. "She committed suicide in September, 1976. I'd like to see the examining officer's notes and the coroner's report."

"What's this one for?"

I didn't tell him, but I was curious to see if Talmadge's name popped up anywhere in the case as a witness or a bystander. He had to be connected to the woman or to Ethan in some way, even if it was only by chance.

* * *

I went back to my office in the Riorley Building and managed to sneak in a couple of hours of sleep on the couch before the phone woke me around one p.m. At least my eyes felt better. I couldn't speak for the rest of my body—it wasn't speaking to me.

The phone call was from Sid McMasters of the CPD. "Al Foster told me to give you a buzz," Sid said. "We got a previous address for Herbert Talmadge."

I picked up a pencil and said, "Go ahead."

"Sixty-seven fifty-five West McMicken. Al said to tell you that Talmadge was a mental case. In and out of Rollman's before he got busted."

Rollman's was a state psychiatric hospital in East Walnut Hills.

"This McMicken address is from '76?"

"Yeah. Al tried to get in touch with the Newport cops to get a current address. But the P.O. in Newport said Talmadge hadn't reported since his release."

"So he's in violation?"

"He will be if he doesn't come in before this Friday. Al also said for you to pick up a report he dug up for you. I'll leave it at the front desk."

"Be right over."

Before I left I called Louise Pearson at the number she'd given me.

"I need you to ask your husband a couple of questions."

"You've made some progress, then?" she said hopefully.

"A little. I've got a name, at least."

"What name?"

"Herbert Talmadge. I think he's the guy that Ethan and Kirsty are looking for."

The woman went off the line briefly. When she came

back on she said, "Could you repeat that? I want to write this down."

"Herbert Talmadge," I said again. "Ask your husband if he recognizes the name. You might also ask him if he worked at Rollman's hospital in the mid-seventies. I'll drop Talmadge's picture off to you later this evening."

"I'm afraid I'm going to the club this evening," the woman said apologetically. "Goddamn cocktail party. I was planning to cancel, but Phil insisted I attend. Perhaps you could meet me in the bar for a drink afterward. Say, around nine?"

"All right."

She gave me the address of the country club and promised to ask Pearson about Talmadge.

After hanging up on Louise I went down to the Fifth Street garage, found my car, and drove over to CPD headquarters on Ezzard Charles. I double-parked in front of a police cruiser, ran in, and picked up the sealed envelope that Sid McMasters had left for me at the front desk. I didn't open the envelope until I got back in the car.

A photo of Estelle Pearson's body, taken at the scene of her death, was the first thing I pulled out. I was sorry I'd looked. If Ethan or Kirsten had seen what was pictured on that riverbank, it was no wonder they'd been severely traumatized. I stuffed the grisly snapshot back in the envelope and tossed it on the front seat. The police and coroner's reports would have to wait—I just didn't have the stomach to go through them at that moment.

Herbert Talmadge's last known address on West McMicken was only about five minutes north of the police station, off Central Parkway in the slum neighborhood called Over-the-Rhine. As far as I knew Over-the-Rhine had always been a slum—crabbed, dismal, little streets lined with brick tenements and abandoned warehouses. A place for German and Irish Catholic immigrants to live at the turn-of-the-last-century. A place for poor blacks and Appalachians to live until the turn-of-the-next.

An elderly black man and a young black woman were sitting on folding chairs in front of 6755. A couple of children were playing in a patch of snow on a nearby stoop. From the way the kids kept glancing at the man and woman, I figured they were more or less tethered there, waiting for the big folks to call them in. I parked across the street from the brownstone, got out into the sun, and crossed over to the shaded side of McMicken.

The man and woman watched me closely. The kids dropped their snowballs and stared.

"I'm looking for somebody who used to live here," I said to the old man.

The woman snorted disgustedly and turned her chair away from me, as if she was blocking me from her mind.

The man said, "You with the Welfare?"

" 'Course he with the Welfare, foo," the young woman said over her shoulder. She looked rather pretty in profile, in spite of the huff she was in. Pretty and tough and proud.

The man had a porkpie hat tilted back on his head and a checked overcoat wrapped around his body. His skin was very black, and his yellowed eyes had the rheumy, unfocused look of old age. His voice was deep and deliberate, while the woman's was all speed and contempt.

"I'm not with the Welfare, and I'm not a cop. I'm just a guy looking for somebody."

"Who'd that be?" the old man said.

"Don' you talk to him, Uncle. Don't you say nothin'," the young woman snapped.

"His name is Herbert Talmadge. He used to live here back in the seventies."

"Sho," the man said. "I remember Herbie." He looked at the girl. "You 'member Herbie, Lorraine."

Lorraine continued to stare indignantly off into space.

"Ain't seen Herbie in ten, twelve years," the man said.

"Ain't none of my business," Lorraine said in a singsong voice. "Ain't none of yours neither."

"Don' know where he went to," he said, ignoring her. "Herbie had him a temper, though. I can tell you that."

"He was crazy," the girl said suddenly and decisively, as if that was her only word on the subject.

"She's right," the man said. "Herbie *was* crazy. Think he might have had him some trouble with the law."

"He was in jail," I said. "He was released last week."

"That so? And you huntin' for him, huh?"

I nodded.

"Tell you what. You go look up some of his old girlfriends, 'cause that's where Herbie gone to. He liked the ladies."

"Anybody in particular?"

"Woman who used to own this house, Miz Thelma Jackson. He liked her pretty good. You go on and talk to her."

"Know where I can find her?"

"She moved out to Carthage, I think. Don' come by here no more."

I reached in my pocket for my wallet and started to take a ten out. The old man looked offended.

"Ain't no call for that," he said. "We just talkin' like folks. Don' pay folks for talkin', do you?"

"Thanks," I said.

As I walked back across the street to my car I heard the girl say to him, "You *is* a foo," in a loud, contemptuous voice.

13

I stopped at a phone booth in Clifton and looked up Thelma Jackson in the phone book. I didn't find a "Thelma" proper, but there were several listings for T. Jackson, and one of them lived on Anthony Wayne in Carthage.

I dialed the number and a woman with a deep, friendly voice answered.

"Thelma Jackson?" I asked.

"That's me, sugar. Who's callin'?"

"My name is Stoner, Ms. Jackson. I was wondering if I could talk to you."

"You sellin' something, sugar?" she said cheerfully.

"I'm not selling anything. I'm looking for somebody you used to know."

"Now who'd that be?"

"Herbert Talmadge."

There was a momentary silence on the line.

"You a police officer, ain't you?" she said in a slightly less cheerful voice, as if the mention of Talmadge had knocked some of the fun out of her.

"I'm a private detective."

She laughed. "Like Magnum?"

"Like Magnum. I'm just looking to find Talmadge, Ms. Jackson. I'm not going to arrest him."

"Shoot! It wouldn't bother me any if you did arrest him. Herbie was a mean little son of a gun. But the truth is I ain't seen him in going on fourteen years. Don't want to see him again, neither."

"You think I could come out and talk to you about him? I promise not to take much of your time."

"I guess that'd be all right," she said, "seeing how I ain't never met no detective before."

I could smell Carthage as soon as I got to North Bend Road. The juniper scent of gin, the cooked fruit smell of brandy. The huge brick smokestacks of National Distillers, on the south side of Carthage, left liquor on its breath every afternoon.

Thelma Jackson's house was near the distillery, where the liquor smell was thickest. Perhaps that was what accounted for her good humor. You could see the smokestacks from her front yard. You could also hear the traffic on the express-way, below the retaining wall on the opposite side of Anthony Wayne.

She was sitting on the porch of her bungalow when I pulled up. A plump, sixtyish black woman with short grey hair and a pretty brown face. She was wearing a housedress with a heavy knit sweater over the shoulders.

"You're the detective, ain't you?" she called out as I walked into the small front yard.

"Yep."

"You don't look like Magnum," she said with mock disappointment. "You ain't got no moustache. You big enough though. And good-looking."

She gave me a bold look, for a sixty-year-old woman.

"Come on inside. Too damn cold out here."

Thelma Jackson got up, and I followed her through the front door into a prim living room filled with floral-print furniture. I sat down on an overstuffed couch. A vase full of artificial flowers sat on a coffee table in front of me. The room smelled sweetly of air freshener and the brandy smell of the distillery.

The woman tugged at her girdle before settling on a chair across from me. "Why you all looking for Herbie?"

"Somebody hired me to find him."

"In other words, it ain't none of my business, right?"

I smiled at her. "It isn't a criminal matter—I can tell you that."

"Have to be criminal if it come to that nigger. Either that or he got himself locked up in the crazy house again."

The woman's pretty face turned sober-looking. "Herbie wasn't never right in the head. He'd fool you, though, being so quiet all the time."

"What was his problem?"

"Got no idea. He had brains. Been in the service a couple of years, I think. And he was good-looking, too. Had him plenty of women."

Thelma Jackson glanced at me and laughed.

"You heard somethin' about him and me, didn't you?"

Whether she'd read it in my face or just guessed that that was the gossip which had led me to her house, I didn't know. "I heard you used to be his landlady, yes."

"Heard more than that," she said shrewdly. "But it ain't so. I never did take up with Herbie Talmadge, 'cept once. And that once was enough."

The woman yanked at her girdle again. "Never was no prude. I like men. Always will. But Herbie . . ." She shook her head decisively. "Uhm-uh. Girl could get killed by a man like that. Isn't that what he went to jail for—messing with some woman over in Newport?"

"Yes. Rape and murder."

"Being with Herbie," she said in a dead serious voice, "was always what you call 'rape and murder.' You lucky if you *didn't* die, you spent a night with him. Police had him in and out of Rollman's 'bout every month 'cause he done some woman wrong. Sent him there myself, once. They couldn't do nothing to change him though. He wanted to change. Used to cry about it when he got high. But the doctors said there just wasn't nothing they could do for him."

"When was the last time you saw him, Ms. Jackson?"

She squinted her eyes, thinking back. "Seems like that would be the summer of '76. Right before he moved to Newport. He got out of Rollman's in the spring and started taking up with some white girl. Herbie followed that ofay 'round like a dog on a chain. Only time I ever seen him act that way."

"Do you remember what this woman looked like?"

"Not much. She never come in the house. She was always waiting on him out in the car. She'd honk and he come running. She had blond hair, I 'member that. Might be she was a nurse, 'cause I 'member she wore a white uniform once. Herbie just crazy about that ofay woman."

"You don't know her name, do you?"

She shook her head. "Didn't want to know. Didn't want to have nothing to do with Herbie, after that one time."

"Is there anyone who might know? A friend of his from back then?"

"Herbie didn't have no friends," the woman said with a dry laugh. "He just have himself."

"Did he have a job?"

"Got him some money from the Vets, I think. Most times he got hard up, he'd just go on back to the hospital. Rest of the times he'd lay up in his room, stoned on them painkillers he got from the doctors."

"Finding him is important, Ms. Jackson. Is there anything else you can remember that would help me?"

"I can poke around," she said gamely. "See what I can dig up. Meantime, you check with that hospital. They gotta know something 'bout him, seeing how he was practically a permanent guest."

* * *

I didn't take Thelma's advice about checking at Rollman's. Not that it wasn't a good idea. I just knew from
experience that no one at a hospital was going to talk to a
private cop without word from somebody higher up. So I
went searching for that word at Sheldon Sacks' office on
Burnett, a couple blocks east of the psychiatric hospital and
just a few blocks north of where I used to live in the
Delores.

Sacks' office was on the second floor of a duplex he shared
with another psychiatrist. There was a hall at the top of the
stairs, with office doors opening off it to the left and a small,
glassed-in receptionist's room to the right. I gave the secretary my name and she told me that she'd buzz Sacks when
his four o'clock appointment was up. In the meantime I
took a seat in a wainscoted waiting room, beside a couple of
middle-aged women who were doing their best to keep
from screaming.

Just sitting there made me queasy. When the secretary
finally called my name, I jumped. She led me back down
the hall to one of the office doors and knocked. Sacks called
out, "Come in."

"Sorry to have kept you waiting, Stoner," he said as I
came through the door.

He waved me over to a stuffed leather chair then sat
down behind a large desk. There was a half-empty box of
Kleenex on an end table by the chair. Half-full or half-
empty—I could never see the fucking difference.

There were a dozen Kleenex on the floor, as if his last
patient had had a real crying jag.

The room was paneled in oak and lined with bookshelves
on two walls. There was a psychiatrist's couch on the third
wall with a framed steamship floating above it. Sacks' desk
was on the far wall, in front of a bank of louvered windows.

Just enough sunlight was filtering through the slats to back-light his head and throw his face into shadow.

"What can I do for you?" he asked.

I told him about Herbert Talmadge. He listened intently, moving forward in his chair so that a bit of his round face came into the desk light.

"When did you say he was treated at Rollman's?"

"1976. Possibly earlier."

"That's odd," he said thoughtfully. "I think Phil did part of his residency at Rollman's, in '75."

"Perhaps he treated Talmadge?"

"It's possible," Sacks said, joining his hands.

I waited for him to say something more, but he didn't. He just sat there with his hands knitted together and a blank look on his face, as if he hadn't drawn any conclusions from what he'd said.

"You and Pearson are close friends?"

He nodded. "Since med school. He and Stelle and I were in the same graduating class."

"She was a psychiatrist, too?"

"She never started her internship. She married Phil in 1966 right after we graduated. She had Ethan at the end of that year."

"She didn't go back to school?"

He shook his head. "She wanted to, but her emotional problems made it impossible."

"She was never hospitalized at Rollman's, was she?"

"No. At Jewish and at Holmes."

He wasn't comfortable talking about the woman, and he wasn't trying to disguise it. Given the circumstances, his reticence irritated me.

"Is there a reason you don't want to talk to me about Estelle Pearson?" I said.

The man sighed. "No one likes to talk about his failures,

Mr. Stoner. Especially when that failure involves people whom you love."

He leaned back in his chair, tenting his fingers in front of his face. "It has been thirteen years since Estelle died, and in all those years I don't think a day has passed that I haven't thought about her. Estelle wasn't just my patient. She was my friend."

I was wrong about Sacks. It wasn't professional reticence, at all.

"I am sorry," I said.

"You have no reason to be. You're just doing your job. But for Philip and Louise and me, this is a very painful thing. A tragic thing."

"Pearson seems to blame himself for what's happened," I said.

"He has his reasons, Mr. Stoner," Sheldon Sacks said without elaborating.

I changed the subject back to Ethan and Kirsten. "The picture that Ethan drew in 1976 looks very much like this man Talmadge."

"Perhaps it was Talmadge," the doctor said. "Ethan may have visited his father at Rollman's. He may have seen Talmadge in the halls or on the grounds."

"Yes, but why would he associate the man with his mother's death?"

"Ethan was very close to Estelle. And she, to him. Right before her death Estelle went through an extended manic period, which lasted almost two months. During that time she appeared to regain a good deal of her energy and focus. To the boy it must have seemed as if she was recovering— that he himself had made a difference in her recovery, as in fact he probably did. The manic stage ended abruptly and the depression returned with a vengeance. Estelle's death following so hard upon that brief period of apparent recov-

ery made Ethan feel as if he had somehow failed his
mother. It was my feeling then, and it is my feeling now,
that his obsession is his way of making amends for letting his
mother down. He has sublimated his own guilt and pro-
jected it onto this man, Herbert Talmadge."

"But why Talmadge?"

"Why not?" Sacks said. "His face may have frightened
Ethan. It stuck in his memory. In his confusion over the loss
of his mother he made it the face of his own guilt."

It was neat and logical. But I wasn't sure I believed it. In
my experience people didn't generally remember anonymous faces in that kind of detail—not unless there was a
strong emotional spur to prod their imagination. Like a
loaded gun, or the threat of one.

I didn't debate it with him. I didn't feel confident enough
to debate. But I did ask him if he could arrange for me to
talk with the staff at Rollman's about Talmadge. And he said
that he would call them immediately.

Before leaving I asked one last question. It had bothered
me since Marnee Thompson had mentioned it, and although Kirsten was still his patient I asked him anyway.

"Kirsten told a friend of hers that you gave her some
Pentothal this summer while she was in therapy. Apparently the drug made her remember something about Estelle—something that really shook her up."

"But her memory wasn't about Estelle," the man said
with an open look of fascination. "It was about Philip."

"I don't suppose you'd like to tell me what it was?"

The open look vanished like a dent closing in dough.

"I guess not," I said.

"She's my patient, Mr. Stoner," Sacks said.

I nodded. "She may not be anyone's patient much longer,
Dr. Sacks."

But he didn't say anything.

14

I gave Sacks about half an hour to make his calls to Rollman's. At five-forty I walked across Burnett to the Rollman
grounds. Up in one of the barred third-story windows I
could see a bald man in a white hospital gown watching me
cross the lawn. His queer, drugged-looking face was lit
strangely by the last of the sunset. Even at that distance I
could see his dead eyes following me as I walked into the
shadows at the front of the building.

I wondered if I could remember that face in detail, a few
weeks or months from that moment. Maybe if I was an
impressionable ten-year-old kid, I could have. Maybe I
could have anyway.

From the front Rollman's looked like a high school—red-
brick facade, oblong windows with white trim and glass
double-doors. But the windows were barred and meshed,
and the doors had buzzers on them. I pressed one of the
buzzers and an orderly peered out.

"Visiting hours over, mister," he said.

"My name's Harry Stoner," I said. "Your director should
know who I am."

The orderly gave me a suspicious look, as if he thought I
might be an escapee. He closed the door and walked down
the hall. When he reappeared, the suspicion was gone from
his face.

"Come on," he said, holding the door open. "Dr. McCall
says you can go up."

I followed him down the tile hall. There were tall barred
windows at the end of it. The last daylight pouring through

them was so bright that both of us had to shield our eyes against the glare.

"You take this elevator up to three," he said, pointing to a grey elevator beside the windows. "Nurse upstairs, show you where to go."

I got in the elevator and pressed three. I hadn't noticed it in the lobby hall, but the elevator smelled ripely of disinfectant and stale, recirculated air.

The third floor was an administrative area, judging from the empty typing carrels off the elevator. I followed an arrow sign around a bend in the hallway to the Director's Office. An elderly nurse with grey hair and a stern, wrinkled face was sitting at a desk in front of the office door. A Norfolk pine decorated with tinsel and greeting cards sat on the floor beside her.

"You're Mr. Stoner?" she said, looking up at me.

I nodded.

"Dr. McCall will see you. Just go through there."

I went into the office. It was a large room, mostly taken up with file cabinets and bookshelves. A red-haired man with a horsey face, horn-rim glasses, and buck teeth was sitting behind a desk at the far wall. He was wearing a doctor's smock with a stethoscope hanging from one of the side pockets. His pale skin was lumpy with ancient acne scars. He fingered one of the lumps idly as I walked up to him.

"You're Stoner?" the man said in a businesslike voice.

"Yes."

"Sam McCall."

McCall motioned me to a wooden chair.

There was a manila folder on his desktop. He put two fingers on top of it as if he was taking its pulse.

"This is what you came for, I think," he said, jabbing the folder. "You know we're not supposed to let you see this.

We're not supposed to show it to anyone other than a physician."

"I guess Dr. Sacks told you it's an unusual case."

McCall nodded. "I'm a friend of Phil Pearson's, too. That's why I'm going to let you read through this. But if the matter should somehow end up in court, nothing that you see in here is admissible evidence. Nothing."

He jabbed the folder hard to emphasize his point.

He came out from behind the desk. "I'm going to make nightly rounds. That usually takes a couple of hours. When I come back, the folder goes in the file cabinet. Agreed?"

"Agreed," I said.

"If you need anything else, ask my receptionist, Nurse Rostow."

He went out of the room, leaving the manila folder on his desk.

It took me about an hour and a half to go through Herbert Talmadge's file. Parts of it I couldn't decipher—pages of notes written like a prescription in a doctor's crabbed hand. But a good deal of it had been transcribed by a typist, and those parts made chilling reading.

Talmadge had first been admitted to Rollman's in December 1974, after beating and sodomizing a teenage girlfriend. The examining doctor's diagnosis was acute schizophrenia.

Subject is an intelligent black man, 28 years old, a high school graduate with three years military service. Subject released from military in 1974, after suffering anxiety attacks and hallucinatory episodes. Subject referred to Veterans Administration Hospital, November 1974, diagnosed as schizophrenic, and allowed disability pension.

Subject was remanded to RPI by court order, 3 December, 1974, after attacking a woman friend with a handsaw. Subject has no memory of the attack. Subject maintains the woman is lying, that he has never harmed a woman . . .

Subject fantasizes himself a ladies' man and claims he only does what women want him to do. Subject refuses to speak in detail about hallucinatory episodes.

Talmadge was committed to Rollman's four more times over the next year—each time following a sadistic attack on a woman friend. He was invariably released after a week of observation—perhaps because the girlfriends had dropped the charges against him, perhaps because they had no room for him at Rollman's or no real interest in his care and cure.

In August of 1975, he was committed to Rollman's for a fifth time by Thelma Jackson, his landlady. The interesting part of the '75 episode was the fact that the attending psychiatrist was Phil Pearson, then a senior resident at Rollman's.

Pearson's notes weren't any different from any of the other examining psychiatrists'. He referred to Talmadge's intelligence, his denial of guilt, his refusal to speak in detail about psychotic episodes. There was some speculation about Talmadge's childhood, with the strong suggestion that incest with his mother may have precipitated his psychosis.

I had hoped to find that Pearson was still the attending psychiatrist during Talmadge's last stay at Rollman's, in the spring of 1976. But he wasn't. A Dr. Isaac Goldman had taken over the case.

Either Goldman was more persistent than Pearson or just plain smarter, because for the first time in three years of being shuffled in and out of psychiatric wards Herbert Talmadge spoke freely about himself. Most of his confession seemed to have been dictated to Goldman and another doctor with the initials R.S.

HT: I ain't got nothing against woman in general. But some women just ain't right.

IG: How do you know when they're "not right"?

HT: You shouldn't try to trick me into talking about her.

RS: We're not trying to trick you, Herbert. You told me you wanted to talk about her.

HT: She won't like it.

RS: I would though.

HT: All right. It's my mama that tells me these things. She knows.

IG: Why does she know?

HT: 'Cause of her own wickedness.

IG: Your mother was wicked?

HT: What you call it? Making me do that stuff to her?

IG: What stuff?

HT: You damn well know what stuff. You read my mind, anyway. You see it yourself. I see it in you.

IG: What do you see in me?

HT: Same wickedness in me. I see some bitch wanta spend my money, take my manhood. Party! Well, all right, then. Let's party. I put that fist in her ass, she don't party so good. When it start to hurt, I get . . .

IG: What?

HT: I just want to . . . go all the way, man. Rip it up. All the way.

There were six or seven more pages like that, some of it a lot worse.

After plowing through thirty or forty pages of denials and silence I was astonished that Talmadge had opened up as he had. Perhaps Goldman or the other doctor, R.S., had given him Pentothal. I didn't know. But once he started talking Talmadge didn't want to stop. And what he had to say should have been enough to have him committed for life— sent to Longview or some state hospital for the criminally insane.

And yet he hadn't been committed. Instead he'd been released by Goldman a month later. I stared at the release form, signed by Goldman, initialed by R.S., and couldn't quite believe my eyes.

Six or seven months after that Talmadge had brutally murdered a woman in Newport, and this time he didn't get sent to Rollman's. This time he'd gone to a Kentucky prison for thirteen years. Thirteen years in a cell, with all that craziness cooking inside him.

I was no longer bothered by why Ethan Pearson had happened to pick Herbert Talmadge's face out of the crowd. A child would have had no trouble sensing what was going on behind that face, even if he'd only seen it staring at him, dead-eyed and numb, from behind a barred window. What bothered me a lot was that he *had* chanced to pick that face—that he and his sister were now looking for the man with that face. I could only hope they didn't find him or that the cops or I found him first.

15

When I finished I took Talmadge's folder out to the reception desk and handed it to McCall's grey-haired secretary, Ms. Rostow.

"Thank your boss for me."

"I will," she said.

She spun around in her chair and socked the folder away in a drawer, slamming it shut as if she was filing her resignation.

"How long have you worked here, Ms. Rostow?"

"Since 1965," she said, swiveling back around to face me.

"Do you know Dr. Isaac Goldman?"

"Certainly."

"Is he still on staff here?"

"He never was," she said. "Dr. Goldman and several of his colleagues rotated through here in the mid-seventies, as part of an intern-exchange program with Washington University in St. Louis."

"Do you happen to remember if either of his colleagues had the initials R.S.?"

"No, they did not. The other two interns from St. Louis were Stanley Lee and Calvin Minard."

"Can you think of another staffer from around that time with those initials?"

The woman laughed fecklessly. "We've had a lot of staff changes in thirteen years, Mr. Stoner. You can't expect me to remember all of them. Is it important?"

"Probably not. Did Goldman go back to St. Louis after interning here?"

"Yes. He has a practice in Creve Coeur. We get a card from him each year at the holidays."

The woman pointed to the tinseled dwarf pine decorated with Christmas cards.

"All of our doctors remember us at Christmas," she said with a pleasant smile.

It was almost eight o'clock when I left Rollman's. I headed east to I-71 and Indian Hill. It was a thirty-minute drive to Louise Pearson's country club on Camargo, which meant I was going to be a bit early for our meeting. But I didn't feel like sitting in a chili parlor for an extra half hour, brooding about Herbert Talmadge. I needed to move around, I also needed a drink.

The club was in a woods off Camargo Pike. I had probably passed it a couple of hundred times the day before, when I was looking for Woodbine Lane. The guy manning the gate had my name—and my number, judging from the way he eyed me and the beat-up Pinto. He made me show ID before waving the car through.

The clubhouse was about a half-mile past the gate, down a tar road that cut between the ninth and tenth holes of a moonlit golf course. I heard music before I saw the building —a jazz combo playing "Sentimental Journey." The horn echoed across the golf course, cutting through the cold clear night like taps in a drill yard.

I parked the Pinto in a crowded lot, squeezing in between a Mercedes and a Bentley. As I walked up to the clubhouse I passed a couple making out in a dark car. He was wearing a tux and she was wearing a chiffon evening gown, pearls, and a fur wrap. Aside from that they were doing it pretty much like the rest of us do. Though when I went by the woman winked invitingly—so I might have been wrong.

The club was large and preposterous-looking, half field-stone Romanesque and half redwood A-frame, like a dowager with a fade haircut. The stone and masonry part abutted the golf course. It had been around for a long while, probably since the twenties. The A-frame part, where all the music was coming from, fronted the road and was obviously a new addition. Two silver spruces, twinkling with colored Christmas lights, flanked the tall A-frame door.

I stepped through that door into a Christmas party. The vaulted atrium was decorated with streamers and filled with men and women in evening dress. They didn't exactly stare as one when I came in. But I got enough funny looks to send me scurrying to the far end of the room, where the glow of a lighted bar caught my eye.

The bar was actually in a separate room, through smoked-glass doors that shut out most of the buzz of conversation and too much of the music. It was dark and cozy and empty in the bar. I sat down on a leather stool and asked the red-vested bartender for The Glenlivet, straight up. Up the rail from me a tall, stocky, red-faced man in a tux, the only other person in the place, toyed with a bowl of Spanish peanuts and stared at me openly.

I'd been in enough bars in my life to know when a guy was looking for trouble. The one in the tux was.

"You're not a member here, are you?" he said after a time. His voice was loud and officious-sounding.

I turned in his direction. "You taking a poll?"

He pretended to laugh. "I'm just wondering what you're doing here, that's all."

He was probably having trouble with a woman. And if he wasn't he deserved to be. But it was his bar, so I kept it polite.

"I'm waiting for someone."

The man parked his elbows on the bar behind him and stared at me across his left shoulder. "Who?"

"Who, what?"

"Who are you waiting for?"

I glanced at the bartender but he looked away quickly, as if he didn't want any part of trouble with the guy in the tux.

"I'm waiting for Louise Pearson. Dr. Phil Pearson's wife."

The man threw his head back slightly and opened his mouth as if he was going to laugh. But no sound came out. He stood like that for half a second, gape-mouthed, staring at the ceiling. Then he closed his mouth and looked back across his shoulder at me.

"Are you her new one?"

I started to get angry. "What's that supposed to mean?"

"Her new stud. Mister December."

"What's the matter, fella? She didn't like you hitting on her?"

He swung around on his left elbow, so he was facing me. "Louise likes to be hit on, *fella*. Don't you know that?"

I stared at him.

The bartender slapped his towel on the bar. He was an older man with a grey moustache and a heavily lined face.

"Take it outside, mister," he said to me. "Take it outside or I call the cops."

The guy in the tux laughed. "Forget about it, Pete. He's not going to try anything."

But the bartender knew better. "Take it outside," he said again.

I swallowed the rest of my drink and left.

I was working my way through the crowd, looking for Louise Pearson, when she found me. I heard a woman call my name, turned around, and saw her standing a few feet away, smiling.

"Hi," I said, smiling back.

"Hi, yourself."

She was wearing a midnight-blue evening gown with a modest slit in the leg and a modest plunge at the breast. She looked terrific.

"I thought I saw you go into the bar. In fact I was going to go in after you."

"I think we better steer clear of the bar."

She gave me a confused look. "Why?"

"Not important. I don't have anything new to report anyway. Go back to your party."

"I don't feel like partying." She stared at me for a second curiously, trying to make out what it was that was bothering me about the bar. Then she shrugged. "If you're going to leave I'll come with you. You can drive me home."

"You're not going to like my car."

"I'll take that chance."

Louise picked up a mink wrap in a cloakroom by the door. Together we walked out to the lot. As we made our way through the parked cars she passed her arm through mine.

"What's the matter?" she asked. "Did somebody say something to you in the bar?"

"Nope. It's just been a long day, and I didn't feel like a party."

"Neither did I," she said with a dismal laugh. "I shouldn't have come. I wouldn't have come if Phil hadn't insisted."

She got a peevish look on her face. "Phil always knows what's best for other people. That's why he's in such good shape right now."

Her mood had obviously changed since the morning, back to the tensions of the previous day.

"How's he holding up?"

"About the same," she said indifferently.

Louise eased her arm away from mine as if talking about her husband had made her feel self-conscious. She didn't say anything for a while.

"You must already know that we're not the perfect couple. I mean you must have sensed that."

I didn't say anything.

When she saw the car she started to laugh. "God, you weren't kidding about this thing."

"It's old, but it's game."

I opened the passenger side door and she slipped in. I got in on my side, started the engine, and headed up the access road to Madeira. Neither of us said a word as we drove back to Woodbine Lane.

I pulled up in the driveway behind her husband's Mercedes. Louise turned in the seat to face me.

"Come in," she said in her peremptory way. "We'll have that drink."

"All right."

None of the downstairs lights was lit, but there was a lamp on upstairs in a front room. Louise glanced at it.

"He should be asleep," she said irritably. "He promised me he'd try to sleep."

"He's worried," I said.

"He's panicking," she said with a trace of disgust.

Louise unlocked the door and flipped on a hall light. "I'll go up and put him to bed. You might as well make us some drinks. The lights in the living room are on the left and the liquor is in a red Chinese cabinet by the sideboard. Fix yourself whatever you want, and fix me a martini."

She didn't wait for an answer. She went up the stairs to tend her husband.

I walked down to the living room, found the lights and the liquor, and made a couple of drinks. I took them over to the red leather chairs by the fireplace, putting the martini down on an oval end table. The fire had almost burned out. I stirred it with a poker and got it going again, like the man of the house.

Ten minutes passed before Louise came into the room. She had changed back to the outfit she'd been wearing that afternoon—white blouse and jeans. She looked just as good as she had in the evening gown. Maybe a little better because the denim suited her ripe body.

"I think I've calmed him down," she said, sitting across from me. She picked up the martini and took a sip, staring at me over the rim of the glass. "He won't get much sleep, though. I don't think he'll really sleep until this is over."

I said, "You do know that there's a strong chance it won't work out."

"I've known that for years."

"I meant finding Ethan and Kirsty."

"I know what you meant," Louise said drily. "By the way, Phil did remember that man, Talmadge. He was a patient at Rollman's when Phil did his residency there in '75. Phil couldn't remember anything specific about the case though."

"I looked into it this afternoon. Talmadge is dangerous."

She looked alarmed. "You mean dangerous to Phil?"

"To the children."

"Christ, I pray it doesn't come to that," she said. "I'm half hoping that they're just doing this to make Phil and me sweat."

"Why would they do that to you?"

"Because they don't like me very much," she said with an unhappy smile. "Neither one has ever really forgiven me for trying to play Mom after Estelle died. I don't really blame them, given the circumstances."

But her voice sounded resentful. She heard it herself and

made a contrite face. "You didn't bargain on a family like this one, did you, Stoner? We must look like lunatics to you."

"You have problems," I said.

"It's worse than that, and you know it. We've screwed it all up, Phil and I." Her beautiful face filled with disgust, and she took a quick drink to cover her revulsion. "This thing has sent us back thirteen years. Back to a place where I didn't want to go. Back to feelings I don't want to relive."

"You want to talk about it?"

"You mean you want to hear more Pearson craziness?"

"I want to hear about you."

She lowered the martini glass down and ran a finger around the edge, making it sing.

"All right," she said after a time. "I feel like talking. Just don't analyze, okay? I've had my fill of that for one lifetime."

Louise set the glass down at her feet. "I wasn't what you would call inexperienced when I met Philip. I'd been married before—to the wrong man. Frank was a beauty but he didn't believe in work. At least, he didn't believe that *he* should have to work. He wasn't so fussy when it came to my time. After the divorce I started looking for someone else. Someone with a different set of priorities. Someone I could build a new life with. This kind of life."

She glanced approvingly around the handsome, genteel room.

"Philip seemed like the one. He came from a wealthy family. He had a promising career. He could be sweet and smart and sensitive, even if he did sometimes act as if he owned the keys to everyone else's psyche. And he was terribly unhappy with his marriage and talking divorce. He'd already gone through several affairs when we met. On the surface he looked like the perfect catch."

She sat back in the chair with a sigh. "But Phil wasn't the

strong, competent, sensitive guru he pretended to be. That part of his personality was designed to impress his clients for one hour a week. The rest of him, the part I had to learn to live with, was still stuck in childhood like everybody else."

Her face bunched up, as if she didn't like the carping sound of her voice. "Oh, hell, that's not fair. It's not Phil's fault that he's built the way he is. The past's not anyone's fault. It's just there, like the moon and the stars. Phil's good, rich family wasn't a very happy one, that's all. You've met Cora. She's a prissy, spoiled woman, but she can be dealt with. At least, I can deal with her. It was her husband, Phil's father, Arthur, who was the real joker."

"He's dead?"

"For years. Art was a weak, wifty drunk. He keeled over when Phil was just a teenager. But not before leaving his mark on Phil."

"His mark?"

Louise looked over at the fire. "I'm not a hundred percent positive of this. I mean nobody's ever said it outright, but I'm reasonably sure that Phil was abused by his father."

She shuddered down her spine. "Pretty awful, huh?"

"It happens," I said. "Even in good families."

"I'm sure it does. But when you marry someone who's hiding that sort of thing in his past . . . it has an effect. Living with a man like Phil—a man with an overwhelming need to dominate in small matters and to be constantly reassured about the important ones—can wear you down, especially if you're not well equipped to handle your own needs. I guess I'm strong enough to take it. At least, everyone has automatically made that assumption about me. But his first wife, Estelle, wasn't."

"Did you know her?"

"I feel like I did through talking to Phil and the kids,

through living the same kind of life. Poor Estelle, she tried to accommodate Phil—dropping out of school, abandoning her career before it even got started, having children she probably didn't want, nurturing Phil when he needed nurturing, eating his all-knowing psychiatrist's crap when he didn't. After ten years of that she finally broke apart."

She made it sound as if Pearson had caused the woman's breakdown. "Estelle had emotional troubles all her life, didn't she?"

"That's what Dr. Shelley Sacks would have us believe. But Phil was his friend, too, you know."

"Meaning?"

"Meaning maybe there was a little ex post facto rationalization there, to spare Phil some guilt. I don't know. I know it hasn't spared me any. You see Phil and I had just started our affair when . . ."

Her face reddened, and she looked away from me.

"When Estelle died." I said it for her.

She nodded, her face still turned. "She didn't know, of course. She was too far gone by then to care, anyway. About me, or any of the others that had preceded me. The nurses and secretaries. But *I* knew. I was actually with Phil when he heard that her body had been found."

She shuddered again. "For a year or so after that we really did need each after. Then it was all guilt. We married to assuage the guilt. We've stayed together to hide it."

Louise turned back to me. "And now you know another one of our little secrets. I've tried to be a good wife, a good stepmother. I got what I wanted, didn't I? All this." She waved her hand around the room, then dropped it in her lap. "I have affairs. He has his work. You know the funny thing is he's extremely good at his job—he has an instinct about other people's weaknesses. It gives him the chance to be strong, to dominate." She made a muscle and laughed ironically. "It isn't like that upstairs."

She hadn't mentioned the children. So I did. "His concern for Ethan and Kirsty seems genuine."

She nodded. "It is. Ethan wasn't his fault. He lost him to Estelle when she died. It was her revenge on him, I think. But Kirsty . . . God, how he's tried to make amends to her."

"Amends for what?"

She shook her head. "Enough family history."

Leaning forward she kissed me softly on the mouth. I started to draw her to me, but she pulled away. She put a finger to my lips and ran it slowly down to my chin.

"I like you," she whispered. "After this is over we'll have to do something about that. Until then . . ."

She came close again. "Keep this in mind."

She kissed me again passionately. Then she got up and walked out of the room, leaving me and the fire slowly burning down.

16

It was a long drive back to the apartment on Ohio Avenue. I tried not to think about Louise. But it was hopeless. For better or worse she was part of it for me now—part of the strange legacy of the Pearson case. The case I wasn't going to make personal.

It was past twelve when I got to Ohio Avenue. As I was getting out of the car I remembered the envelope Sid had left for me, Estelle Pearson's last remains. I picked it up off the backseat and took it inside, tossing it on the couch in the living room.

The light on my answering machine was lit, but I didn't play the messages back. I was too tired for business. I was too tired to think about anything. I sat on the couch, with poor Estelle sitting there beside me, and dreamed about the other Mrs. Pearson—the one who'd never quite been able to take her place.

Sometime during the night I must have wandered into the bedroom, because that's where I found myself when the telephone woke me. It was still dark outside, and it had turned very cold. Shivering, I fumbled for the receiver on the nightstand.

"Stoner?" a half-familiar voice said. "It's Al Foster."

"Yeah, Al," I said groggily.

"We've got something for you."

I struggled to sit up. I was still wearing my clothes—or trapped in them. My shirttail was wrapped in the bedding and I had to wrench it loose to straighten up. I glanced at the clock, which was showing 6:15.

"You listening, Harry?" Al said.

"I'm here, for chrissake. What?"

"We found the car—the grey Volare. The Miamitown police came across it about fifteen minutes ago. It was parked on an embankment of the Miami River."

It took me a second to remember that Estelle Pearson's body had been found in the Miami River. It took me another second to realize that Al hadn't mentioned Kirsty and Ethan, that he'd only mentioned the car.

"What about the Pearson children?" I asked.

Al fetched a sigh that sent a chill down my back.

"There's some indication they may have run into trouble."

"What indication?"

"Harry, I'm just relaying what I was told when this was called in a few minutes ago. If you want details you're going to have to go out there yourself and talk to the examining officers."

He gave me an address on Miamitown Road and the name of a cop—Sergeant Larry Parker. Before hanging up I asked whether the Pearsons had been notified.

"I don't know what the Miamitown cops have done," Al said. "But you're the only person we've contacted."

"Keep it that way," I told him. "At least until after I've had a chance to talk to Parker."

"It's your case," he said.

It took me about thirty minutes to drive to Miamitown on the western side of Hamilton County near the Indiana line. It really wasn't much of a town—just a flat stretch of road dotted with Quonset bars, brick storefronts, and one squat diamond-shaped municipal building with a flagpole and a plugged howitzer arranged in front of it like a place setting.

There was enough light growing in the sky to backlight

the pines on top of the tall forested ridge east of town. I knew that the Great Miami ran beneath the ridge, in a steep, overgrown embankment that was still sunk in darkness. The flashing squad car lights led me to the right spot, a cluster of them blinking like tiny blue Christmas ornaments netted in the pines. I had to turn onto a gravel access road to get to where the cops were parked, past a tin-roofed bait shop, down a short bumpy slope to a dirt clearing above the river.

The Volare was at the back of the clearing—its front wheel resting on some rocks beyond the dirt, where the hill began its slide to the embankment. The car canted down slightly as if someone had parked it there in a rush. Two Miamitown police cruisers were parked on either side of it, and a third cop cruiser was parked behind. I pulled in next to the third cruiser and got out.

Even in the darkness I could see pale foot trails leading away from the clearing, down the hillside to the river. The packed dirt glistened in the half light like a length of bone. A couple of officers with flashlights were making their ways along the trails. The dirt must have been slippery, because the flashlight beams bounced and whirled crazily in the dark—lighting tree trunks, bits of scrap iron, the red staring eyes of a possum. I could hear the river beneath the clearing, coursing over rocks and fallen limbs, running fast and deep with winter snow.

A third cop, a tall stocky man wearing a billed cap and gold patches on his down coat, was standing at the lip of the hill, directing the other two down the trails. He'd stopped to watch me when I got out of the car. After a time he walked over to where I was standing.

"Unless you've got a reason to be here," he said, "you'd best leave."

He had a deep voice—a tough voice. But some of its effect

was lost to the bitter cold. He shivered as he stood there, shifting from foot to foot like a man holding his water.

"My name's Stoner," I said to him. "I'm a P.I. Al Foster of the CPD just called about the Volare. The car is part of a missing persons case I'm working on."

"I thought the name was Pearson," the man said suspiciously. "That's the name we got on the APB."

"That's the name of the family I'm working for. You can get in touch with Mrs. Pearson if you want to check me out."

"Already talked to her," the man said, shifting feet.

"Christ," I said to myself. To the cop, I said, "Exactly what did you tell her?"

He thought about it for a moment. "Better see some ID first." He glanced over at the squad car, as if it were a photo of home. "Maybe we should do it inside, where it's light."

And warm, I said to myself.

I followed him to the cruiser and got in on the passenger side. The man started the engine and flipped on the heater and the overhead light. I could see his name tag for the first time. It read "L. Parker."

I gave Parker my ID. He studied it for a moment then handed it back, flipping off the courtesy light with his other hand.

"We found the car about a hour ago," he said, nodding at the Plymouth. "One of the men was making a routine run down Miamitown when he saw headlights here in the hollow."

"The headlights were left on?"

"A pretty good time, too," the cop said. " 'Cause when he tried to start the car up she wouldn't turn over."

"I take it the keys were in the car."

He nodded. "And these."

He reached into the backseat and pulled out a clear

plastic evidence bag with a pair of stained panties in it. I couldn't tell in the darkness, but the stains looked like blood.

My heart sank. "These were in the Plymouth?"

"On the floor in the back. The panties got a tag in them from a Chicago store—Milady's."

"The missing girl went to school in Chicago."

"That's what the wife said." He ducked his head guiltily. "She seemed like a nice woman. I hated like hell to break this news to her."

I hated it like hell, too. I could scarcely imagine how Phil Pearson had reacted to the news.

"Have you dusted the car for prints?" I asked Parker.

"We're waiting for the State Patrol to send down a criminalistics team. Called it in a goddamn hour ago." He shrugged. "But that's State for you."

He reached into his jacket and pulled out a pack of cigarettes, shaking one out and sticking it in his mouth in a single motion. He offered the pack to me and I said no.

"I guess I should quit," he said, flipping open a silver Zippo and lighting up.

I stared through the windshield at the twisting flashlight beams, shooting up from below the lip of the hill. In the distance the dawn was starting to break above the ridge, purpling the horizon like a fresh, spreading bruise.

"There was nothing else in the car?" I said. "Nothing that a *man* might have carried or worn?"

Parker shook his head, breathing out a thick cloud of grey tobacco smoke. "Just the panties." He gestured toward the windshield. "We're looking down there now for anything else we can turn up. I doubt we'll find much in the dark." He squinted into the dawn light. "When the sun comes up we'll call in some help."

17

I drove straight from Miamitown to Indian Hill. By the time I got to Camargo Pike, it was full morning, grey and turbulent, with a sting of snow already in the air. As I neared Woodbine Lane, an ambulance blew past me, turning west on Camargo, blinkers flashing. I couldn't see inside the ambulance, but I had the awful feeling it was racing Phil Pearson to the hospital.

I knew I was right when I got closer to the Pearson house. Another ambulance—a red emergency vehicle—was parked in the driveway behind a green Porsche 935 and a tan Merc. The tan car belonged to Cora Pearson. I didn't know who belonged to the Porsche.

I parked on the street to keep from blocking the driveway, and walked slowly up to the front door. A tall, handsome man with tan skin and thick grey hair answered my knock. Behind him, down the hall, I could hear Cora Pearson crying.

"I'm Harry Stoner," I said to the grey-haired man. "I work for the Pearsons."

The man smiled as if he recognized my name, flashing a set of teeth so large and white and perfect-looking that I thought, at once, they must be caps. "I'm Saul Lasker," he said in a deep, genial voice. "A friend of Louise and Phil's. Friend and neighbor."

He nodded up the street to another estate house. All I could see of it was the red tile of its roof, billowing like a circus tent behind a protective screen of spruce.

I'd heard of Lasker—at least, I'd seen his name on the financial pages. He was very big in real estate and investment banking. Very big, very rich, very Reagan-Republican. I didn't like him on principle. His kind of money was always tainted with someone else's pain.

"What happened here, Lasker?"

The man tried to stop smiling. But his face wasn't used to bad news. "Phil had an attack about ten minutes ago." He touched the place on his chest where his heart was supposed to be and fought with the smile some more. "I heard the ambulances and came over. He was in the living room when it happened."

"Do you have any idea how bad the attack was?"

"Not good. Louise went with him to the hospital. I'm going to drive Cora over there in a few minutes and try to lend some support, although I guess there's nothing we can do now but pray."

He said it as if it was something he'd heard in a movie.

"What hospital did they take him to?"

"Bethesda North, I think."

"You're not sure?"

"Bethesda North," he said, sounding a little more like twenty million bucks.

I caught the expressway to Reed-Hartman. The hospital was on the east side of the highway—a big glass-and-steel tower, rising out of an ocean of blacktop. I parked as close as I could to the emergency room, but it was still a good walk across the lot to the automatic doors.

I didn't see Louise inside. I figured she was in one of the examination rooms with her husband. I double-checked with a nurse to make sure that Pearson had been admitted, then went over to a waiting area and sat down with three anxious-looking strangers.

Half an hour must have passed before Louise came out. I

could tell from her ashen look that Pearson was in bad shape.

"Oh, God, Harry," she said, slumping beside me in a chair. She covered her face with her hands.

"It's my fault," she said hoarsely. "It's my fault."

"No, it's not," I said.

"You don't understand. They found Ethan's car. I had to tell him they found Ethan's car."

"I know. I talked to the cops."

"You know?" Louise said with surprise. "Then why didn't *you* call me? Why did you let me hear that from a stranger?"

"I got there too late, Louise," I said, feeling bad. "They'd already made the call."

She dropped her hands from her cheeks and stared queerly into space. "I didn't want to tell him, but he knew it was the police. He heard me talking to them." She turned to me with a guilty look. "What was I supposed to do?"

"You had to tell him."

"He went crazy," she said with a trace of horror in her voice. "I've never seen him get that upset, even when . . . even after Estelle. He said things to me. Dreadful things. We fought."

Her head fell to her chest and she sobbed. "They say he may die."

I sat there with Louise for about ten minutes, holding her hand tightly in mine. Lasker finally arrived with Cora Pearson. The woman looked awful, her face blasted, her gait doddering, as if she'd aged twenty years since the day before. Louise got up immediately, walked over to her mother-in-law, and took her in her arms.

Cora Pearson sobbed. "He's not going to die?"

"It's not in our hands anymore," Lasker said.

Louise flashed an angry look at him over Cora's shoulder, and the man's face reddened as if he'd been slapped.

"No, he's not going to die," Louise said to her mother-in-law. She pushed Cora Pearson back and straightened her white hair as if she were grooming a child.

The older woman smiled at her weakly. "You're so good to me, Louise," she said with deep feeling. "Always so good."

Cora walked unsteadily over to the waiting area and sat down on one of the plastic chairs.

I couldn't hear him, but Lasker apparently said something else to Louise, something well-intentioned and inept. She frowned dismissively, and he backed out of the emergency room like he was leaving royalty.

After Lasker left Louise came over to us. "Did you call Shelley?" she asked Cora.

The older woman nodded. "He's on his way."

Louise sat down beside Cora and put an arm around her shoulder. The woman leaned against her heavily. "Don't worry, Mother," Louise whispered. "I'm here with you."

It had come to me when I'd first met Pearson that Louise anchored his life. I was beginning to realize that she anchored the whole family—probably the children too, insofar as they could be reached. It was what she had meant the night before when she'd complained about people automatically relying upon her strength. But that strength was no illusion—it was real and impressive, especially at that moment.

A nurse came into the hall and called Louise's name.

She patted her mother-in-law's shoulder and stood up. "I've got to go," she said to Cora.

"Will I be able to see him?" the woman asked plaintively.

"In a little while," Louise said.

She went over to where the nurse was standing and together they walked off down the hall to the emergency rooms.

I didn't want to leave Cora Pearson alone, so I waited for Shelley Sacks to arrive. The woman didn't say much to me. Her shock was too deep, and there wasn't anything to say.

When Sacks came in, I got to my feet.

The woman looked up at me suddenly. Her face was already red from crying, but the color that rose in her cheeks was more than despair or grief. "*They* did this to him!" she said in a strangled voice. "I hope they die for this—for what they've done."

She didn't mean what she'd said. She might not have realized she was saying it. But the truth was that her curse could already have come true.

18

Before leaving the hospital I called Sergeant Larry Parker from a pay phone in the lobby to see if the State Patrol forensic team had turned up anything new.

"We haven't found a body in the river," he said grimly. "But State confirmed that the stains on the panties were blood. Type O negative. You might want to check with the Pearsons about the girl's blood type. We've also got some positive lifts off the Plymouth's steering wheel."

"Do you have a make on the prints?"

Parker sighed. "Yeah, but you're not going to like it. The prints belong to a convicted felon named Herbert Talmadge."

"Jesus," I said aloud. The very fact that Ethan and Kirsty had ended up in that clearing with Talmadge—in the same spot where Estelle Pearson had taken her own life—defied logic.

"You know the guy?" Parker said, responding to the pained sound of my voice.

I thought about going into Pearson family history with Parker, then decided against it. It wasn't going to help him find Talmadge. "No, I don't know him."

"Well, he's an honest-to-God bad man, Stoner. If your MPs ran into him, I'm afraid they chanced into serious trouble. State's already put an APB out on him. So has Kentucky. The son of a bitch was released from Lexington the week before last. Ten days and he's already . . ."

He didn't finish the sentence, but I knew what he was thinking. Ten days and he'd already committed murder—or attempted to.

"You don't have any leads yet, do you?"

"None. How 'bout you—did you check on that Chicago store?"

"Not yet."

"Well, I'd appreciate you finding out. And find out about the blood type, too. I'll get in touch if anything else turns up."

I was in a bad mood when I hung up on Parker. And the mood kept deepening on the drive downtown to the office.

Herbert Talmadge wasn't the kind of guy who would take hostages or halfway measures. If the Pearson kids had found him as they apparently had, he'd brought their revenge fantasies to a quick, pitiless end—at best. I didn't want to think about what he might have done at worst.

The very fact that Kirsty and Ethan *had* found Talmadge galled me. They'd found him, and I hadn't. All they'd had to go on was the newspaper article in the *Post,* and yet they'd found him in less than a day, while I was chasing blind leads and making time with Louise Pearson.

I didn't understand how it had happened, how the last chapter of Kirsten's life might have ended up being written by a man with no connection to her own past, a man with no real connection to Ethan's past—save for the brief moment that the boy might have seen him in the hospital ward where his father had once worked. And yet they'd all wound up in that clearing above the river like they were holding communion for the dead mother. For the second time in two days I had the weird feeling that there really was a sinister fatality at work in the Pearsons' lives, leading them on to violent death.

When I got to the office I picked up the phone and started making calls. I went back through the people I'd talked to in Chicago one by one. Art Heldman at the university. Jay

Stein. Marnee Thompson at the girls' apartment. And
Hedda Pearson at her end-of-the-road motel. Not one of
them had ever heard of Herbert Talmadge. Not one of
them could explain how Kirsten or Ethan had known
where to find him. The only thing I managed to learn was
that Kirsty had in fact bought underclothes from Milady's
Shop in the Kenwood Plaza in Hyde Park.

"Why is that important?" Marnee asked uneasily.
"What's happened to Kirsty?"

I didn't tell her what I knew. I didn't tell any of them
about the abandoned car and the bloody underwear. Not
even Hedda Pearson, who had a right to know. I just didn't
have it in me to speak the truth.

After finishing the Chicago calls I ran through my local
connections again. Al Foster at CPD. The Kentucky cops.
The State Patrol.

By eleven-thirty I'd run out of people to call. I felt like I'd
run out of luck too, like poor Kirsty and her brother. Then
Lee Wilson, the manager at Ethan's Ft. Thomas motel,
phoned me. And things began to change.

The Blue Grass Motel and Motor Court was on Hidden
Fork Road, about fifteen miles south of the city off I-471. It
was a well-tended place in spite of its out-of-the-way loca-
tion. The stucco-and-glass office building looked newly
painted. The dozen stucco cottages arrayed in a semicircle
behind were just as fresh-faced and neat. A heart-shaped
swimming pool sat to the side, covered with a tarp for the
winter.

I parked in a space by the pool and caught a whiff of stale
chlorine as I walked over to the office building. Wilson was
waiting for me inside—a dapper, balding man in his mid-
forties with the pink, prissy face of a toady.

"You must be Mr. Stoner," Wilson said as I came up to the counter. "I'm Lee Wilson, the proprietor here."

He held out his hand and I shook with him.

"I woulda called you sooner about this, Mr. Stoner, if I'd been on duty last night. I left your message with Roy, my clerk, but he didn't bother telling me until today. That's the trouble with hired help—you can't trust them to follow up on things."

Wilson laughed mechanically. And when I didn't laugh he stopped laughing too, as if he didn't think it was funny either.

"If I hadn't been going through the receipts, I doubt as I would have seen it. Right there in black and white in the registration book."

I had the feeling that this one went through the receipts every hour on the hour. But I pretended it was the blessing he wanted me to think it was and asked to see the book.

Wilson glanced down at the open register on the counter-top, scanning it critically as if he were totaling figures. His eyes stopped on a line midway down the page, and he pinned a finger to it like he was poking Roy the clerk in the eye.

"Here it is."

He swiveled the book around to me, using his finger as a fulcrum.

I glanced at the book, at the line above Wilson's finger. "Ethan Pearson" was written on it in longhand, along with a check-in time of four p.m. Monday.

"Why did Ethan bother to sign in?" I asked, looking up at Wilson. "I mean he lives here, doesn't he?"

"We like to keep track of our guests," the man said stiffly. "We always ask our semipermanent residents to sign in fresh if they been away for more than a day or two. Saves us some problems and them some potential embarrassment. I mean lights come on in somebody's cottage when they're supposed to be out of town . . . well, you can see my point."

I glanced at the polished wood letterboxes behind the counter. Most of the cubbyholes had room keys dangling from them. But a few had notes and letters in them.

"Did Ethan pick up any messages when he checked in?"

"I asked myself the same thing this morning," Wilson said with a self-congratulatory smile—the amateur detective. "But Roy says there weren't no letters. Ethan did get a phone call, though. And I believe he made one himself."

There was a PBX to the right of the letterboxes, an old-fashioned switchboard with a dial receiver at the base and a headset and plug-in lines. Like everything else in the place it was shiny and neat.

"No way to know who was calling in, is there?" I asked Wilson.

He shook his head, no. "Roy said it was a woman, and the call came around eleven-thirty. That's all I can tell you."

"Do you know who Ethan phoned?"

The man smiled triumphantly, as if he'd caught me in a little trap of his own devising. "Got the number right here," he said, pulling a piece of neatly folded paper out of his shirt pocket. "Don't know who it is, but I got the number."

"When did the call go out?"

The look of triumph faded a bit. "Ain't exactly sure of that. Sometime before he left, I reckon."

"He left again around midnight?"

Wilson nodded. "Like I told you on the phone. Right around midnight. 'Least that's what Roy told me."

The man gave me a conspiratorial look. "He had a woman with him," he whispered. "And it wasn't his wife."

"Did Roy tell you what she looked like?"

"A young girl. Brown hair, glasses. She stayed in the car,
Roy said, when the boy signed in."

It sounded like Kirsten, but it didn't have to be her.

I studied the man for a moment—his prissy face. "Think I
could take a look in their room?"

Wilson pretended to be shocked. Or maybe he wasn't
pretending. He took himself fairly seriously.

"It would save me calling the cops," I said. "Getting a
warrant."

The man's shocked look deepened momentarily.

"I guess I could show you the room."

I took out my wallet, pulled two twenties out, and laid
them on the counter. "For your trouble."

That swayed him. "We'll go on down there right now. Just
let me put the 'Closed' sign in the window."

He picked up the twenties and started to turn away. I
caught him by the shirt sleeve and he burped with fright, as
if he thought I was about to arrest him for taking a bribe.

"The phone number?" I said, rubbing my fingers together.

Lee Wilson smiled with relief. " 'Course," he said, handing me the square of paper. "Don't want to forget that."

19

Wilson walked me down to the Pearsons' cottage, unlocked the door with a passkey, then backed away discreetly, as if he was leaving me alone with the casket. I pushed the door open and looked inside.

The motel room was dark, except for the arc of sunlight coming through the door. The sun lit up a slice of carpet, the top halves of two unmade beds, and a corner of blank white wall. What looked like fast-food wrappers were scattered on the sheets of the nearest bed. A tin ashtray glittered on the pillows of the far bed. The room stank of cigarette smoke and stale grease—like the smell of Kirsten Pearson's bedroom in Chicago. I flipped on a table light and went inside, closing the door behind me.

It was a tiny room. Just the two twin beds. A nightstand between them. The lamp table by the door. A wooden bureau-desk on the far wall across from the bed. A door to a bathroom beyond the bureau.

I'd been expecting a few personal items. Photographs. Mementos. Books. But the only artifact in the room was the cheap oil painting of a farmhouse that Lee Wilson had hung above the beds. How Ethan and his wife could have called that spare, denuded place home, I couldn't imagine.

I went through the room carefully, starting with the bureau-desk. There was a phone on top and a pad for messages. One of the sheets from the pad lay crumpled up at the foot of the desk chair. I picked it up and smoothed it out. Someone had written the word "Small" on it with a capital S, followed by a slash mark and the number 5. A phone number was printed underneath:

Small/5

555-1543

I wasn't sure what "Small/5" meant. It could have been a dress or blouse size. If so, maybe the number was for a clothing store. It wasn't the same phone number that Ethan had dialed the night before—that was certain. The one that Wilson had written down for me was 555-8200.

I pocketed the sheet of notepaper with the cryptic message on it and turned to the bureau drawers. There were still a few items of clothing in them. Some men's underwear, a couple of tank-top T-shirts, several loose unmatched socks. A pair of boy's pajamas for David. One of Hedda Pearson's blouses, neatly pressed and wrapped in a Brockhaus Dry Cleaner's paper band. I checked the size of the blouse, but it wasn't a small and it wasn't a 5.

I wondered if Kirsten Pearson wore a size 5.

I went through the nightstand drawer next and found a Gideon Bible, a passbook from First National here in the city, and a Greater Cincinnati phone directory with a pencil stuck in the Yellow Pages. The passbook was in the name of E. Pearson—a savings account with deposits made to it every three months for over ten years, from the time Ethan was about fourteen to less than a few weeks before he disappeared. The deposits were always the same—a thousand dollars—and the entire amount was always withdrawn a month or so after it had been put in the account. It was undoubtedly a record of the "blood money" that Louise had told me about—Phil Pearson's pathetic attempt to buy his son's affection and to assuage his own guilt. It was the only item in the room that connected Ethan with his family, a bankbook that the boy hadn't even thought to take with him.

I put the book back in the drawer and opened the phone directory to the page marked by the pencil. It was a page full of RNs' ads and listings. One of the ads had been circled —The Medical Pool with an address on Oak Street near the city hospitals in Clifton. Very near Rollman's, too.

I started to jot The Medical Pool listing down when I realized that it was the same number that Wilson had given me. The same number that Ethan had called the night before. 555-8200. For some reason Ethan had phoned a nursing agency.

I went through the bedclothes and looked under the beds, but aside from a few wilted french fries I didn't find anything. The cigarette butts in the ashtray were Winstons, Kirsty's brand.

The bathroom was next. There was no medicine cabinet, just a flat mirror over the vanitory, a towel rack across from that, and a shower stall on the right. Someone had used the shower fairly recently, because there were fresh waterspots on the tile and long brown hairs in the drain. The plastic trash can by the vanitory had several Kleenex in it. I wouldn't have noticed the tissues if a few of them hadn't been stained with blood. There was also a small smear of blood in the porcelain washbasin, as if Ethan had knicked himself shaving.

I stopped at the motel office on the way out. Wilson was back at work, going through the books again with a vigilant look on his face. I pitied poor Roy the night clerk. His mistakes were Wilson's meat.

"Thanks," I said to the man, handing him the passkey.

"*Por nada,* as our friends south of the border say."

I forced a smile.

"When does your clerk, Roy, come back on?"

"Tomorrow afternoon," Wilson said despairingly. "I just can't be here all the time."

"Ask him to give me a call, will you? And, of course, phone me if Ethan comes back."

"Will do," the man said with a grin and a Boy Scout salute.

He held the salute a moment too long. When I didn't return it he dropped his hand quickly and wiped it on his pants leg, as if his fingers were wet with embarrassment.

As soon as I got back to the office I took out the crumpled piece of notepaper and called the number on it, 555-1543. I was half expecting to get the women's wear department at K mart—some clerk who could explain the "Small/5" notation. But if it was a K mart they were damn busy, because no one answered the phone.

I put that call on hold and dialed the other number, the one that Ethan had called from the motel room, the one for The Medical Pool.

A woman answered as sweetly as if she were already sitting there by the rented bed, mopping my brow.

"You have reached The Medical Pool. How may we help you?"

"Hi," I said to her. "My name's Ethan Pearson. I called you last night, remember?"

"Of course, I remember, Mr. Pearson," the woman said reassuringly. "Was Rita available?"

"I beg your pardon?"

"Rita Scarne. The nurse you requested for emergency service. We paged her at home and transferred your call, don't you remember?"

It appeared that Ethan had made two calls for the price of one.

"Yes, I did talk to her," I said, jotting down the name "Rita Scarne" on a yellow pad. "But I seem to have misplaced her home number."

"Not to worry. I can find it for you." She went off the line for a second. "Are you ready?"

"All set," I said.

"555-1543. Remember, if she's not home, try at Holmes Hospital."

"Thanks again," I said, hanging up.

I'd just tried the number, thinking it was K mart. But it wasn't K mart. It was a nurse named Rita Scarne. Since she obviously wasn't at home I called Holmes Hospital. The patient information service told me that Rita Scarne wasn't on duty that afternoon. They suggested I try Rollman's, where Nurse Scarne also worked part-time.

Rather than phoning Rollman's I drove over to the hospital on Burnett. The attendant at the door recognized me from the day before.

"If you come back to see Dr. McCall, he ain't here. Had a meeting to go to."

"Nurse Rostow will do," I told him.

He checked to make sure Nurse Rostow was at her station, then passed me through. I took the elevator up to the third floor and followed the arrows around the typing carrels to Sam McCall's office. Ms. Rostow smiled at me as I walked up to her desk.

"I hadn't expected to see you again so soon, Mr. Stoner."

"I hadn't expected to be back."

The woman nodded at McCall's door. "He's gone to a board of directors meeting and won't return today."

"This may be something *you* can help me with."

Ms. Rostow's face lit up pleasantly. "I'll certainly try. Have a seat."

I sat down across the desk from her. "Do you know a nurse named Rita Scarne?"

"Of course," she said smartly, as if it was the first round of a quiz show. "Miss Scarne has worked here since late 1974. On and off."

"You mean she's part-time?"

"I meant precisely what I said," the woman said. "Miss Scarne was a full-time nurse here. In fact, she was chief of the nursing staff for a short while.

"A very short while," she added.

"Something happened?"

Nurse Rostow hesitated this time before hitting the buzzer. I had the distinct impression that she didn't care for Rita Scarne and would have told me why if her professional ethics hadn't blocked the way.

"There was some trouble," she said, feeling her way around the block.

"With a doctor?" I asked curiously.

"No," she said. "Miss Scarne had . . . she didn't behave professionally on the wards."

Judging from the blush in old Ms. Rostow's cheeks I had the feeling that the trouble had been sexual.

"I shouldn't have told you that," she said, looking embarrassed. "Rita's an excellent nurse, who has been quite successful in private practice. She is very much in demand. The problem I referred to is old business. Very old."

I changed the subject to spare her any more embarrassment. "When was Rita Scarne head nurse here?"

"In late 1975 and '76."

"So she might have had contact with Herbert Talmadge?"

"I couldn't say for sure. She *was* head nurse, so it's quite possible."

I was thinking of the transcript I'd read—the interview from 1976 in which Talmadge had made his awful confession. Isaac Goldman, the intern from St. Louis, had been Talmadge's psychiatrist at the time. But throughout the interview Goldman had been assisted by someone else, someone with the initials R. S. I'd assumed R. S. was another psychiatrist, now it occurred to me that it might have been head nurse Rita Scarne. She had to have some connection with Talmadge—some connection that was obvious to Ethan Pearson—or I couldn't see why Ethan would have phoned for her.

"Is Miss Scarne on duty today?" I asked.

"I'm not sure. I can check, if you'd like."

"Please."

She picked up a phone, pressed a couple of buttons, and asked, "Is Nurse Scarne on duty?"

After a moment she hung the phone up daintily and said, "No, Miss Scarne is not here today."

I sighed. "It's important that I get hold of her."

"Have you tried Holmes Hospital? Or her house?"

"She's not at Holmes, and I don't have her address."

"I can help you with that," Ms. Rostow said. She flipped through a Rolodex and scribbled an address down on a notepad. "Here."

Rita Scarne must have made a good living, because her home was on Ridge Road in Amberley Village. That's where I decided to go next.

20

▪▪

Rita Scarne's house was in a wooded dell on the east side of Ridge Road—a two-story Colonial with rounded doors, Dutch windows, and a steep cross gable in front. A black-topped driveway led down to it through a small stand of oak trees. It was just a little past three when I got there, but the sun was already beginning to set. The slanting light caught in the bare limbs of the oaks, turning them gold. Heavy shadows enveloped the trunks, stretching across the yard and up the brick walls of the house.

The driveway terminated in front of a built-in garage. The garage door was open and a green Audi was parked inside. There was a sticker on the rear bumper—"Nurses Are the Best Medicine."

It was a very expensive place—a little too expensive for an unmarried nurse, I thought. But for all I knew she had other sources of income.

I got out of the Pinto and followed a cement walkway to the front door. It was cold in the shady dale and so quiet I could hear the wind creaking in the maples like house noises in the night.

I peered through the small leaded-glass window in the front door before ringing the bell. All I could see was sunlight pouring through French windows at the end of a tiled hallway. When I pressed the buzzer, a woman appeared in the hall. I backed away from the window as she came up to the door and opened it.

"Yes?" she said in a husky, sensuous voice.

Rita Scarne, if that was who the woman was, was a tall, hefty blonde in her mid-forties, with an attractive sun-beaten face and slanting, plum-colored eyes. She was wearing a white mu-mu without much on underneath it, judging from the way the fabric clung to her large breasts and heavy hips. She'd made an early start on the evening, because her breath smelled of bourbon. Her sexy blue eyes looked a little clabbered with it.

"Rita Scarne?"

"That's me. Who are you?"

"My name is Stoner, Ms. Scarne. I wonder if I could talk to you for a minute."

"About what?" the woman said with half a smile. She ran one hand up the jamb of the door, rested the other on her hip and stared at me afresh, as if she liked my looks and didn't care if I knew it.

"It's a personal matter. I promise not to take up much of your time."

"You're not selling something, are you? Like encyclopedias?"

I smiled. "No. I just want to ask you a few questions."

"All right. Go ahead."

"Maybe we could talk inside? It's pretty cold out here."

She closed her eyes thoughtfully then said, "Why not?" And waved me through the door.

"If you're selling insurance, Mr. Stoner, I'm going to be very disappointed," she said as we walked down the hallway to the back of the house. She turned right at a doorway, and I followed her into an enclosed patio, full of cane furniture. The back wall was all glass, and the sun pouring through it filled the room with light.

The woman sat down on a fan-back chair. I sat on a small pillowed sofa across from her. There was a bottle of Old Grand-dad on a small table to her right. Just the bottle—no glasses.

"So what is it you *are* selling, Mr. Stoner?" she said wryly.

"Nothing. I'm a private detective."

"You're kidding," the woman said, looking aghast. She almost reached for the bottle but caught herself.

I took out my wallet and showed her the photostat of my license.

"I'm working for a man named Phil Pearson. A psychiatrist—"

"I know who he is," the woman said sharply.

Rita Scarne gave me a cold, suspicious look—a far cry from the bedroom eyes she'd been making at the front door. "Why would Phil send you to me?"

"He didn't send me. I came because of his kids, Ethan and Kirsty. They've been missing since last Thursday. Pearson hired me to find them."

"I still don't understand why you came to me."

"There's a strong possibility that Ethan Pearson tried to call you last night, Ms. Scarne. At least, he called your agency, The Medical Pool, and they transferred his call to your number. He also received a return phone call from a woman."

"Why would he call me? I haven't seen Ethan or his sister or Phil in years."

"He didn't call?"

"I wasn't even here last night. My sister was house-sitting for me."

"She left no messages?"

"No."

"And you didn't call Ethan?"

She just stared at me.

"Do you have any idea why he would have called The Medical Pool for your number?"

She thought about it for a second. "I did work for Phil once. But that was a long time ago."

"Doing what?"

Rita Scarne gave me an irritated look, as if she were offended by the question—by the idea of being questioned at all. "He hired me to look after his wife, Estelle, if it's any of your business. The experience left a very bad taste."

The woman pursed her lips as if she could still taste it.

"Was Estelle Pearson in your care in 1976?"

Rita Scarne hesitated a moment then nodded, yes.

"That would have been right before she died?"

"Yes," she said bitterly, as if I'd pulled the admission out of her like a tooth. "I was her nurse when she died."

"So Ethan would have remembered you from that time?"

"Oh, yes," the woman said with a dull laugh. "He would have remembered me."

"You had problems with him?"

"You could safely say that. Ethan was a very disturbed kid. It was difficult for me to do my job with him around. He was always spying on me, bossing me about, trying to catch me up. And when he wasn't snooping he was getting in the way. He scarcely left me or his mother alone for a minute. It was exhausting—that kind of attention. And counter-productive."

"You mean he kept you from doing your job."

"I mean he kept driving his mother crazy," she said, losing patience. "Look, the little bastard didn't want Estelle to recover. If she recovered he wouldn't have had her all to himself. When she was depressed she used to dote on his attentions. As she got better she had less time for him. And that really pissed him off. You could see it in his face—a cold, venomous rage."

After thirteen years Rita Scarne's revulsion for Ethan Pearson was still as intense as if he'd just insulted her the day before. I figured that that kind of hatred had to be mutually felt, which made Ethan's apparent desire to get in touch with the woman inexplicable. Unless he and Kirsty felt that they had no choice—that Rita Scarne knew something that no one else could tell them.

I said, "Do you remember another patient of yours from the mid-seventies. A man named Herbert Talmadge?"

Rita Scarne's blue eyes went dead. "Herbert Talmadge?"

"He was a patient at Rollman's when you were head nurse there. Ethan has been looking for him for years now. It could be that was why he contacted you. He may have thought you knew how to find Talmadge."

"That's ridiculous!" The woman's face filled with high spots of color. "I don't even remember this man. Why would I know where he is? What do I have to do with it?"

She brushed her cheeks with the palms of her hands as if she was trying to wipe the blush away. "I think you better leave," she said angrily. "I don't care to talk about this. I don't care to be reassociated with that family's problems. I'm not guilty of anything."

But she certainly didn't act that way. She acted as if she were guilty as sin—and Herbert Talmadge was part of it.

I got up from the chair. "I may want to talk to you again, Ms. Scarne."

"Souls in hell want ice water, too." This time she did pick up the bottle and took a swig. "Get out of my house before I call the cops."

I walked up the hall and out the front door.

As I got in the car I thought about the blond nurse that Talmadge had been seen with—the one that Thelma Jackson had mentioned. On the surface of it I couldn't see why a woman like Rita Scarne would have toyed with a brutal, dangerous man like Talmadge. But if she had it would certainly bring a blush to her cheeks, even after thirteen years. It was something worth looking into.

* * *

I drove away from the house but I didn't go far—just a few blocks north on Ridge to a convenience store with a phone booth on its side wall. I parked by the booth, got out, and started to make calls, looking for someone who could confirm a connection between Rita Scarne and Herbert Talmadge.

I dialed Thelma Jackson first—to see if Rita's name rang a bell. But it didn't.

"Wish I could tell you she was the right one," Thelma said apologetically. "But I don't remember nothing 'bout that nurse, 'cept her blond hair. Can't find nobody else who does, neither. I been asking though."

I told her to keep trying, hung up, and dialed Rollman's.

Nurse Rostow was still on duty. "Could you do me one more favor?" I asked her.

"Again, Mr. Stoner?" she said in a long-suffering voice.

"Do you still have Rita Scarne's employment record from back in the mid-seventies?"

"Mr. Stoner," the woman said. "That's not something I can show you, and you know it."

"I don't want you to show it to me. I just want to find out where Rita was living in 1976."

"I guess the address would be all right," she said after thinking about it. "I mean an address from that long ago would hardly be restricted information."

She went off the line for a second. "Two thirty-four Terrace Avenue. There's also an address for her family in Dayton, Ohio—516 Minton. I believe she was from Dayton originally."

I jotted both addresses down.

"The Terrace residence is in Clifton?"

The woman said, yes.

I had to call long-distance information to make my last call—to Creve Coeur, Missouri. Luckily, Dr. Isaac Goldman had a published number for his psychiatric clinic on Westmoreland Boulevard. I got a secretary who wasn't about to put me through until I told her I was a cop, working on a life-and-death matter.

Goldman came on the line huffily, as if life-and-death matters didn't much impress him unless someone was paying for his time.

"I'm with a patient so please make this brief."

"You were an intern at Rollman's Hospital, here in Cincinnati in 1976. One of your patients was a black man named Herbert Talmadge."

"Yes," he said after a long moment. "I vaguely remember Talmadge. I think I recommended that he be sent to Longview for further treatment."

"As a matter of fact you authorized his release."

"You must be wrong about that. Talmadge had a severe psychosis."

I let that much pass and asked him about Nurse Rita Scarne. "Did she work with Talmadge while you were treating him?"

"Yes. She worked with all the patients on the ward."

"Would she have participated in interviews or tests?"

"Probably. I really don't recall."

"She had no special relationship with Talmadge?"

"Not that I knew of. Anything else?"

"No," I said, letting the disappointment sour my voice.

The man hung up as if he couldn't care less about my disappointments.

I'd accomplished next to nothing with the phone calls, except for worming Rita's old addresses out of Nurse Rostow. And that was a long shot. But it was the best shot I had at the moment. So I got back in the car and headed for 234

Terrace Avenue—looking to find somebody who'd lived there a long while, someone who was a bit of a gossip and a bit of a snoop. Someone who might have seen young, round-heels Rita with a solemn, ferret-faced black man with a terrible kink in his psyche.

21

▮▮▮

Terrace Avenue was a short, narrow side street off Clifton Avenue, full of old yellow-brick apartment houses and red-brick duplexes. Like most of the side streets in that neighborhood it was sedate, proper, and a little decrepit-looking —a home for students who could afford high rents and for older couples who couldn't. Two thirty-four was the first duplex on the south side of the street, a two-story bungalow with a bricked-in front porch and a cracked driveway on its side. A fat old man with a square-jawed face and short iron-grey hair was sitting in a rusty lawnchair in the partial shade of the porch overhang. He was wearing a lumberjack shirt, chinos, and a Reds baseball cap. The setting sun lit his face from below like a monument.

"Howdy," I said as I came up the walk. "You know the owner of this place?"

The man nodded. "Sure do. *I'm* the owner. Owned it for the last twenty-three years. Why? You looking to rent?"

"No, I'm trying to find an old friend of mine who used to live here."

"Now who would that be?"

"A nurse named Rita Scarne."

The man laughed hoarsely, falling forward over his gut and grasping his legs as if that was a real knee-slapper. I laughed, too, to make him feel at home.

"Christ, son, where've you been?" he said, still laughing. "That girl, Rita, hasn't lived here since . . . oh, hell, must've been '76 or '77."

"I moved out of town," I told him. "This was the last place she lived before I went away. I sure would like to find her."

"Rita was a hot ticket, all right. She and her roommate. You know them nurses—had men coming and going."

He waved his right hand as if he'd burned it on Rita Scarne's ass. It wouldn't have surprised me if he had. Up close he was a bit disreputable-looking. Shirt misbuttoned, salt-and-pepper beard on his chin, a nose that was a little too red even for that kind of weather.

"Couldn't begin to count the visitors Rita had," he said, rubbing it in.

"Guess I was just one of a crowd."

"You were, son."

"Come to think of it, I do remember one other guy that Rita ran with. I think his name was Talmadge, Herb Talmadge. Feisty little black fella with a goatee?"

The man shook his head decisively. "Nope. No niggers. Not in this house."

"Maybe I got it confused."

"Most like."

He stared at me suspiciously, as if I was that odd breed of animal—a white man who palled with blacks. Or maybe he was wondering whether Rita had actually pirated a black man into the house, like a puppy or a hot plate.

"Well, I don't know where the girl's gone to," he said, still eyeing me. "Christ, we must have rented that upstairs apartment ten or fifteen times since then. Me and the missus."

The man nodded at the stout, iron-bound door to the house as if it were a portrait of the wife. He raised up and sat down again like an automatic pin-setter. I assumed that was my cue to leave.

"You know I'd completely forgotten Rita had a roommate," I said, trying a new tack.

"How could you forget that one?" He pursed his thin lips

and made a silent whistle. "Man, she was pretty. Only lived here a few months, back in '75. But I never forgot her."

"You don't remember her name do you?"

"Carla Chaney," he said nostalgically. "She wasn't real fast or flashy like Rita. But she was a beauty. She and Rita were both beauties."

"You don't know where Carla went, do you? Maybe I could get in touch with Rita through her."

The man lifted his cap and raked his hair with the tips of his fingers. "I think she moved back to Albuquerque," he said, pulling the hat back down over his forehead smartly. "Leastways that's where she was from. Albuquerque, New Mexico."

I thanked the man and started back to the street. About halfway down the walk I looked back at him and said, "You know I think I remember Carla after all. She was a blond girl, wasn't she?"

"Blond and blue-eyed," the man called out. "Just like Rita."

I drove half a block to a Steak N' Egg on Clifton and phoned Albuquerque information from a booth in the corner. They had no listing for a Carla Chaney. But there was a listing for a Nola Chaney on Mesa Drive. I dialed it and had to wait ten rings before a woman answered. It was hard to tell over the phone, but she sounded drunk. Her voice was slurred and brassy, like a muted horn.

"Yes? What is it?" she said irritably.

"Mrs. Chaney?"

"Yeah. This is Nola Chaney."

"I'm an old friend of Carla's, Mrs. Chaney, calling from Cincinnati, Ohio. I've been trying to get in touch with Carla, but I don't know where she's living now. I was hoping you could tell me."

The woman laughed bitterly. "That's a rich one." She laughed again, stretching it out for effect. "Mister, I haven't seen Carla in sixteen years."

"You haven't seen her since 1973?"

"How about that?" Nola Chaney said as if it was even more preposterous when I said it. "Hasn't even called me on the phone. Her own mother. Her own flesh and blood."

"She was doing some nursing the last time I saw her."

"Well, I wouldn't know about that," the woman said. "Carla was a smart girl—maybe she did become a nurse. I always thought she'd end up in L.A. Become a model or something. Had her take tap lessons and elocution and everything."

The woman sighed heavily.

"But she pissed it away getting married so young. Just like me. I fell for a no-good one when I was no more than seventeen. Carla saw what happened. Lord knows, she saw what happened when a girl makes that kind of mistake. So what does she go and do when she's just barely out of high school? Runs off with another pissant son of a bitch no better than her dad Paul was. Not a dime in his pocket. Mean as a snake. But Bobby had the looks all right—and I guess that's all that counts when you're young."

"I didn't realize Carla was married."

"Might not be anymore, if I know my own blood."

"Her husband's name was Bobby?"

"Bobby Tallwood. Airman at the air force base out here." The woman's brassy voice mellowed slightly, as if she was reliving the distant past. "She and Bobby lived in a nice little house out near the base for a couple, three years. Had a kid named Joey. Cute little kid. Bobby didn't treat him right though, and I told him so. Hell, when he got drunk Bob was just as mean as Paul—always used his fists, you know? Don't know how many times Carla come running on home with the baby after Bobby gone on a rampage. But she always went back to him after a day or two. When you're getting it that good, I guess you go back no matter what. Anyway Bobby got transferred to Wright-Patterson in Dayton in '73. Moved down there to Ohio. And that's the last goddamn thing I heard from either one of them."

"Maybe I'll try up in Dayton," I said. "Could be she's still living there?"

"If you find her let me know, huh?"

But she'd hung before I could say that I would.

I called Dayton information, asked for listings for Bobby Tallwood or Carla Chaney, and drew a blank. I tried Cincinnati information on the same two names and didn't do any better. Wherever Carla Chaney was, it didn't look as if I was going to find her easily.

It was close to six when I got off the phone. I hadn't touched base with Louise Pearson in several hours, so I decided to drive to the hospital before going home. In the back of my mind I was thinking that Shelley Sacks might still be in the Bethesda emergency room. Since the Scarne woman had admitted to looking after Estelle Pearson in 1976, Sacks would certainly have known her at that time. And there was an off chance that Louise knew something about her too.

I knew it was a terrible day for the Pearsons—family and friends—and I hated to pester them with questions. But until I was certain that Kirsty was dead I was going to continue to track her. Even if she was dead in the river I knew I'd stay with it. I owed the girl that chance.

22

It was almost six when I pulled into the Bethesda North lot. By then the sun was setting in earnest in high bands of color across the western sky. It made me think of the sunrise that morning, hours earlier. Of the cold desolate clearing with the river running beneath it. They'd been dragging that river all day—Parker and his men—looking to catch something paler than fish belly, puffed up like risen dough.

I went down to the emergency room and was told that Phil Pearson had been transferred to ECU on the top floor. I took the elevator back up.

Shelley Sacks was sitting with Cora Pearson in a white shoebox of a waiting room, just outside the ECU door. Through the picture window on the far wall you could see the parking lot, dotted with mercury lamps that had begun to burn like little torches in the sunset. High on the right wall a television set flashed pictures of a game show.

The woman didn't see me as I came into the room, but Sacks did. He stood up with effort and walked over to where I was standing.

"Hello, Stoner," he said. His round face was grey with fatigue. His voice spiritless.

"How is he?" I asked.

Sacks shook his head. "Not good. He's in a coma, just barely clinging to life."

"I'm sorry."

He nodded sadly. "So am I. Terribly sorry for all of this." He glanced at the mother, sitting glassy-eyed and still in a far corner of the room. "Cora is going to need a great deal of support before this is through."

"How's Louise doing?"

"A rock," he said admiringly. "As always. She's in with Phil. Did you want to see her?"

He gave me a funny look that almost made me blush.

"No," I said, feeling guilty because I *did* want to see the woman—and a little paranoid because I thought Sacks knew why. Louise was fairly open about her love affairs, and I felt as if he'd somehow guessed that I was standing next in line. "I don't need to disturb them right now. You could relay a couple of messages for me, if you would."

"Certainly."

"The police need to know Kirsty's blood type." I thought of the cryptic message on the crumpled notepaper and added: "They need to know her blouse and dress size, too."

Sacks grimaced. "Louise told me about the car and the clothing. The police think that Ethan and Kirsty may be . . . ?"

"Nobody's sure, yet."

He sighed heavily. "I don't suppose there's any good news?"

"I'm afraid not. I have learned that Kirsty and Ethan stopped at Ethan's motel room yesterday. Apparently Ethan tried to get in touch with a psychiatric nurse named Rita Scarne."

"Rita Scarne?" Sacks said with mild surprise. "She was the nurse who took care of Estelle."

"So I understand. I talked to her this afternoon. She seemed to feel a lot of bitterness toward the Pearsons—especially Ethan."

"That's not entirely surprising. Part of Rita's job was to keep Ethan apart from his mother for a few hours every day. In fact *I* suggested that she do that."

"Why?"

"Because he was smothering his mother with attention—

and making Rita's life miserable. Estelle was simply too
weak to say no to Ethan, so I instructed Rita to say no for
her. Ethan became quite upset with Rita because of that—
and with me, too, I think. When Stelle died he blamed both
of us."

"*Was* she in any way to blame for the woman's suicide?"

"Of course not. In fact, she wasn't even at the house on
the day it happened. She'd called in sick with flu early that
morning."

Sacks' round blue eyes clouded up, and his voice caught
in his throat. I knew the excess of emotion wasn't just because of the past—it was partly because his friend was dying
a few feet away from us. But it was also because of the
woman, Estelle Pearson. He must have cared a great deal
for her.

"I thought Stelle would be all right without supervision
for one day, especially since she was scheduled to see me
that afternoon. I phoned her twice that morning, once right
before she was getting ready to leave for the appointment."
He raised an arm as if he were reaching out to guide the
dead woman through his office door, then dropped his hand
heavily against his side. "As you know, she never made it to
the office. She drove to the river instead."

He took a deep breath and brushed at his wet eyes. "Her
VW was found very near the place where Ethan's car was
found. They didn't find her body until several days later."

The fact that Ethan's Volare had ended up near the same
spot as his mother's VW, thirteen years after her death, was
a damn strange coincidence, if it *was* coincidence and not
something else. It had bothered me since Parker had tied
Talmadge to the car. I could see Ethan driving to the river
with Kirsty. What I couldn't see was Herbert Talmadge
going along for that ride. Not unless he'd been tricked or
forced into coming along—or had followed the kids there

on his own. But if he'd followed Kirsty and Ethan to the clearing, then my whole line of speculation went out the window. If he'd followed them, then it was conceivable they hadn't found Herbie—Herbie had somehow found them.

There was a third possibility—one that I'd been trying to shoot down since I first saw Ethan's collection of clippings. But it kept popping back up like a duck in a gallery. Whether they'd found him or he'd found them, it was conceivable that Herbert Talmadge had ended up in that clearing because he'd been there before. Appearances to the contrary, suicides could be faked, although that raised a helluva lot more questions than it answered.

"How soon after his mother's disappearance did Ethan start talking about a murderer?" I asked Sacks.

"Immediately, as far as I know. In fact, Phil called me on the day Stelle dropped out of sight to tell me that Ethan was throwing a violent tantrum. We both agreed it was a hysterical reaction."

"Did Pearson tell you what Ethan was *actually* saying about his mother's disappearance?"

Sacks drew back a little, as if he'd been offended by my question. "Ethan said he'd been watching Stelle from an upstairs window. He saw a man come out of the trees and get in the car with her."

"Talmadge?"

"He had no name for this bogeyman."

"He didn't associate Rita Scarne with the killer, did he?"

The man sighed. "Frankly, Stoner, I never heard the boy talk about any of this. He didn't like me, remember. He blamed me for not taking better care of his mother. I blamed me too. It was a terribly confusing time for all of us."

"Did the cops follow up on the kid's story?"

"I'm not sure."

It was easy enough to check. All I had to do was read through the police reports on Estelle Pearson's suicide when I got back to the apartment.

Sacks was beginning to look a little worn down by the conversation—by the terrible memories it invoked. He had too much else to cope with, so I decided to drop the subject of Estelle Pearson's death.

Before leaving I did ask him how it happened that Rita Scarne had been hired as Estelle Pearson's nurse. Given the woman's spotty employment record it was something that had bothered me.

"Phil liked her," he said simply. "So did Stelle. Rita has a no-nonsense manner that appeals to many people. And then Stelle worked with her once."

"I thought Estelle never practiced medicine."

"She didn't. But for a couple of years she worked as a nurse. Phil was interning, and they needed the money desperately."

"She didn't work at Rollman's, did she?" I said, taking a wild shot. "Say in the mid-seventies?"

"No. Stelle was a surgical nurse at General. In '68 and '69, I believe."

I sighed. For all I knew Talmadge was still in the army in '68 and '69.

"Were you aware that Rita Scarne had some trouble at Rollman's Hospital—trouble that got her fired in 1976?"

"No, I wasn't," Sacks said, looking surprised. "Phil did part of his residence at Rollman's. If there was trouble, it couldn't have been the kind that reflected on Rita's professional competence or he would certainly have known about it."

"I guess that's it then," I said, starting for the door. "Tell Louise I'll be in touch."

23

██

Cold night had fallen by the time I got to my car in the hospital lot. Beyond the haze of the mercury lamps and the fluorescent glare of the fast-food joints on Reed-Hartman, a full moon, red as October, climbed the eastern sky. Shivering in the wind I stared at it for a moment—a harvest moon in a winter sky.

I thought about paying Rita Scarne another visit. But until I could confront her with solid evidence connecting her to Talmadge she wasn't about to talk to me. I headed back to my apartment instead—to see if I couldn't find some of that evidence buried in the police reports of Estelle Pearson's suicide, buried in the past.

The manila envelope containing the photos of Estelle Pearson's last remains was sitting on the living room couch —just where I'd left it the night before. Throwing off my topcoat I scooped the folder up, sat down at the trestle table in the bay window, and began to go through its contents, starting with the investigating officer's first report. I was looking specifically for Ethan Pearson's testimony—anything he might have said tying Rita Scarne to the man who'd kidnapped his mother.

I didn't expect to find much—maybe a sentence or two that would look different in light of what had happened over the past few days. But the cold fact was I didn't find anything at all. Nothing about a black man hiding in the trees. Nothing about Estelle being kidnapped. Nothing about Rita Scarne. Nothing about Ethan himself.

The cops had obviously taken their cues from Phil Pear-

son and Shelley Sacks and ignored the boy. I couldn't blame
them. The boy *was* hysterical, and there was real tragedy
going on all around them. And yet cops were creatures of
habit. Crazy or not, Ethan's accusations should have been
routinely logged if only to be dismissed. Which meant that
someone had specifically requested that the boy's testimony be omitted from the record—someone with a powerful interest in the case. Given the circumstances I figured
that someone had to be Papa Phil Pearson.

I could see it happening. If Ethan had been making a
violent scene, Phil might have been small enough to feel it
personally, as he had when Kirsty had her breakdown thirteen years later, as he had when he'd hired me. Moreover,
he had reasons of his own for not wanting his kid to shoot his
mouth off around the police. If the cops had been led too far
afield, the investigation could have spilled over into the rest
of Pearson's life—exposing his affair with Louise, exposing
any number of ugly family secrets. Louise had hinted that
Phil had played a larger part in driving his wife crazy than
anyone realized. Even if she'd been exaggerating, it would
have been one more reason for Phil to hold the line, to limit
the investigation to a suicide watch.

Of course, it was just as possible that Phil Pearson had
been trying to protect his son on that terrible September
afternoon, doing the best that a man with his heightened
sense of shame could do to keep Ethan out of the public
eye. The truth was probably somewhere in between—
where it usually was.

I took a look at the coroner's report after I finished with
the police folder. A couple of grisly pictures of Estelle Pearson's body were clipped to the front—one taken at the
river, one at the morgue. After ten days in the Miami River
the woman's nude body was badly decomposed. The coroner found deep cuts on the face and neck and what he

termed "severe accidents" to buttocks, anus, pubes, and pelvis. The injuries might have raised suspicions of rape—especially when coupled with the fact that her body had been found nude—had the woman not jumped into a flooding river. The Miami's current was particularly strong that September, following a week of stormy weather. According to the coroner, driftwood and rock had done the damage to Estelle Pearson's body and the strong current had torn away her clothes. Shreds of her skirt and blouse were later found downstream in a backwater.

The coroner's autopsy revealed traces of Thorazine and alcohol in Estelle Pearson's blood. The Thorazine had been prescribed by Sacks. The booze was her own idea. After the autopsy the cops ran a cursory check of the bars in the Miamitown area on the off chance that someone had spotted Estelle tanking up. But she'd apparently done her drinking alone—perhaps as she sat in her car in the deserted field above the river. According to the coroner, the combination of Thorazine and liquor was probably potent enough to kill her. However, there was water in her lungs, so she was alive when she jumped—even if she'd been close to unconsciousness.

The only question raised at the coroner's inquest was why Estelle had killed herself on that particular afternoon. Shelley Sacks testified that the woman had been making progress since her breakdown in June. But he went on to say that violent mood swings were typical of her manic-depressive illness, and that the combination of alcohol and Thorazine had probably precipitated a psychotic reaction.

He was begging the question of why she'd taken all those drugs in the first place, but the coroner didn't pursue it. It was pretty clear from the rest of his testimony that Sacks didn't really know what had prompted Estelle Pearson to get high and throw herself in the river. As he'd once said to me and said to the coroner, she was simply "doomed" to take her own life.

I didn't know what to think when I finished the folder. By definition suicides always leave unanswered questions behind them, and Estelle Pearson was no exception. If you were convinced from the start that she'd killed herself, then you accepted the fact that those questions would never be satisfactorily answered. Which was precisely what the cops and the coroner had done. If like Ethan Pearson you were convinced that the woman had been kidnapped and murdered, the least you could say, on reading through the reports, was that the evidence didn't rule out the possibility.

The coroner hadn't been thinking rape and assault when he examined the corpse, so some of the tests that would have normally been administered in a criminal investigation—tests for semen, tests for blood type, tests that would have been consistent with the woman's injuries—simply weren't performed. The cops hadn't been thinking homicide either, which is why they hadn't bothered to record Ethan's testimony or come up with anything other than a spotty timetable of Estelle Pearson's last few hours on earth. Perhaps self-protectively Shelley Sacks had convinced himself that his friend was hopelessly psychotic, so he didn't really have to face the question of why, after several months of progress, the woman had suddenly decided to end her life.

There was room for doubt, all right. And yet, even playing devil's advocate, I couldn't honestly say I believed Estelle Pearson had been murdered by Herbert Talmadge. The woman's mental balance *was* very fragile. And even if the evidence of her suicide had a few holes in it, it was still persuasive. While Talmadge would help to explain the unexpected suddenness and violence of her death, his pattern of assaults didn't really fit the case. He'd always picked on girlfriends—women he knew. If he'd attacked Estelle Pearson he'd stepped out of character and assaulted a virtual stranger. On the basis of the evidence I couldn't see any reason why.

I'd just finished with the transcripts when the phone rang. I was glad of the interruption—glad to get away from the pictures and the autopsy report. I dropped the folder on the table and walked over to the wallphone in the kitchen. It was Louise Pearson at the other end.

"How's Phil?" I asked after saying hello.

"He gets a bypass tomorrow morning."

"And the chances . . . ?"

"Not good," she said.

"I'm sorry to hear it."

"So am I," Louise said sadly. "We haven't had a happy marriage, Phil and I. Not a . . . happy marriage. But we're tied to one another, nevertheless."

She cleared her throat. "Shelley said you needed to talk to me?"

"A couple of questions about the kids."

"Why bother? It's pretty clear that Kirsty and Ethan aren't coming home, isn't it?"

"It looks that way," I admitted.

"Then why bother? Why bother about any of this hopeless mess?"

I didn't say anything.

"I'm sorry," Louise said after a moment. "It's been awful being in this goddamn hospital for ten hours. Dead time—time to think about all the mistakes. Phil and the kids. Frank."

"Your first husband."

"I was trying to remember why I married him."

"What did you come up with?"

"I loved him, I guess," she said with mild astonishment, as if it surprised her to admit it, as if the love itself surprised her. "At least I don't have to cope with that anymore. It was pure business with Phil. He got what he wanted—me. And I got the life of the country club. It was a fair trade, I suppose. The country club set for Frank."

She cleared her throat again. "What is it you wanted to ask me?"

Rita Scarne was on my mind—because of the police report—so I asked about her.

"How in the world did you come up with that woman's name?" Louise said with a laugh.

"I didn't. Ethan did. He tried to call her last night. At least, I think he did—sometime before he and Kirsty ended up with Talmadge in that clearing above the river. The Scarne woman claims he didn't call."

"You've talked to her?"

"Several hours ago."

"Rita was a hot ticket back in the old days," Louise said.

"You knew her?"

"Phil and I would occasionally run into her at parties after we were married. She was always with someone new —and young. Rita had a bit of a reputation with the hospital personnel."

"For what?"

"For being wild. You know, sexually uninhibited. It was rumored that she liked her sex rough."

"Rough enough to interest a man like Talmadge?"

"I wouldn't know. I shouldn't have been repeating thirteen-year-old gossip in the first place."

"Phil hired her to look after Estelle, didn't he?"

"Yes. He'd worked with Rita at Rollman's and thought

she was a competent nurse. I guess she was—I never heard anyone say different. I can't see why Ethan and Kirsty went looking for her unless they associate her with Estelle."

"Or with Talmadge," I said. "Herbie had a white girl-friend who was a nurse."

"It's possible, I guess. What do you think?"

"I think I'm going to have to talk to her again. Soon."

Before hanging up I told Louise that the cops wanted to know Kirsty's blood type. "I know," she said. "I've already spoken with them."

"When?"

"Lieutenant Parker called here at the hospital about an hour ago. He also wanted to talk to you."

"Did he say what about?"

"That man, Talmadge, I think."

24

After finishing with Louise I phoned Parker at the Miamitown PD—and got one of his deputies.

"This is Stoner. I hear your boss is looking for me."

"Yeah, he is," the cop said. "You got a pencil?"

I took out my notebook.

"Six forty-four Reading Road, Apartment five. Park's there, and so are the Cincinnati police."

"What happened?" I said, writing the address down.

"This guy you're looking for—Talmadge. They found him about an hour ago."

Six forty-four Reading Road was right in the heart of the Avondale ghetto—a grimy four-story apartment house with a thirties Moderne facade of black marble window bands and smooth grey block. Small spotlights lit the walkway and the door. The building itself was dark, save for scattered lights in the apartments.

It was past nine when I got there—full dark and cold. But in spite of the bitter weather a small crowd of onlookers had gathered in front of the building—men and women, all black, peering curiously at the cops in the foyer. There were cops everywhere, and patrol cars up and down the street.

I made my way through the crowd into the apartment house lobby. A cop I knew—a patrolman named Klein—pointed me toward Sergeant Larry Parker.

"He's up on the second floor. Apartment five. That's where most of them are."

I went up the staircase to the second floor. The stairwell

smelled of the dry rot that was eating into the banisters; the stairposts shifted in their sockets like loose teeth. From the landing I spotted Parker and Al Foster of the CPD, leaning against the wall outside number 5. There were several other cops in the hall—forensic specialists with evidence kits. A dozen neighbors crowded in doorways and stared wide-eyed at the activity.

Inside apartment 5 a photographic strobe went off with a brilliant flash, spilling harsh white light through the open door. For a split second everyone in the hall was frozen in the glare. The detectives, the wide-eyed bystanders. Like one of Weegee's midnight crime-scene specials. I didn't want to think about what the cops inside the apartment might be photographing.

I walked up to Parker and Foster.

"I been trying to get you for an hour," Parker said when he spotted me.

"You've been here that long?"

He glanced at a wristwatch. "Since a quarter of eight." He looked at Al. "Isn't that when the call first came in?"

Al nodded. "Around then."

I said, "What have you got?"

"What we got," Al said, pushing away from the wall with his elbows and turning to the door, "is Herbert Talmadge's apartment."

"What about Talmadge himself?"

"Take a look," he said, waving me in like an impresario.

I walked through the door into a foursquare room, empty except for a single folding chair and a new-looking portable TV. The pine floors were swollen in ridges where the hot water pipes ran underneath them, giving the place a wavy, seasick feel. There was a stench, too. Not the dry rot smell of the stairs but a fecal smell of decay, like a dead animal in a wall. I didn't know where the stink was coming from until I glanced to my left through a portal leading to a small kitchen.

I couldn't see him clearly because of the criminalistics men surrounding him like mourners at a visitation. But when one of the cops moved, I caught a glimpse of his legs, sprawled at angles as if he'd been struggling to get up. Then I saw his face—that devilish, V-shaped face—grotesquely purpled and swollen in rigor. Herbert Talmadge. Streaks of blood, turned thick brown like molasses, flowed from his body, from a wound I couldn't see.

I looked away, at the seasick room. There were no decorations on the peeling yellow walls. No pictures or papers. A bare mantel to the right with a small dusty mirror above it and a dead fireplace below, charred like a burnt pot. Blinded windows on the far wall, with a stertorous hot water radiator rattling beneath them. Like Ethan Pearson's barren motel room it was the end of the road for Herbert Talmadge.

When the smell began to get to me, I went back into the hall. Al was standing just outside the door.

"You saw?"

I nodded. "How long has he been dead?"

"We won't know for sure until the coroner gets him. But forensic is guessing about twelve hours—maybe a little less."

"So he died around six this morning?"

Foster nodded. "Give or take an hour."

The Pearson kids had left the motel room at midnight Monday. Their abandoned car had been found at six that morning—and it had been in the clearing for an hour or two more than that, judging by the dead battery. That meant that Talmadge could have left his prints in the Volare anytime between midnight and four or five a.m. After that he'd apparently come home to be murdered himself.

I stared uneasily through the door at the circle of cops standing around Herbert Talmadge's corpse. "How did he die?"

"Again, we're not sure," Foster said. "Drug overdose, we think. At least we found an empty bottle of Demerol on the floor—and enough drugs in the bathroom to have put him to sleep forever. But there's a wound, too."

"What kind of wound?"

"Somebody stabbed him in the heart. What we don't know is whether the stabbing occurred before or after Talmadge was dead. Whoever stabbed him didn't like him— that's for sure. They twisted the blade back and forth several dozen times, like a drill bit."

In spite of myself I thought of Ethan and Kirsty Pearson. They had motive, God knew. And Talmadge had died as Ethan foretold in his poem—*a knife blade in the darkness.* "Did you find any evidence connecting Talmadge to the Pearson kids?"

"We found a woman's shoe in the fireplace," Parker said. "Size eight. There was some blood on it. Right now we're not sure whose blood it is. There was some other stuff in the fireplace, some paper—apparently he tried to burn it."

"Any idea what it was?"

"Forensic's got it. We'll know in a day or so." Parker took a breath. "There's something else."

From the look on his face I knew I wasn't going to like it. "What?"

"The back room. There's a mattress and . . . well, it looks like someone was tied down to it and pretty badly used. We found blood, hair, ropes, and a gag. Harry, the blood is type O negative. Same as on the panties."

"Kirsty," I said.

Parker nodded. "They must've found him in the apartment. He overpowered them and. . . . When he was done he drove them out to the Miami and tossed them in like a sack of kittens. It almost looks like Talmadge was waiting for them. I mean, the ropes and gags."

I said, "Didn't anyone in the building hear anything, for chrissake?"

Parker shook his head. "No. At least no one's saying they did."

"Who called the thing in?"

"A neighbor-woman up the hall," Al said. He pulled a notebook from his coat, flipped it open, and glanced at his notes. "When she got home from work today, she smelled that stink in Small's room and phoned us."

"Small?" I said.

"I mean Talmadge," Al said, flipping the note pad shut. "Small's the name she and the neighbors knew him by—the name he rented the apartment under. Herbert Small."

I glanced at the door to the apartment where a pitted brass number dangled from a nail. Number 5. *Small/5.*

"How the hell did they find him?" Parker said with exasperation. "Why did he kill them? Why did he drive them to the river?"

The only question I could answer was the first one—they'd found him because someone had phoned them at the motel and told them where to look. I didn't let Parker know that. I didn't want to.

"The woman who called this in," I said to Al. "You think I could talk to her?"

He nodded. "Across the hall. Number seven."

Her name was Moira Richardson, and she worked as a cleaning woman in Roselawn. She claimed to have no particular interest in Herbert Talmadge, but after I started talking to her I got the feeling that she took an interest in everything that went on in the building—or on the block.

She was a buxom woman with a shrewd, mobile, care-worn face. She spoke very slowly as people do when they want to be taken seriously, when they take themselves seriously. A younger woman, her daughter I thought, sat in a rocking chair in a far corner of the room.

I asked Moira Richardson when Talmadge/Small had moved in.

"Monday a week," she said. "Didn't have no belongings. No furniture."

"Do you know if he had a job?"

"That kind don't never work," the woman said, scowling. "In fact, I couldn't figure out where he got money for rent. Bought him a TV, too. And a car. Now where's a jailbird like that gonna get a TV, less he's pushing drugs or got some woman on the street."

It was an interesting question.

"Did he have any friends in the building?"

"He didn't ever say no more than two or three words to no one. Just come and go—mostly late at night. Girl down the hall said he asked to use her phone once. But she wouldn't let him in. She was scared of him." The woman threw her hand at me dismissively. "I ain't scared of no woolly-headed monkey like that."

"Did you let him use your phone?"

"He never asked me. Knew better than to ask me anything."

"Did you ever see him with anyone outside the building?"

The woman shook her head. "No sir, I didn't."

"I did," the one in the rocking chair chirruped.

She was a plump, pretty girl with soft brown eyes and a tiny, sparrow voice.

"Wha'chu mean 'you did'?" her mother said with massive suspicion.

The girl squirmed in the rocker. At first I thought she was frightened, then I realized she was simply excited at being the center of attention—mine and her mother's.

"I did too see, Mama," she said, twisting her head around and pouting at the far wall with her lower lip. "Saw him in the park with a white lady, last night."

The older woman fell back in her chair, stunned. "Well, I'll be."

"What time last night?" I asked.

"Time I'm coming home on the bus," the girl said. " 'Bout six o'clock. They was in Prospect Park. Way back in the shadows, toward the apartment house."

"You're sure it was Tal . . . Small?"

"Purty sure."

As if someone had snapped his fingers, the mother came rocketing out of her trance, lunging forward in her chair and fixing her daughter with a savage look.

"You didn't see nobody in no park."

"Did too," the girl said, shrinking beneath her mother's doubt.

"You wasting this man's time with your foolishness."

The girl's big brown eyes began to water. "I saw him," she said with trembly lips. "With a white lady."

"What that lady look like?" the mother said, as if she had her now.

The girl's head sank to her breast. "Couldn't see her face. It was too dark."

"You see," the mother said to me triumphantly. "She didn't see nothing. That's why she didn't tell them cops. She knew they'd catch her up on her lies."

"I ain't lying," the girl said, in tears now. "She was a white lady in a long brown coat. And she had on a white dress and white stockings and white shoes."

"Like a nurse?" I said, feeling a chill.

"Yes, sir," the girl said plaintively and looked up at me like I was her savior. "That's what I said to myself. He gone and got him a nurse from the hospital. You believe me, don't you? Tell Mama you believe me."

"Yes," I said. "I do."

25

I didn't tell Parker or Al Foster where I was going when I left the apartment house. I wasn't ready to tell them anything, yet. Not until I'd had the chance to talk to Rita Scarne without the law looking over my shoulder. I could always contact Parker—or threaten to contact him—if Rita wouldn't cooperate. But in the mood I was in I didn't think that was going to be necessary.

It was almost ten-thirty when I turned into the driveway leading to Rita Scarne's handsome house. I flipped off the headlights and coasted slowly down the hill, through the oak grove where the dark trees rustled in the wind. There was enough windowlight coming from the front of the house to guide me toward the garage. I parked the car at an angle in front of it, blocking off any exit. Getting out I walked up to the door, pressed the bell, stepped back into the shadows, and waited. After a time I heard someone fiddling with a bolt lock. The bolt slid free and the door opened a crack. I stepped forward immediately, leaning against the door with my shoulder and forcing it all the way open.

Rita Scarne was standing just inside the hall. She was wearing a brown topcoat over a nurse's uniform—the same outfit she'd worn for her meeting with Talmadge in Prospect Park. A small black leather satchel, like a doctor's bag, sat on the hall floor where she'd dropped it.

"What the hell is this?" she said, looking startled. "You're not welcome here. I thought I made that clear."

"We're going to talk, Rita," I said, grabbing her by the arm.

She tried to jerk away from me, but I pulled her back hard. "Don't," I said, waving a warning finger in her face.

"You can't do this!" she shouted.

"Watch me."

Dragging the woman behind me I walked quickly down the hall to the glassed-in terrace. I yanked Rita Scarne through the door, spun her around and sat her down on the fan-back chair. She stared up at me savagely.

"Now we're going to talk Rita," I said, bending over her. "No bullshit. The truth this time."

"The truth about what?"

"About last night. You remember yesterday evening, don't you? When Ethan called?"

"He didn't call."

"Don't say that! I don't want to hear that! Or about your sister who was house-sitting."

The woman's face reddened furiously. "Well, what the hell do you want to hear? Tell me so we can get this melodrama over with."

"You called the motel and sent those kids to that fucking maniac's apartment, Rita. You may even have told the son of a bitch they were coming. I want to know why. I want to know what those kids knew about you and Herbert Talmadge that made you send them to their deaths."

"Nothing!" she shouted. "There was nothing between me and Herbert Talmadge. I've already told you that."

"You were lying then. And you're lying now. You were seen with Talmadge on McMicken Street before Estelle Pearson died and again Monday night in Prospect Park."

"That's preposterous. Where are you getting your information—from that screwball Pearson kid?"

"I'll make this easy for you. You were fucking Talmadge back in '76, and Ethan found out. A snoopy kid who hated your guts, he saw you and Herbie doing it in the backyard, or the patio, on your lunchbreak, while Estelle was zonked out on Thorazine. Anyway he saw you."

Rita Scarne sneered at me. "Why would I screw a man like that?"

"Because you like men like that, Rita. You always have. Big, brutal, dangerous men. Men who can make it hurt the way you like it. Men like Herbie."

Rita Scarne sat back in the chair and laughed contemptuously. "You've got me confused with somebody else, Stoner."

"Like who?"

"Like you figure it out. Only you're not talking about me."

She reached over to the table where the fifth of Old Grand-dad was still sitting. There was a scant shot left inside, and she swallowed it straight. The whiskey made her face flush again, all the way to the roots of her loose blond hair.

"I don't know anything about Talmadge or the Pearson kids." She settled back in the chair, hugging the bottle to her breasts like a stuffed toy. "You can keep this up all night, and it won't change that."

"You don't understand, Rita. The cops have a witness who'll swear she saw you in Prospect Park with Herbert Talmadge. They've got a record of the call Ethan Pearson made from his motel room to your agency—the call the agency forwarded to your house. They've got drugs that can probably be traced to that bag of yours. A TV your money paid for. And they've got a dead man in an Avondale apartment with a big hole in his chest that you made with your own little hands."

"A dead man?" Rita Scarne said. The fight drained out of her face, leaving the naked fear. "Who's dead?"

"Talmadge, Rita. Herb Talmadge. And Ethan and Kirsty

Pearson. You killed them all this morning, don't you remember? Herb did two for you, and you did Herb." I bent
down so my face was only a few inches from hers. "You
killed them all and you're going to die for it."

"Bastard!" Raising both hands, she tried to claw my face. I
grabbed her wrists and pinned them to the arms of the
chair.

"He came after you, didn't he, Rita? Thirteen years and
he came after you the day he got out of Lex. What did he
want? Drugs? Money? Some of that good, old-fashioned,
hardball sex you specialize in? You couldn't say no, could
you? Not to Herb. What did he have on you? Something
from your days at Rollman's? Something about Estelle?"

The woman looked away.

I stared at her for a moment—at her red, averted face. "It
was Estelle, wasn't it? What did Talmadge do to Estelle?"

And, suddenly, I didn't have to ask anymore. "Good
Christ."

I started to laugh.

I let go of the woman's hands—she wasn't going anywhere—and sat down across from her on the couch, still
laughing. It was such a grand joke. "Ethan was telling the
truth. Your crazy, drugged-out boyfriend *did* show up at the
house, looking for you. Only you weren't there. You were
sick. That's it, isn't it? What happened then, Rita? Did
Herbie grab Estelle instead? Grab her, pour liquor into her,
and rape her. Is that why she killed herself? Or did Herb do
that, too?"

Rita Scarne's head sank slowly to her chest.

I sat back in the chair, letting the last of my laughter die
away. "And you were afraid to say anything—afraid you'd
catch the blame. After all you'd just been fired from Rollman's, so your credibility wasn't so hot. Or maybe Herbie

was the reason you got fired in the first place. A little hanky-panky on the psych ward. It's easy enough to check out."

The woman raised her head weakly. "Getting fired had nothing to do with sex," she said in a whisper. "I was fired because of . . . I did a favor for someone."

"What favor?"

She looked at me squarely for the first time since I'd mentioned Estelle Pearson's death. "I got the bastard released. Okay? They were going to send him away for good, and I got him released." She looked down again—at the bottle in her arms. "I stole some drugs from the dispensary, too."

When I'd talked to him on the phone, Dr. Isaac Goldman had claimed he hadn't authorized Talmadge's release—that he'd recommended confinement at Longview. I thought he'd simply forgotten the facts. Now it seemed he'd never known them.

"You forged Goldman's signature?"

"I waited until he left town, so they never knew about the release. It was the drugs that cost me the job. The old biddy, Rostow, found out I'd been taking them from the dispensary. The hospital board agreed not to press charges if I resigned my post."

"What kind of drugs did you steal?"

"Painkillers. Demerol. Talmadge loved the shit. And . . . it made him manageable."

"Manageable? Manageable by whom?"

Rita Scarne sighed heavily. "A friend. She was . . . involved with him. She wanted him out of the hospital."

"Your friend was a nurse?"

"Yes."

"Carla Chaney?" It was the only name that made sense.

The woman jerked as if she'd been prodded. "You know about Carla?"

"Just her name and the fact that she was your room-mate."

Rita Scarne stared at me searchingly, then shook her head as if she hadn't found what she'd been looking for. "You don't know anything. You couldn't."

She said it, but she didn't sound convinced.

"What is it I don't know?" I asked. "Why did Carla want Talmadge out of the hospital? What did it have to do with last night?"

"Last night?" She wasn't paying attention to me any-more. She sat in the chair and stared fearfully out the win-dow at the cold December dark.

"What really happened thirteen years ago?"

Rita Scarne blinked stupidly and stood up. The whiskey bottle slid off her lap, clattering to the floor. "I've got to get out of here," she said in a desperate voice.

"Not until we're finished."

The woman clasped her hands together as if she was praying. "You don't understand. It's falling apart. All of it. I should have known when you first showed up." She glanced through the window again at the dark woods behind the house. "I'm next. It won't stop until no one's left to tell."

"To tell what? For chrissake, make sense."

"I can't," she said. "Not now. Not until I'm sure it's safe. Not until I've made it safe."

"How will you do that?"

But she didn't answer me. "Give me a few hours. Please, Stoner? A few hours to make it safe. Then I'll talk to you about Carla . . . about all of it."

"What's to keep you from running away?"

"Where to?" she said. "I've got no place to run." She sat back down on the chair and raised her clasped hands. "Please, Stoner. Just a few hours."

I glanced at my watch which was showing ten-thirty. "I'll

give you until two-thirty this morning. Then we talk about you, Herb, Carla, Estelle, this whole damn thing."

She nodded, yes.

I started for the hall.

"Stoner," the woman called out. I looked back at her. "You were right—Ethan must have seen me with Talmadge."

"I thought you said you had nothing to do with Herb."

"He picked me up at work a couple of times in Carla's car." The woman laughed dully. "Who knows? Maybe it was planned that way."

26

██

I left the house but I didn't go far. Up Ridge to a gravel turnaround about fifty yards from the head of Rita Scarne's driveway. I sat there among the maple trees and the road-side hackberry bushes, listening to the tail end of a basketball game on the car radio, and waiting.

Around eleven-thirty I saw headlights coming up the driveway. A moment later Rita's car—the green Audi—cleared the crest of the hill and nosed out onto Ridge. Turning left the woman blew past me, heading west toward Roselawn. I waited until the taillights disappeared over a small rise, then put the Pinto in gear and started after her.

The night was clear and there wasn't any traffic on the road, so I had no trouble following even at a distance. And then Rita Scarne wasn't making any tricky maneuvers—a left on Section, a right at the Paddock entrance ramp to the interstate. She got on I-75, and I did too, settling back a couple hundred yards behind her as she sped north toward Dayton.

It began to flurry about a half hour after we got on the interstate—big flakes that fluttered lazily in the beams of the headlights and blew back against the windshield in sudden, undulant gusts. Through the side window I watched the dark, featureless hills along the expressway take shape beneath the snow—the stands of trees grow crooked limbs, white and fantastic-looking. Straight in front of me the twin red dots of Rita Scarne's taillights marked the miles.

About forty minutes outside of Cincinnati we hit the Dayton corporation limit. According to Nurse Rostow, Rita

Scarne was from Dayton, Ohio, and I had the feeling that she was headed home.

But she didn't take the first Dayton exit. In fact she went all the way through the city before slowing down and pulling off the interstate on the north side of town. The exit ramp emptied into a working-class suburb of two-story brick houses and foursquare lawns. Red and green Christmas lights were strung on most of the porches. Here and there nativity scenes burned like lighted billboards in the slanting snow.

Rita worked her way through a maze of side streets before finally pulling over in front of a staid red-brick St. Louis with no strings of Christmas lights on its porch, no nativity scene on its narrow lawn. I pulled over across from her and watched through the windshield as she got out of the Audi and walked up to the house. She was carrying the black leather satchel I'd seen in the hall.

The St. Louis had front stoops on either side. Rita walked over to the right-hand stoop and up the stairs to the door. Someone opened the door immediately, as if she was expected.

The door led to a living room with a picture window in front. The window was lighted and the blinds were up. After a time Rita came into view in the window, with a second woman trailing behind her. I couldn't make out the second woman's face because of the falling snow, but she was wearing a nurse's uniform, just like Rita's. The two women embraced for a moment, then walked off into another part of the house, disappearing from sight.

At precisely one a.m., Rita Talmadge came back out onto the stoop at the side of the house. The snowstorm had blown over by then, leaving the night sky spangled with cold, distant stars. I heard Rita say, "Good-bye," to someone inside the doorway, and watched as she walked down to the street and over to the Audi. She wasn't carrying the satchel anymore.

I waited until she drove away, then got out of the Pinto and walked up to the brick St. Louis. The front window was still lit. Through it I could see the second woman standing in the living room, staring queerly off into space. She was a tall buxom blonde like Rita. Only younger than Rita by five or so years and less weathered-looking. I went around to the right side of the house and climbed the stoop. There was a mailbox by the door with a name and number. I'd expected to find "Carla Chaney" written on it, but the placard read "Charlotte Scarne, 516 Minton." I assumed Charlotte was Rita's sister. It was unquestionably Rita's old address. I knocked on the door.

Charlotte Scarne must have thought Rita had come back a second time, for she was smiling when she opened the door. Her smile wilted when she saw me.

"Yes?"

"My name's Stoner, Ms. Scarne. I'd like to talk to you about Rita."

The woman didn't look surprised. She didn't invite me in, either.

"You know who I am?" I asked.

She nodded. "I know. Rita told me."

"Did she tell you what kind of trouble she's in?"

She nodded again.

"If you want to help her, you'll talk to me."

"You're not trying to help her," the woman said scornfully. "You're trying to put her in jail."

"I'm trying to find out what happened to two lost kids, Ms. Scarne. And I don't want to send anyone to jail—especially the wrong person. But if you and Rita don't cooperate, you're not going to leave me a choice."

"I don't know anything," the woman said. But she was a poor, inexperienced liar, and the words caught in her throat.

Charlotte Scarne was definitely not the hard character that her sister was. Everything about her was softer, less coarsened by experience—her voice, her face, her manner. I knew I'd have no trouble working on her—whatever her sister had left behind was visibly weighing her down.

I said, "Ms. Scarne, help me put this thing together before someone else ends up dead."

The woman started as if I'd touched the right nerve. "Rita's afraid of that."

"Can you tell me why?"

"Something from the past—something she shouldn't have done."

Charlotte Scarne stepped back from the door. It was as much of an invitation as I was going to get and I took it, stepping quickly into the room.

It was an old-fashioned parlor full of dusty knickknacks and dark mahogany furniture. Framed photographs of Mom, Pop, and the girls lined the mantel. Other pieces of ancient memorabilia were scattered on end tables and sideboards—china plates from a postwar exposition, a Steuben trout blowing crystal bubbles in a crystal cube, one lorn tin trophy that Dad had won at a company picnic, a wedding picture of the folks fading to yellow in its glass frame.

The room had the feel of arrested development—of life gone sad and sour and still. The whole house was probably the same. A woman like Rita Scarne could never live in a place like that. I had the feeling that her sister, Charlotte, was trapped in it.

"I haven't cleaned yet," the woman said guiltily, as if that explained the dismal room. "I was on duty tonight, and I didn't have a chance to clean."

"It's fine," I said to her.

She laughed dully. "No, it's not." And that was all she said.

I sat down on a dusty tuxedo couch, and the woman wandered over to a chair. "What can you tell me, Charlotte? What's got your sister so frightened?"

Charlotte Scarne looked down at the floor. "All she said was that it had to do with Carla—something she'd done for Carla a long time ago. She wouldn't say any more than that. She told me it was better if I didn't know."

"Carla, meaning Carla Chaney?"

The woman nodded.

"They were like sisters," she said, then flushed a little at the irony in her words. "Carla rented the upstairs rooms for a few months in the winter of '74 and spring of '75, while she was working as a nurse. Rita was a nurse, too. So they just naturally got along."

From the sound of her voice I had the feeling that she hadn't shared her sister's feeling for Nurse Chaney. "You didn't like Carla?"

"I liked her okay," Charlotte said without conviction. "It was just that she was always so . . . ambitious. Carla wanted things, and she didn't seem to care what it took to get them. She kind of infected Rita with her thinking. At least, I felt she did. It was a fact that Rita stopped coming to see us once the two of them moved to Cincinnati. She didn't visit us for almost two years after they left town."

Charlotte Scarne frowned bitterly, as if those two years alone with the folks had cost her something she'd never been paid for. "Rita finally came back in '77 when Dad died. By then she had everything she wanted—car, clothes, money. She paid for Dad's funeral out of her own pocket— several thousand dollars. She paid the last of the mortgage off, too. It was a humbling experience. Especially for Mom. I mean she thought Rita was going straight to hell when she left with Carla. I guess Rita showed her—and me, too."

"How did Rita make so much money in two years, Charlotte?"

"She had a good job. She said she'd saved it. Now I'm not sure."

The woman got up and went over to a mahogany breakfront. Opening a drawer, she lifted out the black leather satchel. "This is what Rita came for. She wanted me to have it, in case . . ." She stared blankly at the satchel, as if it wasn't the legacy she'd expected from her sister.

"What's inside?"

"Money. Ten thousand dollars." She handed the bag to me. "There are some bankbooks, too."

"Did Rita say where she got the money?"

"Some of it was left over from a long time ago. Blood money, she called it. Some of it she said she'd saved on her own. She told me I was to use it to buy myself a new chance at life—I mean if something happened to her." Charlotte Scarne shuddered violently. "I don't want it. I don't want any part of it. Someone died because of it."

"Did Rita say who?"

Charlotte took a deep breath. "Carla, I think."

I stared at the woman for a long moment. "What makes you say that?"

"Because we never saw Carla again after she and Rita left town. Rita never even spoke about her. I mean the two of them were inseparable friends. And then it was as if Carla never existed."

"Maybe she moved away from Cincinnati?"

"I don't think so," Charlotte said. "Whenever I'd ask Rita about Carla, she'd act like it was something she couldn't talk about. Something bad, you know? Carla could be pretty bad. I used to think that something must have happened to her when she was a kid—something really dreadful—to make her that way."

"What way is that?" I asked.

"Just . . . brutal," she said, flushing again. "Except for Rita she didn't really seem to care about anything or anyone—like what was inside her, the caring part, had curled up and died. I sneaked up to her room once while she was living here and found this stuff—leather-and-metal stuff. I didn't know what it meant then, just that it was bad. Later I realized that Carla liked to be hurt and to hurt other people."

I thought of Herbert Talmadge—a man after Carla's own heart.

"Your sister said she did a favor for Carla that she'd been paid money for. Did she give you any hint what that favor was—if it might have involved a man named Talmadge?"

"All she said was that someone had died as a result. And that she was afraid she might die, too."

"Why?"

"I don't know," the woman said helplessly.

"Did she mention Kirsty and Ethan Pearson?"

"Who are they?"

"The children of a woman Rita once worked for. A phone call from them last night might have triggered this whole thing. You don't know anything about that, do you?"

"Why would I know anything?" the woman said, looking confused.

"Your sister claimed you were house-sitting for her last night. And the agency Rita works for forwarded the Pearson kid's call to Rita's house."

"I don't know anything about any call," she said flatly.

"And Rita never mentioned the Pearsons to you?"

"She didn't mention them." Charlotte Scarne shuddered from head to foot. "Mr. Stoner, Rita acted as if she deserved to die. Whatever she did, it must have been a pretty terrible thing to make her feel that way."

Although the woman was talking about something in Rita's past, I couldn't help thinking of Herbert Talmadge, lying on that kitchen floor with his heart cut out. Of the deserted, blood-spattered Plymouth, sitting above the river where Estelle Pearson had died. Terrible things indeed.

27

Charlotte was still staring dully at Rita Scarne's satchel when I left the house on Minton Street. To her the money was tainted by death. Tainted also by her own ambivalence toward Rita—the prodigal who had run away from home, leaving Charlotte to live a life of dismal rectitude in that dismal house. No matter that it was probably the life that suited her best. It was less painful to blame Rita. And perhaps Rita had felt some of that blame was deserved. Ten thousand tax-free dollars certainly would have given Charlotte a fresh chance.

It took me forty minutes to get back to Cincinnati and another ten to wend my way up the snowy Amberley Village side streets to Ridge Road and Rita Scarne's house. It was after three in the morning by then, past the time I had set for my meeting with the woman. No matter the time I intended to talk to her.

Because of the snowfall I had trouble finding the entrance to the driveway. I might not have found it at all if it weren't for a pair of fresh tire tracks veering off Ridge and leading down the hill to the house. The treadmarks were a doubly good sign—they meant Rita Scarne had come home. After she'd run to her sister's house in Dayton, I was a little worried that she might keep going—out of the city, out of the state. But she'd decided to come back. With all those bad memories in her head, maybe she didn't have it in her to go anywhere else.

I followed the tire tracks through the oak grove into the snowy dell, and found the green Audi parked in front of the garage. At least I thought it was parked there. But as I got closer I saw grey smoke trailing from the tailpipe. The engine had been left running. The parking lights were on too, throwing a faint yellow wash up the side of the dark house. The fact that there weren't any lights on in the house itself bothered me. Even if the woman had dashed inside, intending to come right back out, there should have been lights on somewhere.

I pulled up behind the Audi and realized with a start that Rita Scarne was still sitting in the car. I could see her head and shoulders in the beam of my headlights. I could see something else too. The passenger-side window of the Audi had a spiderweb fracture—the kind that comes from a gun shot.

"Christ," I said aloud.

Leaving my headlights on I got out into the cold and walked slowly up to the woman's car. The Audi's radio had been left on. I could hear it singing softly over the idling engine. There was a sharp smell of cordite in the air, and something else. Something that wasn't gunpowder or exhaust fumes. Taking a breath I bent down and looked inside the car.

The driver-side window was open, and a bit of snow had blown through it, dusting the shoulder of Rita Scarne's coat and what was left of her face.

She'd been shot in the temple—at very close range because the powder burns had singed her blond hair above the left ear. The bullet had apparently gone through her skull, exiting the right side of her head and breaking the passenger-side window. There was no question Rita Scarne was dead. Half her brain was lying beside her in the passenger seat.

There was enough light coming from my headlights and the Audi's dashboard instruments for me to make out a gun

—a snub-nosed .38—lying in the woman's lap next to her outstretched hand. There was a sealed envelope on her lap too, spotted with blood.

I stood up and looked around the car. Two sets of footprints, a woman's shoe, stretched from the driver-side door to the front door of the house and back again—as if Rita had gone inside for a moment. There were no other footprints, man's or woman's, in the front yard snow and no other tire tracks in the driveway, save for those from the Audi and my Pinto.

I glanced back at the woman—at the blood-spattered envelope in her lap. She'd been deeply depressed that night. Talmadge was dead, probably at her hands. The Pearson kids were also dead with her connivance. An ugly thirteen-year-old secret—a secret full of blood and money —was coming back to haunt her. With me and the cops breathing down her neck, she could easily have decided to end it. In fact she'd told her sister she'd deserved to die no more than an hour before, after giving away all she had left to give.

It was probably a suicide, all right. And yet I couldn't quite buy it. Maybe because I hadn't been prepared to find her dead. Maybe because she'd left me with too many unanswered questions. Maybe because I'd half believed her earlier that night when she'd begged me to give her time to make things right. She'd been afraid of someone. Not me or the cops but someone from her past, someone who had paid her the "blood money," someone who had marked her— and Estelle, Talmadge, and the two Pearson kids—for death.

Suicides could be faked—it was like a theme running through the case. The open car window could have meant that she'd been approached in the driveway by someone who had carefully covered his tracks. It could also have meant that she'd wanted a breath of air before pulling the trigger—a breath of air and some elbow room to hold the gun to her head. Finding the truth of it was a job for a forensic team and a coroner.

Reaching through the window I flipped off the engine and pulled the keys out of the ignition. The sudden silence in the dell was dramatic enough to send a chill down my back. I looked around the yard again at the dark house and darker woods beyond it. If there was someone out there looking back at me, I couldn't see him. But I wanted to get inside the house anyway—away from that car and my own paranoia.

The house key was on the ring with the car keys. I found it, unlocked the front door, and went inside.

There was a phone on a stand in the hallway. I picked the receiver up and dialed Al Foster at the CPD. While I waited for him to come on the line I thought about going back outside and getting the envelope from the car. But I knew the forensic cops wouldn't like me tampering with evidence. I had enough to answer for already.

We were in the kitchen on the south side of the house—Parker, Foster, and I. Through the icy windows we could see the forensic men packing up their gear. It was almost six-thirty, and grey morning light had just begun to spill down the hillside, wrapping itself around the oak trunks and turning the pitted snow in the yard to lead.

The coroner had taken Rita Scarne's body away about ten minutes before. And now it was just the routine work of cleaning up after a suicide. That was what the coroner called it when he'd finished the preliminary exam. The woman's prints were on the gun butt. A paraffin test had turned up gunpowder on her fingers. The angle of the bullet was such that only she—or someone bending down beside her and holding the gun right to her skull through the open window—could have pulled the trigger. And there were no other footprints by the car. The ones leading to and from the door were definitely Rita's. And if that wasn't enough there was the note, sealed in the envelope.

I got to see it myself after Parker and Foster had read it— a typed confession on a page of Rita's stationery. It sat between us on the kitchen table, like a dividing line. I picked it up and read it again while we waited for the forensic team to finish—Rita Scarne's last testament.

I am responsible for the deaths of Herbert Talmadge and Estelle, Ethan and Kirsty Pearson. May God forgive me for what I've done and what I'm about to do.

There was no signature. She'd signed it in that car with the gun.

I laid the thing back down on the table. I didn't feel any different than I had the first time I'd read it. Which was to say I didn't know what to think. She hadn't explained anything. And I said so out loud.

Larry Parker eyed me balefully across the kitchen table. "What is your problem, Stoner? This wasn't her life story. It was a suicide note. She'd been caught red-handed committing murder, for chrissake. Or she would have been caught if you'd obeyed the law."

It wasn't the first time we'd gone over that ground in the past few hours, and I was getting a little tired of it and of Parker, who'd started to act very much like a small-town cop.

"There was someone else involved," I said to him. "Someone who'd paid Rita off thirteen years ago. Someone she was afraid of."

"Like who?" Parker said irritably. "And what difference would it make? You heard the coroner. The Scarne woman wasn't murdered—she killed herself."

"It makes a difference if you're interested in why she did it."

"I'm interested in solving three murders. Period. And we've got the evidence to do that."

He held up his right hand and started ticking things off on his fingers. "The shoe we found in Talmadge's apartment is the same size that the Scarne woman wears. There are a couple of bottles of Demerol in her medicine cabinet upstairs just like the ones we found in Herbie's apartment. We got a witness who saw her talking to Talmadge on Monday night. We got a phone call from Ethan to her agency, as well as a note from the motel room, with a name and address that could only come from her. And, lest we forget, we have a fucking confession, typed on her typewriter, on her stationery." Parker dropped his hand to the table. "We got it all."

"Except for the reasons why."

Parker got a pained look on his face. "She'd been making time with this guy, Talmadge, thirteen years ago. The Pearson kid saw them together and remembered Herbie's face. Thirteen years later Talmadge gets out of jail and looks old friend Rita up. She can't say no to him because he's dangerous. Plus he's got something on her—something connected to Estelle Pearson's suicide or to that other woman you mentioned, the Chaney girl."

"Like what?" I asked.

"How do I know what?" he snapped. "Christ, it was your idea. You tell me what. Whatever the reason Rita's scared to death of Talmadge but doesn't know how to get rid of him until the Pearson kids blunder onto the scene. The boy calls her up, and she sics them on Herbie. And when that back-fires she gets Talmadge stoned and does the job herself. Case closed."

"What about the ten thousand bucks? Who paid her that kind of money, Parker? And why? She said someone died because of it."

"She said a lot of things," Parker said uneasily. "Christ Almighty, she was headed for death row. She got fired for stealing drugs, didn't she? Maybe the money came from drugs—or from some other deal she cooked up. Who the hell knows?"

"Or ever will," I said, "if you don't ask a few more questions."

He glared at me. "Well, we can't ask Rita now, can we? Thanks to you."

"We can try to find Carla Chaney," I said. "At least we can try to find out what happened to her."

"*You* try to find her." Parker got up and lumbered over to the door. "I'm going home to get some sleep." He glanced back over his shoulder at me and Foster. "It'll come to-gether. Over the next few days, it'll all fit. Even the money thing. We'll keep dredging the river, but I already know what we're going to find."

"We don't know they're dead," I said.

"I do," Parker said. "The blood on the panties we found in the Plymouth and the blood on the bed in the apartment was Kirsten's. We've confirmed it."

"How?"

"The stepmother gave me the girl's blood type last night when I called the hospital looking for you. Type O nega-tive."

He opened the door then looked back over his shoulder. "You know those papers in the fireplace? Forensic says they could be pages from a diary. Some kind of manuscript, anyway. Does that ring any bells for you?"

"The Pearson girl was writing a book about her life. She was looking for an ending."

"Well, she found one," he said as he went out the door.

28

I spent a few more minutes talking to Foster before going home. He knew the case wasn't as cut-and-dry as Parker wanted it to be. But he also knew that most of the questions I'd raised would never be answered. There was no one left to answer them.

"Thirteen years is a long time, Harry," he said. "There are bound to be loose ends when a thing stretches back that far. Parker's got to make a case for the coroner's jury. And there's enough circumstantial evidence to do that."

"It isn't right, Al," I said, shaking my head.

"Maybe not. But unless you come up with something more than hearsay or a hunch, I'm going to have to stick with Park."

"Do me one favor, will you? Just run the Chaney girl through CID. Okay? Carla Chaney." I gave him her old addresses on Minton Street in Dayton and on Terrace in Cincinnati. "See if you come up with anything."

Al sighed. "Like what?"

"I'd settle for a current address."

He wrote down the girl's name, then got up and went to the door. "You better start resigning yourself to the fact that the Pearson case is history. Or you're going to end up wasting a lot of your time—and mine."

I should have phoned Louise Pearson as soon as I got back to the apartment. But I was too depressed to make the call. Larry Parker had been right about one thing. If I'd told the cops about Rita Scarne, she'd have been in custody at that moment. Instead I'd played it as if it was my case—mine alone. And now Rita was dead. And whatever she had known had died with her.

I lay down on the bed and eventually fell asleep. But it was troubled sleep—full of my own guilt and other people's deaths. The woman in the car with her head split apart. The grey Plymouth with the dark river below it, making a roar like traffic. Kirsten's book, turning fat and black in the fireplace. Talmadge, leaking blood on a battered kitchen floor. A world without second chances.

The alarm woke me around eleven that Wednesday morning. There was sun outside and cold blue sky. I sat in bed for a while, letting the dreams clear out of my head. Dragging myself into the kitchen I fixed coffee, pouring a little Scotch in the cup to brace myself for what lay ahead.

Officially the Pearson case was almost over for everyone but me and the Pearsons. However many of them were left alive on that winter morning.

I took a hot shower, shaved, dressed, and managed to make it out of the apartment and into the car by noon. Phil Pearson would be coming out of surgery about the time I got to Bethesda North, if he'd survived the bypass. With what I had to say it might have been better for him if he didn't survive.

I got to the hospital at twelve-thirty. The woman at the reception desk on the first floor told me that Pearson, P. was in ICU recovery. His condition was critical.

I took the elevator up to the top floor and followed arrows to ICU. The Pearsons, wife and mother, were sitting in a waiting room outside the recovery room door. Pale sunlight coming through the plate-glass window cut across their feet and climbed the far wall, turning it brilliant white. The air was still and cool and full of that quiet that isn't really quiet, just a holding of breath. I felt like holding my breath, too.

The mother saw me first. She had been crying, and powder had run down her cheeks like salt tears.

"Louise," she said in a deadened voice.

Louise leaned forward in the chair, and her face came into the sun. Like the mother, she looked haggard and sick with waiting.

"Hello, Harry," she said.

"Hello, Louise."

Louise glanced at Cora Pearson then stood up slowly, as if she didn't want to alarm the older woman with sudden movements. She came over to me and took my hands in hers.

"I'm very glad you're here," she said with feeling.

"How is he?"

She shook her head. "We don't know. He just came out of surgery twenty minutes ago. Five hours. That's how long it's been."

"Wasn't anyone else here with you?"

"Shelley. He had an emergency a few hours ago. He said he'd be back as soon as he could." She forced a smile. "Now you're here."

I ducked my head. "I have something to tell you."

"Is it about the kids?"

I nodded.

Louise looked back over her shoulder at Cora. "Mother, I'm going to go talk with Mr. Stoner. I'll be right back."

The older woman didn't move—she didn't hear Louise. All her energies were concentrated on the door to ICU Recovery.

We went down the hall to another empty waiting room. Louise closed the door behind us. Taking my hands in hers she drew me close and laid her head wearily on my shoulder. Outside in the corridor an elevator bell went off melodiously, like a shipboard gong.

"Are you going to be okay?" I asked her.

"I guess I am," Louise said, almost as if it surprised her. "Yes, I am. At least, for now. What is it you want to tell me?"

"It isn't good, Louise. Are you up to it?"

Her face went white. "They found the children's bodies," she said, pulling away from me.

"Not yet. But you better brace yourself for it eventually. Rita Scarne committed suicide last night and left a note implying that Kirsty and Ethan were dead. Murdered by Talmadge."

Louise's eyes filled with tears. "I expected it," she said, fighting to control her voice. "I guess we all did. That's why Phil's lying in there now."

She went over to a chair and sat down heavily. For a while she simply stared at the stippled wall.

"How did Rita know they were dead?" she asked after a time.

I explained the whole thing—at least as much of it as I could explain. I saved the part about Rita, Talmadge, and Estelle's death for last. When I told her what I suspected, her face filled with shocked surprise.

"You mean Ethan was right? Stelle really *was* murdered?"

"I don't know for sure. But there is that possibility. There's something else, too. The cops don't seem to care about it but I do."

"Go on."

"Thirteen years ago Rita Scarne was paid a good deal of money. The cops think it was for a drug sale. But I don't. I think it was connected to someone's death, quite possibly Estelle's."

"Why do you say that?" Louise asked. "Why would someone pay Rita off for what Herbert Talmadge did in a drugged fit?"

"Someone may have wanted to keep the whole thing quiet. To keep what had really happened a secret."

"You're not serious?"

"I'm very serious."

She laughed nervously. "But that's crazy. I mean you sound like Ethan—that's how crazy it is."

When I didn't laugh, she stared at me incredulously. "Even if this was true, who would want to do such a thing? I mean who would profit by it?"

It was something I hadn't wanted to think about, especially that morning. But there was one obvious candidate— a man who had already showed me how readily ashamed he was of his children and his past.

Louise caught what I was thinking, and her eyes went dead. "You're not suggesting that Phil . . . ?"

"It's possible," I said uneasily. "I have a hunch he kept Ethan's testimony about Talmadge out of the police report. It's possible that he paid Rita to shut up, too."

"To cover up murder?" Louise shook her head, no. "It's true that he wanted Estelle out of his life. After all those years of hell he wanted to be done with her and start fresh. But he didn't connive at her death, if that's what you're saying. My God, all he had to do was divorce Stelle to be rid of her. In fact, that's precisely what he intended to do at the end of the year."

I sighed. "Well, someone died because of that money. At least that's what Rita told her sister. And I'll tell you something else—Rita acted as if there was another person involved, somebody who was capable of killing." I stared at Louise for a moment. "The name Carla Chaney has popped up a couple of times. Does it ring any bells for you?"

"I've never heard of her. Who is she?"

"A nurse, a friend of Rita Scarne and Herbert Talmadge.

She might be dead, too, as a result of this thing. If not, she's probably the one person left who can unravel it."

Louise stared at me thoughtfully. "The police are going to try to find her?"

"*I'm* going to find her," I said. "The police think the case is closed."

"Perhaps it should be closed. So much death." She glanced toward the door. "Even Phil. He's going to die—I know it in my gut."

"He may survive."

"No," she said, shaking her head. "I know he won't. I've simply got to prepare myself for it. For all of this."

Someone knocked on the door. Louise straightened up quickly. I straightened up, too. It was Saul Lasker, he of the Porsche and the mansion house and the fixed, paltry smile. He was still smiling when I opened the door, although his grin wavered for a second when he saw me and Louise, as if the current that ran it had momentarily failed.

"I'm not interrupting anything, am I," he said with a smooth sort of nastiness.

"No, Saul," Louise said flatly. "When did you get here?"

"A few minutes ago. I was talking with Cora when the nurse came out of ICU. There's news about Phil." He put the smile away and put on the deeply earnest number. "The surgeon wants to talk to you."

Louise looked at me. For just a second her face trembled with fear.

"Do you want me to come with you?" I said to her.

She shook her head, no. "I've come this far alone. I'll see it through."

She put her hands to her face as if she was gathering her strength, then dropped them to her sides.

"I'll be there in a second," she said to Lasker.

He nodded and walked off down the hall.

Louise came over to me and put a hand to my cheek. "You'll call me tonight?"

I didn't have to think about it. "Yes."

She started for the door, then looked back over her shoulder. "Let the police handle this from now on, Harry. There's been too much death. Stirring things up won't bring Kirsty back to life. Or Ethan. It won't change any of it. From what you've told me, it was too late to change anything, anyway. Too late by thirteen years."

I went back to the office and just sat behind the desk for a while, staring out the frosty window at the sunlit city and the cold blue December sky. There were things I could have done—calls I could have made to jog the cops. Instead I sat there waiting, as if I were still sitting in that muffled hospital room. Around one-thirty Lasker phoned to tell me that Phil Pearson had died in recovery.

"Louise asked me to call," he said.

"How's she taking it?"

"She's fine. It's Cora we're worried about . . . she collapsed when she heard about Phil. They have her in ECU right now."

"Christ," I said.

"They're doing everything they can," he said lamely. "I'll call again if there's any further news."

I hung up the phone and stared stupidly at the desktop. The whole Pearson family was dying or dead. Something out of the past had risen up and killed them, and I hadn't been able to do a thing to stop it. All I'd done was make mistakes.

It was the girl that bothered me most. I'd had a chance with Kirsty—if I'd stayed in Marnee's apartment for a few minutes longer, or come back a few minutes earlier, or found that Evanston motel sooner in the day. But she and her brother had managed to keep a few ticks ahead of me, as if they were operating on a different kind of time than I was—a ruthless, malevolent kind of time. A time with murder in its heart. And now there weren't going to be any second chances for her.

Something was very wrong. I knew it in my gut. Taking Parker's case against Rita as gospel it had all been accident, coincidence, mad, vengeful error. Kirsten Pearson had died because Talmadge had impulsively murdered her mother, because Rita Scarne had hidden a guilty secret rather than go to the cops, because Ethan had seen something that no one believed, because thirteen years later all four of them had collided again like a car wreck, with Kirsten riding in the backseat.

Shelley Sacks would have called it "fate," because it was messy the way fates always are. But it wasn't random enough for me. Not with the whole family lying dead. I had no proof, just a guilty feeling that I'd missed it somehow— that we all had. And I couldn't live with that feeling—even if Louise and Parker could.

29

■■

After Lasker's call, I started making phone calls of my own —to anyone who could possibly help me locate Carla Chaney. I tried the nursing agencies first—to see if she was still working locally—and drew a blank. I tried the hospitals and hospices in both Dayton and Cincinnati, without any luck. I tried Nola Chaney again in New Mexico—and got no answer.

Around two I tried Al at the CPD. All he'd come up with was a driver's license application from 1974. It wasn't much, but it was better than nothing.

The address on the application was 678 Aviation Road in Dayton. It sounded like a Wright-Pat address. According to Carla's mother Nola, '73 was the year Carla had moved to Ohio from New Mexico—the year her husband, Bobby Tallwood, had been assigned to Wright-Patterson AFB. Carla applied for the license in November 1974 under her maiden name, Chaney. Perhaps she'd been divorced by then—that was what Nola Chaney had expected. Charlotte Scarne hadn't mentioned Carla's husband or kid either. I decided to find out what had happened to them.

It took me forty-five minutes to drive to Wright-Pat. I used my old D.A.'s deputy badge to get onto the base, and followed the signs to the headquarters building. One of the streets I passed was Aviation Road. I stopped at the corner, just to take a look.

It was a barracks street lined with neat frame Quonsets, row upon row of them like painted lunchboxes on a shelf. A tall wire fence spackled with ice ran behind the houses, separating them off from the huge cantilevered hangars and long tar airstrips. The roar of jet engines was constant. The ground trembled with it like a low-grade earthquake. I supposed you got used to that after a time. Or maybe you didn't. Maybe all you wanted to do was serve your time and get away from it—and the life inside those nondescript huts.

The yellow-brick headquarters building was a few streets north of Aviation Road. There was a flagpole out front and a stone guardhouse. I showed the MPs the pass I'd been issued at the gate, and they waved me through.

There were more guardposts inside the building—a whole series of them. By the time I got to the adjutant's office, three or four different tags hung like battle ribbons from my coat.

I told the adjutant I was looking for an airman named Tallwood, and he referred me to Personnel. It took a couple of more tags to get into the Personnel Office, and that was where I finally found someone to talk to.

His name was Olkiewcz, and he was a top sergeant with a square-jawed, implacable face straight out of Steve Canyon. He'd been stationed at Wright-Pat since the early seventies, and he knew most of the men who had served there by name.

He remembered Airman Tallwood, all right. But he refused to talk about him until I'd stated my business. Since Olkiewcz thought I was from the Cincinnati D.A.'s office, I figured Tallwood had a reputation for off-the-base trouble. But I was wrong.

"He's not wanted for anything," I told Olkiewcz. "I need to speak to him in connection with a missing persons case."

The sergeant allowed himself a tight little smile the size of a baby's fist. "That's funny," he said without sounding amused. " 'Cause you could say that Bob's a missing person, too."

"He's AWOL?"

"Permanently. He's dead, mister."

"When?"

Olkiewcz ran the fingers of his right hand through his hair like a four-pronged comb. "October 9, 1974."

"What makes you remember the date?"

"It wasn't something you were likely to forget—the way it happened, I mean."

I stared at him curiously. "You want to tell me about it?"

"I don't see no reason why I should," Olkiewcz said. "You got your answer—he's dead."

"Look, Sergeant. His wife, Carla, is in some trouble. I'm trying to locate her, and any information I can get about her past could be crucial."

This time he gave *me* a curious look. "What'd she do? Kill somebody?"

"Possibly." I said it because I had the feeling that was what he wanted to hear. His eyes had filled with hate when I'd mentioned Carla's name.

Olkiewcz leaned back in his chair and stared at me coolly. "I shouldn't tell you this, but I'm going to do it anyway. 'Cause I wouldn't want that two-timing bitch to get away with it again."

"Meaning what?"

"Meaning she killed her husband and her kid."

Olkiewcz smiled his tight smile again, then wiped it off his face with his right hand as if it was something that had dribbled out of the corner of his mouth. "Oh, she didn't actually pull a trigger. But she sure as hell drove that boy over the brink. Made him so crazy he killed that little kid of theirs, then turned a shotgun on himself."

"Tallwood killed his son and himself?" I said.

"That's was the way it looked—and nobody could prove different."

"Did anybody try?"

"Sure. The adjutant tried. We all did. Everybody knew the bitch was running around with a nigger. That it was driving Bobby nuts, the way she and the nigger carried on —right there in front of the kid. Crazy little coon. Just as sick as she was. Got four-effed right after it happened."

"This guy was a soldier on the base?"

Olkiewcz nodded. "A psycho. P.T.'d a half-dozen times for attacking nurses. That's how the bitch met him—on the psych ward at the base hospital."

"Carla worked there as a nurse?"

He nodded. "I don't know what she saw in the nigger— he sure as hell didn't have rank or dough. Everybody told Bobby to kick her ass back to New Mexico. But he wouldn't do it. He just kept looking the other way till the day he snapped. The joke is the bitch ended up with his insurance. Ten thousand dollars' worth." Olkiewcz hawked up an oyster of phlegm and spat it into a trash can beside the desk. "No woman's worth that. I don't care how good the pussy."

"The black soldier Carla was screwing, do you remember his name?"

I just wanted to hear him say it. And he did.

"Talmadge. Airman Third Class Herbert Talmadge."

Olkiewcz's story was so obviously tainted with prejudice that I decided to stop at the base hospital where Carla Chaney had worked to double-check it. One of the doctors on the surgical ward, a major named Carson, remembered Carla Chaney fairly well. Carson was a tall, heavyset man in his mid-forties, with the patchy, red-eyed face of a heavy drinker. He wore a pair of extremely thick, government issue glasses. His bleary eyes swam behind them like huge, bewildered fish.

Carson confirmed the bare bones of Olkiewcz's story. Tallwood had killed himself and his son, in October 1974. But he had a different recollection of the wife.

"Carla," he said nostalgically. "Christ, she was a dish. Half the doctors on the ward followed her around with their tongues hanging out. She could have had any one of them— any of us—in a minute. But she stayed married to Bob Tallwood—why I don't know. The son of a bitch used to beat her up every other day. He beat his son up, too."

"Olkiewcz left that part out," I said.

"Olkiewcz is a racist thug. Just like Bob Tallwood was. And then Carla never gave Olkiewcz a tumble, and that probably stuck in his craw."

"You seemed to have gotten along with her."

Carson smiled. "She didn't give *me* a tumble either, if that's what you mean. But yeah, I wanted her. I guess she liked me well enough. We'd talk occasionally on the ward, and I treated her on the QT a couple of times after Bob beat her up. I even tried to talk her into leaving the son of a bitch. But she said Bob would kill her before he gave her a divorce. And if she left him he'd just come after her—and make things that much worse."

"It was lucky for her that he killed himself then, wasn't it?"

"Some people looked at it that way. I didn't."

I asked Carson about Herb Talmadge, but he couldn't place the name.

"For all the attention paid Carla, I never saw her get halfway serious about anybody except Sy Chase. She spent a lot of time with him on the ward and off."

"Chase was a doctor?"

He nodded. "An intern who served here in '73 and '74.

He was politically connected somehow, or his wife's family was. That's why he ended up at Wright instead of in 'Nam. I thought he was an asshole, but Carla went for him."

"How serious was it on Chase's part?"

"I think he would have divorced his wife and married Carla in a minute if she'd been free. But he never got the chance. His hitch was up in June of '74. He left the base a few months before Tallwood shot himself. Never saw him again after that."

"When Tallwood died, was there any hint that Carla might have had a hand in it?"

"There are always rumors after a suicide," Carson said dismissively. "No one ever uncovered any evidence to support them. Bob Tallwood was a vicious man with a violent temper. He'd beaten Carla and his son up plenty of times before. He just went too far on that particular night and killed the kid. Afterward he started drinking and ended up eating a shotgun. I think the rumors about Carla started because she'd been out that night—because she hadn't been killed too. And then she didn't show much emotion when she was told what had happened. Not even about the little boy." The man shook his head. "I don't think Carla had much feeling left after living with Bob. I think he'd killed that part of her for good."

"Meaning she was a sociopath?"

"Meaning like most people who live with constant abuse she was deeply scarred."

"You said she was out on the night of the suicide. Do you know where?"

"She'd gone to stay at a house of a friend, as I recall. A civilian nurse who occasionally worked here on the base."

"Do you remember this nurse's name?"

Carson scratched his head thoughtfully. "I'm sorry. It's just been too many years."

"It wouldn't have been Rita Scarne, would it?"

His big, bleary eyes lit up with recognition. "I think it was Rita Scarne. At least the name rings a bell. How did you know that?"

"Just a lucky guess," I said grimly.

30

||||||||||||||||||||||||||||||||||||||||||||||||||||||||||||||||||||||

Carson didn't know what had become of Carla Chaney after she left Wright-Pat in late '74. Neither did the Records Department at the base hospital, although they confirmed the facts that she and Rita Scarne had been employed as psychiatric nurses at Wright-Pat and that Airman Herbert Talmadge had been one of their patients. They also managed to dig up an office address for Dr. Sy Chase, the man Carson had linked to Carla Chaney. The address on Gallatin Avenue in Cedar Falls, Ohio, was fourteen years old. But Cedar Falls wasn't far out of my way, and I was willing to make a side trip to find out just how serious Carla had been about Sy Chase—whether she'd been serious enough to commit murder. And a terrible murder, at that.

The possibility was there, undeniably. Another suspicious suicide with the same cast of characters who'd popped up in the Pearson woman's case. Only Tallwood's death had been no accident—not with a ten thousand dollar payoff at the end of it, the very amount that Rita Scarne had collected in blood money. If Tallwood hadn't committed suicide, there was a chance he'd been deliberately murdered by Talmadge at Carla's behest, with Rita providing the alibi. And that chance made me rethink what had happened to Estelle Pearson.

I'd assumed that Herb Talmadge had mistaken Stelle for Rita on that September afternoon in 1976—that whatever he'd done to her had been unplanned mayhem, later covered up by Phil Pearson. But the circumstances surrounding Bob Tallwood's death suggested a more sinister scenario. It now seemed possible that Estelle Pearson had been deliberately murdered, too. It would explain why Carla had gone to such lengths to get her hitman Talmadge out of the hospital in June of '76, why Rita had stolen drugs to keep him "manageable" throughout the summer, why Herb had shown up at the Pearson house on the one day of the year that Rita called in sick.

It was possible, all right. And if it was true there had to be another payoff—for Rita and Carla and Herb. The original ten thousand would hardly cover a second homicide. There had to be a payoff and a man to pay it. The only person I could think of with that kind of money and a connection to Stelle was Phil Pearson. I didn't know why he'd want his wife dead or how he'd come to pick Rita, Carla, and Herb to do the job. But if Estelle *had* been murdered Phil was behind it—no matter what Louise said.

There wasn't much to Cedar Falls, Ohio. Just a numbered exit off 74-West, emptying into a short commercial drag lined with two-story brick storefronts—half of them built in the thirties by the WPA. A frayed red-and-white banner of Santa Claus and his reindeer was strung between telephone poles at the head of Main Street. There were no other decorations in store windows or on the sidewalks. Even the banner didn't look festive. The winter wind had dogged it to tatters.

I drove under the torn-up Santa, around a small, deserted park at the end of Main, into the meager fringe of suburbs outlying the town. A raw-faced boy at a Clark service station directed me to Gallatin Street.

Dr. Sy Chase's office was the very last house on Gallatin, a tired frame bungalow with a converted first floor. Beyond Chase's office building the town simply died off into flat, snowy farmland and distant pines glittering in the sun. I parked in a lot beside the building, got out, and walked up to the porch. A sign with a physician's caduceus on it was hanging above the door. I went in.

There was a small glassed-in office immediately to the right of the door and a waiting area to the left. The waiting area was empty, although someone had left an overcoat and purse on one of the chairs. A red-haired nurse with a freckled, sharply featured face was sitting on a stool inside the office. She watched me intently, as if she was half afraid I planned to snatch the purse.

"I'd like to see Dr. Chase," I said, smiling to soothe her nerves.

The alert look on the woman's face turned to confusion. Wrinkling her nose she said, "Why, don't you know that Dr. Chase doesn't work here anymore?"

"He moved?"

"He died. Thirteen, no, fourteen years ago. He had a car accident and died."

"I see," I said with disappointment.

"You were a friend of his?"

"A friend of a friend's."

"I guess you could talk to Dr. Steele. He used to be Dr. Chase's partner." She glanced down at an appointment book on the ledge in front of her. "Doctor doesn't have any patients for the rest of the afternoon. It's always slow like this around Christmas."

"Dr. Steele would be fine."

"Your name?"

"Harry Stoner."

The nurse showed me down a short hall to a white-walled examination room. After a moment Steele came into the room—a short, bony man in his early fifties, with thin grey hair and a lean, fleshless face, grooved like nutmeat at either cheek. He was wearing a white doctor's smock and carrying a styrofoam cup of coffee in his right hand.

Steele took a sip of coffee and eyed me speculatively.

"So you were a friend of Sy's?"

He had a flat, nasal voice with a trace of caution in it—a good voice for a small-town doctor.

"I never met the man," I told him.

Steele looked taken aback. "I thought Sylvie said—"

"I'm searching for someone Dr. Chase used to know. A woman named Carla Chaney."

Steele gave me a long look. "Are you a policeman?"

"Does her name make you think of cops?"

"Frankly, *you* make me think of cops," Steele said.

I grinned at him. "I'm a P.I. working on a missing persons case. Two kids from Cincinnati."

"And you think Carla is involved?"

I nodded.

He stared at me again. "After fourteen years it's hard to imagine how you would end up in Cedar Falls, looking for Carla Chaney. But I guess that doesn't matter. The short and sweet of it is I have no idea where she is. I haven't seen her since the spring of 1975."

"Then she used to live in Cedar Falls?"

"No. She lived in Dayton and commuted to work for a couple of months back at the end of '74 and the beginning of '75."

I assumed those were the months that Carla had spent at the Minton Street house with Rita and Charlotte Scarne, the months before she'd moved to Terrace Avenue.

"What kind of work did she do here?"

"Officially she was Sydney's nurse."

"And unofficially?"

Steele flushed.

Taking another sip of coffee he sat down on a leather stool beside the mirrored cabinet. "I guess it won't matter if I talk about it now. They're all gone anyway. Dead or gone. Even Jeanne."

"Jeanne?"

"Sy's wife," he said. "She left town about a year after Sy was killed in the accident. And no one seems to know what became of her. It's quite a mystery, really. Her parents even hired a detective like you to look into it but . . . no luck."

He said it with deep regret. He had obviously liked the woman. In fact talking about her disappearance made him eye me anew, as if he was considering asking me to look into Jeanne Chase's disappearance.

I said, "You were going to tell me about Carla," to head him off.

"I guess I was," Steele said. "Not to put too fine a point on it Sy was boffing the hell out of her. I mean they were having a four-star affair. At one stage Sy even hinted that he was going to divorce Jeanne and marry Carla."

"But he didn't get the divorce?"

Steele shook his head. "He talked himself out of the idea —or Jeanne did. The truth was Sy was just a bad little boy, who liked to peek up women's skirts. Jeanne knew that about him. When it came down to it, she also knew that Sy would never leave her."

"Why?"

"Jeanne's family had money. If he divorced her he'd lose his meal ticket. And Sy loved the good life too much to throw it away, even for a beauty like Carla. Jeanne knew that about him, too. We all did, except for Carla."

"So Chase broke the affair off?"

Steele shook his head. "He didn't have the guts to tell Carla it was over, so Jeanne did it for him. There was a scene—right here in the office. An ugly tiff. The next day the girl quit and Jeanne went to work in her place. She was trained as a nurse, but what she really wanted to do was keep Sy away from further temptation."

"Did it work?"

Steele laughed dully. "Eventually. Sy kept seeing Carla for a short time after that. I know he gave the girl money out of the office account—to help her relocate in Cincy. It was the kind of thing Sy was always doing, instead of the right thing."

"You didn't like Chase much, did you?" I said.

"No, I didn't," the man said without reflection. "I took him into the practice as a favor to Jeanne's father. But it was clear from the start that Sy was never interested in the life of a country physician in a town like Cedar Falls. He'd done his internship in psychiatry and fancied himself too well educated for general practice. Hell, he was too well educated to work. He was a weak man. A spoiled, self-indulgent man who thought only of his own needs. Frankly I could never figure out what Jeanne or Carla saw in him."

"Perhaps someone who could be easily manipulated," I said, thinking of the "toys" in Carla's apartment. Toys to punish bad little boys.

"That's not a good enough reason," Steele said. "At least it wouldn't have been for a woman like Jeanne. God, I wonder what really happened to her."

But I was thinking of what had happened to the other one —the one who had gone to Cincinnati.

31

Before leaving the office I asked Steele about the accident that had killed Sy Chase—whether there had been any doubt that it *was* an accident. Suspicious deaths seem to follow Carla Chaney around, whether she'd had a hand in them or not.

But Steele said there'd been nothing suspicious about Sy Chase's death. One December night in 1975, on his way home from Cincinnati, he'd driven his car off an icy road and died instantly in the crash. The only possible connection Carla might have had to the accident was incidental—Steele thought he'd might have gone looking for the girl on the night he died.

"At least Jeanne suspected that was what he was up to. She was pretty damn bitter about it, too. Sy swore to her that he'd given Carla up."

"Carla was still living in Cincinnati at the time of the accident?"

"Yes. Like I said, Sy supported her for a while down there —until Jeanne found out about it. Then the money stopped. Carla took a job and that was the end of their affair." He smiled. "Sy was damn bitter about it. You see, it didn't take Carla long to find someone new. After she got the job she dropped Sy like a hot rock."

"When was this?"

"In the fall of '75, I think."

That meant that Carla had probably been living on Sy Chase's money throughout the summer when she'd roomed with Rita Scarne on Terrace Avenue. In the fall she'd found a different way to support herself—and a different boyfriend.

It occurred to me that it would be damn convenient from my angle if Phil Pearson turned out to be Carla's new employer—and lover. Louise said that Phil had had several lovers before her. Nurses and secretaries. Without question he would have looked like a real catch to Carla. A successful, unhappily married man who was talking divorce—that was how Louise had described him in late '76. He probably wasn't much different in the fall of '75. Another Sy Chase, without a wife to rein him in.

A short, passionate affair with a treacherous girl who loved money and had lethally dangerous friends—it could have led to murder. Although what Phil would have gained from killing off Stelle I didn't know. What Carla had stood to gain was easier to figure: a rich husband. As for Rita, she would have settled for some of Phil's cash.

"Do you happen to know who Carla went to work for in Cincinnati?" I asked Steele.

He rubbed the side of his nose. "Some doctor, I think. Sy probably mentioned his name. But after fourteen years . . ."

"It wasn't a psychiatrist named Pearson, was it? Phil Pearson?"

"Frankly I don't remember. Could be I've got the name written down at home in one of my old date books or calendars."

I took out my card and handed it to him. "If you find it, give me a call."

It was past five when I got back to the office. The first thing I did was phone Nurse Rostow to see if Carla Chaney had gone to work at Rollman's Hospital in late 1975—while Phil Pearson had been finishing his residency.

"The name doesn't ring a bell," Nurse Rostow said. "I could consult our records if you wish."

"That would be fine."

While I was waiting for her call back I went through the messages on my answering machine. There was one from Larry Parker, telling me that the State Patrol hadn't found the children's bodies yet. And one from a man named Elroy Stenger. I dialed him up.

"Elroy Stenger," the man said, as if I should have placed his name immediately. "You know? Roy Stenger, out at The Bluegrass Motel?"

"I thought a guy named Wilson ran the motel."

"He does," Stenger said. "I'm the clerk. Wilson said I should call you."

"That was two days ago."

"I been sick. Ain't gonna come in here sick, you know. No matter what that sumbitch Wilson says. He don't pay me enough that I should come in here running no fever. Hell, I don't feel a hunnert percent yet."

Roy Stenger had the whiney, sullen voice of a born loser, a man whose sole tactic was complaint. I could almost see him standing in front of me—thin as a rail, with an anchor tatooed on his arm, his back teeth pulled, a mean blue eye, and an attitude that never quit. I could understand why Wilson had felt like poking him in the nose.

"All right, Roy," I said wearily. "What's up?"

"Ain't nothing *up*," he said, as if I'd thrown him a curve. "Thought you had some questions you wanted to ask me."

"Not anymore."

"You don't want to know about them phone calls?" He didn't wait for me to answer. "There were two. One going out and one coming in. That kid made that first one a little after he and that girlfriend of his drove in on Monday after-

noon, maybe 'bout five or six o'clock. I got the number if
you want."

"I already have it," I said.

"It was to some nursing agency, I think."

"How did you know that?"

"I listened in on the line. Got nothing better to do 'round
here most evenings."

"Did you listen to the second call, too?" I asked curiously.
"The one coming in?"

"Nope. The goddamn ice machine went on the fritz
again 'round eleven-thirty, so I missed most all of it." He
said it like it was a TV show he'd been planning to watch.
"It was a woman, though. And she asked for Ethan Pearson
by name." He paused to clear his throat. "Maybe it was the
woman who come by that night. She was wearing a nurse's
outfit. So likely it was."

I sat up in my chair. "What are you talking about?"

"A woman come by the office, 'bout ten o'clock Monday
night. She was wearing a nurse's outfit."

"Wilson didn't mention that."

"I didn't tell him is why. Don't tell him everything that
goes on 'round here. No reason to."

"What did this woman look like?"

"Didn't see her face. She had on dark glasses and a scarf
'round her head. But she was a good-size woman with blond
hair."

It sounded like Rita Scarne.

"What did she want?"

"She left a package for the kid. Just an envelope with
some papers or something in it. I rung his room and he
come picked it up a few minutes later, after the nurse done
left."

"What was she driving, this nurse?"

"An old-make Pontiac. Real beat up."

"You're sure of that?" I said, thinking of Rita's Audi.

"Hell, yes I'm sure. Saw her again last night. 'Bout three a.m."

I didn't say anything for a second. "You saw this same car last night? Wednesday morning?"

"Same car, same woman," he said. "That boy must have given her his key, 'cause she went in his room and come out and drove off. Out the back way, 'round past the pool."

"Did you see her face this time?"

"Nope. Is the boy sick or something? Got him the flu, maybe? Man could catch his death in this kind of cold."

I didn't say it out loud, but that was what Ethan had caught all right, and Kirsty too.

It took me thirty minutes to drive to The Bluegrass Motel.

Stenger was waiting at the desk in the office. Tall and lean, with lax black hair combed straight down across his forehead and a scraggly moustache like a pencil scribble above his sullen mouth. He wore an open-collared white shirt with a plastic name tag pinned to the pocket. Elroy.

It cost me forty dollars to get Wilson to give me the passkey to Ethan's bungalow. Stenger came a good deal cheaper. Ten bucks and he slid the key across the counter with his forefinger.

"Figured you'd be interested in that nurse," he said, congratulating himself on his big score.

"You figured right. This package of papers the woman dropped off on Monday—you didn't happen to look inside, did you?"

" 'Course not," Stenger said, feigning outrage. "I don't pry into nobody else's business and I expect no man to pry into mine. She left that package for the Pearson boy and said to tell him it was from Rita. And that's exactly what I done."

"You didn't happen to catch the license number of Rita's car, did you?"

"Nope."

"Not this morning, either?"

Stenger drew back as if I was asking for the world. "You're damn lucky I saw her at all—way she come sneaking 'round the back entrance that early in the morning."

"You're sure it was three?"

"Sure I'm sure. *Love Boat* just come on Nineteen." He nodded behind him at the grey, fulgent eye of a portable TV, sitting on the manager's desk. "Saw her reflection in the tube. That white uniform."

"She the only one who paid Ethan's room a visit this week?"

"Just her and you, far as I know."

"No cops?" I said skeptically.

Elroy Stenger drew back a step farther. "What'd cops want 'round here?"

From the way he said it, I figured he was in a better position to know than I was. Talking about cops killed off the little hospitality the ten dollars had bought me. Pocketing the bill Elroy turned his back on me and flipped on the TV.

"Just drop that key on the counter when you're through," he called out as I left.

I walked down the tar driveway that led from the office to the cottages. The drive ran past the heart-shaped swimming pool and behind the cottages to the highway. There were no overhead lights along the way, so it was just good luck—or Elroy Stenger's persistent nosiness—that had led him to discover his early morning visitor.

Whoever she was, she wasn't Rita Scarne, who had been sitting dead in her car at three a.m.

*   *   *

There was no police seal posted on Ethan Pearson's motel room door—Stenger had been right about that. For Parker, Foster, and the Ohio State Patrol the case had apparently ended at first light with the discovery of Rita's body. No one had even bothered to make a routine check of Ethan's room.

I fit the key in the lock and pushed the door open.

At first glance the place looked the same as it had on Tuesday afternoon. The fast-food wrappers on the bed. The tin ashtray on the pillow. The phonebook sitting where I'd left it on the dresser. Hell, there wasn't that much that could have changed. And yet Carla Chaney, or someone else, had taken a huge risk to revisit that room. I wanted to know why.

I went through the place again. The bed, the bath, the nightstand, the bureau. And that's when I found it.

Ethan's bankbook, the one listing his father's regular thousand-dollar deposits to the savings account at First National, was missing from the bureau drawer. As far as I could tell it was the only thing missing.

I sat down on the corner of the bed and stared stupidly at the bureau. There was no sense to it—to someone risking her life to steal a dead boy's bankbook. There had been no money in the savings account—I'd checked. The last thousand-dollar deposit had been removed two weeks before Ethan disappeared—the money had always been removed several weeks after it was deposited.

I reached over, picked up the phone, and dialed the desk. Elroy answered.

"You gotta pay for any calls you make," he said immediately, as if he could see the money coming out of his ten-dollar bonus.

"I'll pay," I said. I took my notebook out of my jacket and

flipped through it until I found the number for The University Inn in Evanston.

"Long-distance gonna cost you extra," Elroy said after I gave him the number.

"Just dial the fucking thing."

I got The University Inn's version of Elroy Stenger after a couple of rings. He put me though to Hedda Pearson.

I hadn't been sure that the woman was still at the motel. But she was there all right, still holding vigil in that little room, still waiting, as she told me she would wait, for Ethan to return home.

"Is there news?" she asked nervously. "Have they found him?"

"Not yet."

Hedda Pearson laughed a terrible laugh. "They think he's dead, don't they? And for what? For some neurotic, oedipal fantasy."

"Ethan's story about his mother may not have been as fantastic as we thought."

Hedda Pearson sucked in her breath as if I'd slapped her. "Is that what you called for? To tell me that I don't know my husband? That I couldn't tell truth from fantasy?"

"I called because I need to know about Ethan's savings account at First National—the one his dad deposited money to every three months."

The woman laughed wretchedly. "Are you insane? First you say this absurd story of Ethan's is true. Then you ask me about imaginary bankbooks."

I stared down at the bureau, at the empty drawer. "You're telling me that you don't know anything about a savings account or a passbook?"

"Yes. That's what I'm telling you. There was no savings account. No money from Ethan's father. He wouldn't have accepted money from his father if it *had* been offered. Don't *you* know that?"

I told the woman I would call her when I had word about her husband. But from the sound of her voice when she hung up, I knew that she would just as soon never hear from me again—or anyone else who took Ethan's fantasies seriously. She'd been more upset by the possibility that she'd been wrong about them than by the possibility that he was dead. But then his obsession had given form to her life for the past four years—it had shaped her relationship to Ethan. Without it she lost her identity as his victim.

After hanging up on Hedda Pearson I phoned Al Foster at the CPD and asked him to do me another favor.

"I need a check run on a savings account at First National Bank, under the name of E. Pearson. I'd like to know who actually owns the account, who deposits to it, and who withdraws from it."

After that morning's scene with Parker I'd expected him to say no—especially to the bank inquiry, which would require a court order. But he didn't.

"I'll see what I can do."

"Why so cooperative?" I asked curiously.

"Let's just say that things aren't working out exactly as expected at this end."

"You want to explain that?"

"When the time is right," Al said.

32

After Al hung up I sat in the motel room for a little while longer, thinking about the missing bankbook that hadn't belonged to Ethan Pearson. Someone must have given it to him on Monday night—probably the nurse who had come to the motel. The nurse who wasn't Rita Scarne. Presumably the same woman had returned on Wednesday morning, after the boy and his sister were dead, to take the book back. Roy Stenger claimed the nurse had her own key to the motel room, but I didn't know whether to believe him or not. He was pretty damn corruptible when it came to passkeys—that was how I'd gotten in. The only other way Carla—or whoever the nurse was—could have gotten a key was to take it off Ethan Pearson's dead body in Talmadge's apartment. Or off Talmadge's body on Tuesday morning.

Whether Carla had done all that or not, it figured that the account book had something to do with Stelle Pearson's death. Finding and punishing their mother's murderer was all that Ethan and Kirsty had been interested in.

I picked up the phone again and told Roy to dial Dayton information. Rita Scarne's sister, Charlotte, had mentioned bankbooks with money in them—part of the grim inheritance that Rita had left her on Wednesday morning. I wanted to know whether they connected to Ethan's missing account book.

I got Charlotte's number from information and had Roy dial it.

"This is Stoner, Charlotte."

"Yes," she said stiffly. "I recognize your voice."

"I need to talk to you about Rita."

It took her a while to speak. Given my part in the tragedy of her sister's death, I understood why. "What about Rita?"

"You mentioned some bankbooks that she gave you. I'd like to have a look at them."

Charlotte Scarne took a deep breath and let it out slowly. "I think maybe you should," she said, sounding relieved.

"Why do you say that?"

"There was an article in the *Daily News* today—about Rita and those children you were looking for. The Pearson children. It said they were presumed dead and that Rita might have played a part in their murders."

"No one's completely sure."

"It's horrible," the woman said, shaken. "So horrible."

At first I thought she meant the accusation itself, but she didn't. "Mr. Stoner, I think Rita did kill them."

"Why?"

"The bankbooks. The ones that you're talking about. Some of them have Ethan' and Kirsten Pearson's names on them."

I didn't put it together until I got inside the woman's house, past the frozen ice on her stairs—ice that still bore my footprints and Rita's—past the frozen, accusatory stare on Charlotte Scarne's face when she answered the door. The black bag was already sitting on the dusty table in the center of the dusty sitting room. I went straight over to it while Charlotte hovered nervously in the hall. There were four bankbooks inside the bag, two in Ethan's name, one in Kirsty's, one in Rita's. I looked at the ones with Ethan's and Kirsty's names on them first—passbooks for three savings accounts at three different Cincinnati S & L's. City Bank, Constellation, and First National. The one from First National bothered me—it looked like the same book I'd found in Ethan's motel room.

"When did Rita give you this book?" I said to Charlotte.

"Last night. You were here, don't you remember?"

I let that pass and took a look inside the other two books. Like the one I'd found in Ethan's drawer they'd been deposited to at three-month intervals for almost a decade—thousand-dollar deposits, circulated among the three accounts so that one of them always had money in it every month of the year. The cash was regularly withdrawn a week or two after the deposits were made. I only had to glance at the single passbook with Rita's name on it to see where that money had gone. The books balanced perfectly. Every penny from the three Ethan and Kirsten Pearson accounts had ended up in Rita's name. One hundred and twenty thousand dollars, paid out over ten years in one thousand dollar monthly increments.

It helped explain Rita's fancy house and car. It helped explain a lot of things.

"She was stealing from that boy and his sister," Charlotte Scarne said in a feverish whisper.

I shook my head, no. "She wasn't stealing from them."

The woman looked confused. "Then why did Rita have their passbooks—and all that cash!"

I sat down on the tuxedo sofa and stared at the black bag full of money. Blood money. "They weren't Ethan's and Kirsty's passbooks, Charlotte. Ethan and Kirsty didn't know a thing about them—at least, they didn't until a few days ago. Those accounts were established by someone who was using their names to launder money."

"Launder?" the woman said.

"To make the deposits look legitimate. To make it seem as if the money was going to Ethan or Kirsty, when it was really being paid to Rita."

"Over a hundred thousand dollars!" Charlotte cried. "Who would do such a thing?"

I could only think of one person with the means. One person who could plausibly use Ethan's and Kirsty's names to hide illegal transactions. He'd died that afternoon. "Phil Pearson."

Charlotte stopped her pacing and sank into a chair beside an octagonal table full of knickknacks. "I don't understand this at all. Wasn't he the one you were working for? Why would he secretly pay Rita money?"

"For something she did for him thirteen years ago," I said, thinking aloud. "Something she and Carla and Herb Talmadge did."

"What?" the woman said with appetite.

"They planned and covered up a murder. Estelle Pearson's murder."

Charlotte Scarne fell back in the chair with a groan. "Oh, God, I knew it! I just knew Rita killed someone!" She threw her hands to her face and sobbed melodramatically, although I detected a bit of triumph mixed with the tears.

Looking around the room, at the dusty furnishings that hadn't changed in three decades, I could see why. Fourteen years before, Rita had run off with a woman she had loved better than her own sister, leaving Charlotte to lead a drab life with her drab parents in that drab house. The woman was owed a little vindication. Perhaps she had felt she was owed more than that.

"Why didn't you show me these passbooks on Wednesday morning, Charlotte?"

The woman stopped sobbing and pulled her hands slowly away from her eyes, drawing down the pink flesh beneath them.

"I didn't look at them myself until after Rita had died."

I shook my head. "That isn't true. It can't be."

She laughed nervously, dropping her hands from her cheeks to her lap. "Are you accusing me of lying?" she said, as if the very notion was preposterous—as if I had the wrong sister.

I got up and walked over to the doctor's bag. Reaching inside I took out the First National passbook. "I found this in the Pearson boy's motel room on Tuesday afternoon. Someone gave it to him on Monday night and picked it up again early this morning. Someone dressed as a nurse. Now it's here in your house. How'd that happen?"

The woman blanched. "I . . . I don't know. There must have been another book."

I shook my head again. "If there were more than three of these account books, the deposits to them would have been staggered differently. The books wouldn't balance to the penny. There would be missing months, missing deposits made to the fourth book. No, I think there were just three accounts in Ethan's and Kirsty's names. But I can always check with First National—if you force me to."

"Of course, you could," she said dully, as if that was something that hadn't occurred to her. "You could check the bank."

I asked her again, "When did you get this book, Charlotte?"

The woman's face slowly changed. Age and bitterness came over it, greying the pink, girlish flesh, turning the weak smile into something that looked like it might fall out of her mouth and shatter. Raising her right arm woodenly Charlotte Scarne swept the top of the octagonal table beside her, knocking the mementos—the yellowing picture of Mom and Pop, the crystal trout blowing bubbles in its crystal cube—onto the floor. The picture frame cracked in two. The crystal cube exploded with a loud pop, splashing glass shards against the far wall.

Charlotte Scarne brought her arm back across the table, laid it in her lap and stared at it curiously as if it was something not quite under her control. After a time she looked up at me.

"I took the bankbook to the boy's motel on Monday night," she said in a deadened voice. "I was at Rita's house when his call came in. I knew about the accounts with their names on them. I . . . I wanted to help them."

"You knew about Stelle's murder?"

"I knew about the accounts," she said sharply. "I'd known about them for years. I thought Rita was stealing money from that boy and his sister. I mean why else would she have books with his name on it? Why would she have a house like that? And a car? And so much cash to spend? She'd done something terrible to that boy and his sister. She and that dreadful bitch, Carla. For years Rita had gotten away with it. Why should she keep getting away with it? Lording it over me when Dad died. Making me look small with her dirty money. Even Mother . . ."

Choking with anger Charlotte fixed me with a savage stare. "The boy and his sister deserved to know what Rita had done."

But what she really meant was that her sister deserved to be punished. She still felt that way even though Rita was dead.

"So you told Ethan that Rita had been stealing from him."

"I thought he and his sister would take the book to the police. I didn't know that they would end up dead. I swear to Jesus I didn't."

She dropped her head heavily to her chest. "After you came here I got panicky. I was afraid the police would find the passbook and trace it to me. I already had all the money that she'd given me. I thought they might think, that *you* might think I was . . . that I had something to do with the blackmail. So I went back to the motel after you left and got the book."

"How did you get into Ethan's room?"

"The man at the desk," she said miserably. "I gave him money—and he gave me a key."

She looked too damn guilty to be lying. But then she'd lied to me before about the bankbooks and, more importantly, about what she'd suspected Rita and Carla had been up to—thirteen years past.

"I never knew what the money was for, Mr. Stoner," Charlotte Scarne said as if she was reading my mind. "I just knew Rita was getting it for something bad. Rita was bad."

She started to sob. "Bad," she cried again, like a tattling child.

As I watched her weeping bitter tears that weren't for Rita, I wondered just how large a part Charlotte herself had played in her sister's suicide and, maybe, in the Pearson kids' deaths. I couldn't be sure about what she'd said to Rita or to Ethan on Monday night. I did know that someone had told those kids where to find Talmadge—someone who'd known where to find them *and* Herb. And Rita had had that black bag of blood money packed *before* I showed up on Wednesday morning—ready to take to her sister in Dayton. At the very least there was an ugly possibility that Charlotte had done a little blackmailing of her own. But then the Pearson case was full of ugliness and simmering vengeance. And murder.

"Did you tell your sister that the Pearson boy had called her, Charlotte?" I said, when she'd calmed down.

She shook her head. "No. I didn't tell anyone."

"And you didn't call Ethan back on Monday night?"

She said no, again.

"Somebody called them," I said uneasily.

"It wasn't me," Charlotte said, coming out of the chair

with a horrified look on her face. "I didn't know about that man, Talmadge."

"He never showed up at the house, when Carla was living here in '74 and '75?"

"Never. The men she saw—they were always . . . respectable-looking."

"Do you remember any of their names?"

"One of them was a doctor," the woman said. "I think Carla worked for him."

"Sydney Chase?"

"Yes, he came here. A lot."

"Anyone else?"

"There were other men," Charlotte Scarne said vaguely. "It's been so many years."

"Was one of them Phil Pearson?"

"I don't recall the names."

"Tall, dark hair, blue eyes."

The woman stared at me blankly. "I just don't remember."

33

▌▌▌

I took the bankbooks with me when I left the house on Minton Street. I didn't give Charlotte a choice, but the truth was that she didn't really care about the money. Just about Rita—evening things up with Rita. Revenge was almost as much of a theme in her life as it had been in Kirsty's and Ethan's. And it had almost poisoned her life to the same extent.

Before driving off I checked the garage beside the St. Louis. An old brown Pontiac, the car described by Roy Stenger, the motel clerk, was parked inside.

I stopped at a Stuckey's on my way back to Cincinnati and had a cup of coffee and a sandwich. It was past ten and the papery sandwich was the first food I'd eaten all day. I sat there for about fifteen minutes, drinking coffee and thinking about Ethan and Kirsty Pearson.

Getting that bankbook from Charlotte would have confirmed what the kids already suspected—that Rita Scarne was heavily involved in their mother's murder. If they'd used their heads the account book would have told them something else—something they didn't know. That their father had been involved in it, too.

I wasn't sure if Al Foster had looked into the ownership of the savings account yet—I'd check that out when I got back to town. But I would have been very surprised if it didn't belong to Phil Pearson—or jointly to Pearson and Rita. Who else would have used Ethan's and Kirsty's names to cover up a payoff? The names of his kids. It was what Shelley

Sacks would have called "sublimation." It was what I called smart thinking.

Louise had already told me that Phil regularly sent Ethan money—"blood money," she called it ironically. Blood money it was. But not paid for Ethan's imaginary complaints or to assuage Phil's guilt, as Louise had thought. Paid to cover the cost of a very real murder. And the money would have been untraceable, if Charlotte Scarne hadn't taken a hand.

But she had. And the two kids had discovered that Papa Phil was involved in Mama's murder. They might have acted on that discovery if someone hadn't called them at the motel and told them where to find Talmadge. I'd thought that someone had been Rita Scarne. But after talking to Charlotte I was no longer sure. If Charlotte was telling me the truth, Rita really *hadn't* known that the kids had called her on Monday night. She hadn't known that Ethan and Kirsty were at The Bluegrass Motel, plotting revenge.

But someone else had known they were there on Monday —the same person who had known where to find Herb. What I couldn't figure out was how that someone—Carla or whoever she was—had come by that knowledge, if it wasn't through Charlotte or the kids themselves.

It was ten-thirty when I got back to the Riorley Building. The answering machine on my desk was blinking in the twilight, its one yellow eye. I played back the messages while I put Rita Scarne's bagful of money in the office safe. The first one was from Louise, asking me to come to the house later that night.

"I've never felt so alone," she said. "Please come here, after eleven, after the others have left. I need you."

Her voice was weighted down with a desperate loneliness. A burden I was bound to add to if the path I was following led to Phil. I didn't know how I was going to handle telling her that I was still working on the case, still trying to prove her dead husband was a murderer. I didn't know how I was going to handle Louise herself. She wasn't inviting me home to talk. I knew that. I also knew that I wanted her badly enough to go, even on that night.

I played back the other messages and tried not to think about Louise. But it was no good—the sound of her voice had started something inside me. I was reaching for the phone to call her when it rang.

It was Thelma Jackson. Who'd thought I was like Magnum—good, decent, and pure. The sort of man who would never fuck a dead man's wife on the day he died.

"That ofay nurse you asked me about?" She paused dramatically. "I found somebody who remembers her real well. Her and Herbie, both."

"Who is that?" I said.

"Old friend of mine from back on McMicken, used to work in the coffee shop over at Jewish Hospital. She seen this girl with Herbie a couple of times."

"I already know who the girl is," I said wearily. "What I need to know is how to find her."

"Sarah don't know where she is now," the woman said. "She ain't seen her since '76."

I sighed.

"Ain't you gonna come over and chat?" Thelma Jackson said disappointedly, as if she was looking forward to the company.

"I'm pretty tired, Thelma."

Thelma put her hand over the receiver and I heard her say, "He ain't coming," to someone else in the room.

"Tell your friend I'll call her tomorrow about Carla."

"Carla?" Thelma said. "Who's that?"

"Herbie's girlfriend."

"Her name wasn't Carla," the woman said. "Was it, Sarah?"

She went off the line again and I heard her say something to her friend. When she came back on she was full of confidence. "She wasn't no Carla. She was a Jeanne. Jeanne Chase."

It was past eleven by the time I got to Thelma Jackson's bungalow on Anthony Wayne. The air near the distillery smelled of peaches that cold December evening. I took a big whiff of it as I crossed over to the house, and caught a hint of gasoline drifting up from the expressway.

Thelma was standing in the front door as I came onto the porch. Another black woman in her sixties, with a small, gnarled face and a slightly humped back, stood a few feet behind her in the shadows of the living room. The second woman watched shyly while Thelma ushered me in.

"This here's Sarah Washington," Thelma said, turning to the other woman.

"Pleased," Sarah Washington said in a squeaky little voice.

Thelma grinned at her shy friend. "You wouldn't believe it to look at her, but Sarah was wilder than me in her day."

"You hush," Sarah Washington said, looking embarrassed.

I went over to the floral-print couch. The women sat down on chairs opposite me. Both of them were wearing floral-print dresses. Thelma filled hers out impressively, while Sarah's hung from her skinny shoulders like a coat from a hook.

"Ain't he good-looking?" Thelma said to her friend. "Too good-looking for an old woman like me."

She snapped her girdle, and the other one clucked her tongue mournfully. I had the feeling that Thelma Jackson was going to keep snapping and her friend was going to keep clucking all night long—that that was the way they related to each other.

"You remember the nurse that Herbie Talmadge was seeing, Ms. Washington?" I said, trying to steer the conversation toward business.

"Yes, uhm-hm," Sarah Washington said, nodding until I thought her neck might break. "She worked in the Jewish Hospital Doctors' Building back in '75 and '76. I believe her name was Chase. Jeanne Chase."

"You're not sure?"

The woman ducked her tiny head. "Not for absolute sure."

"It couldn't have been Chaney, could it? Carla Chaney?"

"I'm purty sure her last name was Chase. Somebody told me she come down from a Dayton hospital, but I never did know that for a fact."

"She was an RN?"

"No, no." The woman shook her head in the opposite plane. "A receptionist."

"Y'all got to quit that shaking," Thelma said irritably. "Make the rest of us dizzy."

The woman gave her an ugly look.

"Who'd she work for?" I asked.

"I ain't for sure. One of the doctors in the Jewish Hospital Building."

"You tell him what you saw," Thelma prompted.

"I saw her and Herbie Talmadge together," Sarah Washington said, drawing herself up in the chair. "Saw them a couple of times—out in the parking lot."

I said, "By together, you mean . . . ?"

"I mean what I said. They weren't doing more than talking, far as I could see."

She gave Thelma Jackson a quick, sharp look.

"Are you sure this is the same woman that you saw on McMicken Street?" I said to Thelma.

She nodded. "Has to be. Big blond white girl. 'Bout twenty-four, twenty-five years old."

"Is that what she looked like?" I said to Sarah Washington.

The woman bobbed her head like a fighter ducking a bag. "Yes, sir."

Jeanne Chase sounded an awful lot like Carla Chaney, with a new name. Sy Chase's wife's name. It struck me as a kind of grim joke—Carla taking the name of the woman who'd spoiled her chance to become the real Mrs. Chase.

"Did you ever talk to this woman?" I asked Sarah Washington.

"Never did talk to her but once," the woman admitted. "She was in the coffee shop and I waited her table. She acted kind of high-strung, I remember that. Kind of uppity. I figured her for one of those college girls who come and go. You see them all the time. Only reason they work is to snare them some young doctor. And when that don't happen, they just drift on to something else. Stopped seeing her in the spring. And never did see her again after that. Never saw Herbie but one time after that, either. In the fall of that year."

"Where did you see him?"

"Out front of the hospital."

The woman shook her head with what I thought was a dismal accent. It depressed me that I was beginning to understand the code of her gestures. In fact I'd started to bob my head a little, too.

"I thought the boy was waiting on a bus," Sarah Washington said, "but this fancy car come along and picked him up. Big, black car. Doctor's car."

"Did you see who was driving it?"

"Just the license. Had MD on it. I remember that."

34

As soon as I finished with Thelma I went looking for a phone. I found a neon-lit convenience store on North Bend Road, blazing in the dark as if it had been doused with cognac, and called Dr. Steele's office from a booth on the wall. I half expected to get an answering machine, but he answered the phone himself like a good country physician used to night calls.

"Sorry to bother you again," I said, "but I've got a funny situation here. Jeanne Chase, Sy Chase's wife . . . can you describe her for me?"

"Why?" the man said, perking up. "You haven't found her, have you?"

"I've run across her name."

"She was a green-eyed redhead, about five-four, one-twenty. A tough little Irish girl. Real pretty and real smart."

She certainly didn't sound like the woman that Sarah Washington had seen with Talmadge. The woman Sarah Washington had seen still sounded like Carla Chaney.

"Christ," Steele went on eagerly, "if you do find anything about Jeanne you've got to call her folks. When she disappeared their lives virtually ended."

"When did she disappear?"

"In October '76. She'd gone to Cincinnati to interview for a nursing job. She just couldn't stand to work up here anymore without Sy. And she was the type who needed to work. I remember that the detective her folks hired traced her as far as the hospital where the interview took place."

"Do you know which hospital that was?"

"No. It would be in the report the detective made—I'm

sure. I do remember that she called her folks that afternoon and told them that she wouldn't be coming home right away. That she'd run into an old friend and would be staying in town a few more days."

"Did she identify the friend?"

"Not that I recall."

"You think you could get me the name of the detective who worked on the case? I mean without working anybody up."

"Of course. A doctor gets used to watching what he says."

I dug another quarter from my pocket and phoned Al Foster at CPD.

"No," he said. "I don't have any news on the Pearson kid's bank account."

"Well, I do," I told him. "Rita Scarne was drawing money out of it to the tune of a hundred and twenty grand. Someone was paying her off and using the Pearson kid's account to launder the cash."

"Got any idea who?"

I did but I wasn't ready to tell the cops yet—not until I had Pearson's motive for murder pinned down. "It would help if you could find out who was depositing to the account."

"I've done enough work for the day," Al said wearily. "Your friend, Carla, I've dug up something on her. You're not going to like it, though."

"What?"

"You sitting down or standing up?"

"Just tell me."

"She's dead, Harry."

Behind me an ice machine made a thump, like a sack down a laundry chute.

"That can't be true," I said, wishing I was sitting down.

"I don't want it to be true, either. Parker would be pissed

as hell if I told you this but we've got a couple of slots that
your Carla was tailor-made to fit. It turned out that the
nurse in Prospect Park, the one that black kid saw with
Talmadge, definitely *wasn't* Rita Scarne. We did some
checking and the Scarne woman was on private duty until
eleven p.m. Monday night. Plus criminalistics lifted a pair
of prints off the damn shoe we found in Herb's apartment
that don't match Talmadge or Rita. Parker doesn't think it's
enough to queer the case for a grand jury, but it's making
him sweat."

"You're sure the Chaney woman's dead?"

"For thirteen years. Talmadge killed her. It's why he
went to jail. For raping and murdering Nurse Carla Chaney."

It was all there in black and white, in a folder that had
been sitting on a parole officer's desk for better than a week.
Al had found out about it early that evening after running
Carla Chaney's name past Newport CID.

"Hall Scott, Talmadge's parole officer, called to follow up
on Herb's murder," Foster said as we sat across his desk
from each other in the homicide office of the CPD Building.
"We got to talking about the son of a bitch. And the Chaney
girl's name popped up. Talmadge must have hated her
guts, because he really did a number on her. Beat her up so
badly they had to rely on a piece of physical evidence to
identify the corpse—a wedding ring on the woman's hand.
And then she'd been in the Ohio River for three weeks,
which didn't help."

"He dropped her body in the river?"

"Helluva coincidence, huh?" He pushed the manila
folder across his desk to me. "Take a look at who made the
ID."

I flipped open the folder and scanned the report. The

woman's nude body was found on November 10, 1976—
about two months after Estelle Pearson was pulled from the
Miami. The body—what was left of it after three weeks in
the water—was identified by one Rita Scarne, a nurse and
friend of the deceased. According to the report Scarne
claimed Carla Chaney had been Talmadge's lover and that
she'd been missing since mid-October. There were no relatives listed for Carla. Husband and child, mother and father, were said to be deceased. Without Rita and the ring
Carla would have been just another Jane Doe.

"Did Rita testify against Talmadge at the trial?"

"There wasn't any trial," Foster said. "Herb copped a
plea—second-degree murder. That's why he was released
ten days ago instead of spending another ten years in jail.
The Scarne woman must have been scared to death when
she read he was going to be paroled. Scared enough to use
those kids to try to kill him, scared enough to do it herself
when the scheme backfired."

Only Rita Scarne hadn't known about the kids. I was
beginning to wonder whether she'd known about
Talmadge's release. The person she'd been afraid of—the
person who phoned the kids at that motel—was a lot more
dangerous than Herb. And a lot harder to pin down.

"See what you can dig up on an MP named Jeanne
Chase," I said to Al. "She disappeared close to the same
time that Carla went in the water."

"How close?" he said, perking up.

"I'll find out."

I went back to my office and phoned Dr. Steele again. He
had the name of the detective for me by then—Jim Sanchez
out of Dayton. And something else—something I hadn't
expected.

"I came across the name of that doctor that Carla went to
work for in Cincinnati. I'd written it down on an old calen-

dar." Steele laughed. "I keep stuff like that around. My wife says forever. Anyway the name wasn't Pearson. It was Sacks —Sheldon Sacks."

"No shit!" I said with surprise.

Steele laughed. "That's what it says here. Sheldon Sacks, Jewish Hospital Doctors' Building."

That helped to explain how Carla/Jeanne had come in contact with Phil Pearson, Sacks' closest friend. And as receptionist to Shelley Sacks, Carla would have had access to Sacks' files—to all that useful information about Stelle and Phil's rotten marriage. Information that it was high time I had a look at, too.

I phoned Dayton information and got Jim Sanchez's number. I didn't figure he'd be in his office at ten-thirty on a Friday night. But I was wrong. Like me he was working on a case that troubled him—a missing child. Talking about Jeanne Chase didn't improve his mood.

"I tried like hell on that one," Sanchez said unhappily. "I mean I liked the family, the folks. I wanted to deliver for them. But once Jeanne left that hospital she simply dropped off the face of the earth."

"What hospital was that?"

"Holmes. She'd gone there for an interview with a doctor who'd advertised in one of the nursing journals. You know Jeanne was trained as a nurse."

"Do you remember the doctor's name?"

"I've got it in my files. Hold on a minute." He went off the line for a couple of minutes then came back on, with a sound of papers rustling. "The doctor's name was . . . Morse. Carl Morse. He was a psychiatrist, looking for a nurse who could also act as a receptionist and keep the books. He'd had a girl who did those things for him, but she'd retired the month before."

"Dr. Steele told me that Jeanne called her folks after the

interview to tell them she was going to stay in Cincinnati for a few days. She said she'd run into an old friend at the hospital."

"Not a friend. I mean she didn't use the word 'friend.' What she said was . . ." I heard him rustle through the papers again. "She saw somebody at the hospital—someone she knew. Her parents had the impression that seeing this person upset Jeanne. At least, they thought something had upset her."

"Jeanne didn't say who this person was, did she?" I asked.

"No," Sanchez said. "But I tried like hell to find out. The interview was held in the afternoon. And you know how busy hospitals get. There were scores of people around. It could have been any of them."

"Morse didn't have any idea who Jeanne might have seen, did he?"

"No. He claimed no one else came into his office during the interview. I went up and down the hall to every office on the floor and no one recalled seeing her. Christ I got a list of names a mile long. Flaigler, Thomas, Galaty, Pearson—"

"Hold up," I said. "Phil Pearson?"

"Yeah, as a matter of fact. Dr. Philip Pearson. He was down the hall from Stein. Is that material?"

It could have been, if Phil Pearson had been meeting with Sacks' secretary.

"What day did Jeanne disappear?"

"Wednesday, October 19, 1976."

I jotted the date down on my desk blotter. Almost three weeks to the day before "Carla Chaney's" body was found in the Ohio River.

"I may have something for you on this," I said.

"Christ, that would be terrific. The thing has eaten at me for thirteen years."

"What I need is a photograph of the Chase woman, her

dental records, and a description of any distinguishing scars or marks."

"You've found her body?" he asked.

"The cops found *a* body," I said carefully. "Thirteen years ago, three weeks after Jeanne disappeared. At the time the body was identified as someone else, but I've got reason to think that it may have been misidentified. Deliberately."

"Why?" Sanchez said eagerly.

But I didn't know why—not for sure. What I *thought* was that someone had been impersonating Jeanne Chase for almost a year—someone who looked very much like Carla Chaney. If Carla had been visiting Phil Pearson that October afternoon, the Chase woman could have seen her, could have found out that she had a double. A woman masquerading as the late Dr. Chase's tony wife. A woman whom the real Jeanne Chase had a terrific grudge against. If Jeanne had confronted Carla with what she knew, it could have cost her her life.

Stelle was only one month dead at that point, and Carla wouldn't have wanted anyone prying into her affairs—especially someone with a score to settle. Plus eliminating the real Jeanne Chase had some extra benefits: Carla would no longer have to worry about exposure, or about crazy Herb Talmadge, who had obviously been set up to take the rap for Jeanne Chase's murder.

It was beginning to look like Carla Chaney had left a whole string of corpses behind her in her metamorphosis from Nola's squalid daughter to the snooty girl that Sarah Washington had seen in Jewish Hospital to whatever she'd become after Phil dumped her for Louise. All it had taken to turn the tide of the past was a half-dozen murders and two accomplices who were willing, for drugs or sex or money, to go along with the mayhem. And Phil Pearson, of course, to finance the deal.

For thirteen years she'd probably lived comfortably in her new identity—off Phil Pearson's money. Just as Rita had. In fact it wouldn't have surprised me to learn that there were three more phony accounts in the kids' names at three more Cincinnati banks, with regular monthly deposits to and withdrawals from them. It would have stayed a nice life if Herb had not gotten out of prison, bringing the past back with a vengeance. But he had gotten out, dragging the Pearson kids in his wake.

Somehow Carla had found out about Ethan and Kirsty and tracked them down to the motel. Talmadge had already made himself known to her—Carla had even bought him a TV to keep him quiet. Looking for a way out she'd callously pitted Kirsty and Ethan against Herb, and when that didn't work she'd done the job herself with a handful of pills and a butcher knife.

If Carla Chaney hadn't changed her name again I might be able to find her through Shelley Sacks, who'd hired her in the fall of '75 under the name Jeanne Chase. It was time to talk to Sacks, anyway. There was too much that he'd been concealing for too long. Motives and memories that could help me explain why Phil wanted Stelle dead—and why thirteen years later Kirsten Pearson had joined her brother on their strange ride toward death.

35

■■

It was almost one when I finished with Jim Sanchez. I knew that Shelley Sacks wouldn't be in his office. If he was anywhere other than at his own home he'd be with Louise. I went ahead and phoned the Pearson house, knowing full well that she'd expected me to come to her—that she was still expecting it.

Louise answered on the second ring. As soon as I heard her voice I knew why I'd resisted making the call.

"Hello, Louise."

"Hello, Harry," she said stiffly. "It was nice of you to check in."

"I'm sorry, Louise."

She laughed. "Of course you are."

"What do you want me to say?" I said, feeling the same deadly mix of lust and guilt I'd felt about three hours before. Knowing deep down that the lust would win out.

"What I want clearly doesn't make any difference to you."

"That isn't true."

Her voice dropped to a wounded whisper—so full of pain that it hurt me. "I needed you, damn you. And you didn't come. You left me alone."

I didn't answer her. I didn't know how to answer.

After a moment's silence she found her voice again. "What is it you wanted?"

"Shelley Sacks," I said guiltily. "Is he there with you?"

Louise laughed again. "He went home about two hours ago. They've all gone home hours ago."

"Where does he live?"

"Two twenty-five Camargo Pike. Is that it?"
She hung up the phone before I could answer her.

I got in the car and started for Sacks' house. Out I-71 into
that rich preserve of mazey woods and hidden drives. But
somewhere along the way I got lost in the dark, and it was
Pearson's house I found myself parked in front of. There
were no lights on. No other cars in the driveway. I sat there
for a long time, listening to the December wind rattling the
icy branches of the ginko trees, without the guts to go in,
without the guts to leave. I don't know how much time
passed before a light came on above the front door—fierce
and white as a spot.

The door opened and I saw her look out. She was
wrapped in a silk robe that seemed to have no color at all in
the fierce white light. Louise herself didn't look quite real
in the blazing light. She stared out at me for a long moment.
Then the light went out. All I could see in the sudden
darkness was the glimmer of her white wrap, trailing across
the moonlit lawn like an afterimage.

I got out of the car and went after her. She was shivering
when I caught up to her. She looked at me wild-eyed, as if
she didn't recognize my face. All around us the wind
chimed in the trees.

"It's me," I said over the wind. "It's Harry."

"I thought it was someone else," she said, still looking
wild-eyed. "I thought it was . . . someone."

I pulled her close, wrapped my coat around her shoulders, and started her back to the house. She leaned heavily
against me.

As soon as we got in the door I flipped on the hall light.
The wind had disheveled her hair, leaving it tangled about
her face. Shivering all over Louise ducked her head in
embarrassment.

"I took some pills," she said weakly. "I was asleep. I heard the car outside. I thought . . ."

Raising her head she reached for me. I pulled her against my chest.

"I had a bad dream," she whispered. "And I was alone."

"I'm here now," I said.

Holding her tight I guided her down the hall and upstairs. There was an open door next to the landing. The room inside was lit faintly by the moon. A canopied bed with lace valances. A smoothly sculpted Italian bureau. A skeletal chair by the window, casting long barred shadows on the rug.

I guided her over to the bed and laid her down on it. She wouldn't let go of my hand.

"Please don't leave me alone," she whispered. "I don't want to be alone tonight."

"I won't leave you alone."

Working loose from her grasp, I went over to the window, picked up the chair and brought it back to the side of the bed. Sitting down I reached out and took her hand again.

"Are you all right?" I said to her.

"Better," she whispered. "You won't go?"

"No."

She lay back on the pillows and stared up at the canopy above her. "I never liked being alone in the dark. There's something in it, something that always terrifies me. Phil says . . ." Her voice caught in her throat. "He said that someday it would swallow me up."

"Why would he say that?"

"To frighten me." She giggled like a child. It sounded strange coming from her—huddled and sad.

She squeezed my hand, then dropped it and rolled onto her side.

"You don't have to sleep in that chair, you know," she said, sounding more like the woman I knew.

I watched her for a time, then got up and lay down on the bed beside her. She put an arm around me.

"Thanks," she whispered.

When I was sure she was asleep I got up and went downstairs. The flickering red-and-blue Christmas tree lights guided me down the hall to Phil Pearson's study. I opened the door and went inside. Enough moonlight was coming through the French windows for me to make my way over to the glass desk. A small lamp sat on one corner. I flipped it on.

Papers were scattered on the desktop where Pearson had left them. I went through several of them—notes on patients, bills. I was hoping to find something to lead me to Carla. But nothing connected to the woman.

I did find something connected to Kirsten, however. Or disconnected. Facedown in the drawer of the desk I found half of a picture that had been torn in two. It was a picture of Kirsten when she was a little girl, standing on a lawn looking up lovingly at someone in the missing half of the photo. I could have been wrong, but I thought it might be the missing half of the photo I'd found in the girl's room in Chicago—the photo of Pearson.

I was staring at it when Louise came in the room.

She startled me so much that I jumped.

"Sorry," she said. "I woke up and thought you'd gone."

"I told you I wouldn't leave."

"People don't always do what they say." She stared at the torn photo in my hand. "What's that?"

"A picture of Kirsten when she was a little girl."

A dark look passed over Louise's face. "He would keep such a thing. His hair shirt."

"What does that mean?"

Louise shook her head sleepily. "What difference does it make anymore? Come back to bed."

"It makes a difference," I said sharply.

Louise stared at me with new interest. "I thought this thing was over."

"It's not over."

"I told you I didn't want you to keep investigating it."

"I know what you said. I'm not working for you now."

Louise went over to a chair and sat down heavily. "Is there something I should know?"

"I think your late husband murdered his first wife."

"Harry, I've already told you that he had no reason to want Stelle dead."

"There was a reason—one you don't know about."

She shook her head. "It's impossible."

"I've got proof."

"There is no proof," she said dismissively.

"It's in my office safe right now. Bankbooks for accounts that Phil established in Ethan's name. Accounts that were used to pay off Rita Scarne."

"Pay her off for what?"

"For helping to arrange Estelle's murder with the help of a woman named Chaney or Chase."

"Chase?" Louise said, looking surprised.

"You know her?"

"Phil had a secretary named Chase. At least I think that was her name." She ducked her head. "Actually the one I'm thinking of was more than Phil's secretary. She was . . . involved with him right before we met."

"This could be important, Louise."

She stared at me for a long moment. "All right, I'll find out tomorrow. I'll go through his old files. Okay?"

I nodded.

She held out her hand. "Now will you come back to bed?"

I got up from the chair and flipped off the light, dropping the torn photo of Kirsten back in the drawer.

Upstairs we made love, although there wasn't much love in it. I wanted her. And she didn't want to be alone in the dark. That was how it started, and how it finished. Just a one-night stand with the beautiful widow.

"Don't brood," she said, running a hand down my chest. "You helped me tonight."

I shook my head. "Did I?"

"Yes," she said, touching my cheek. "Sometimes it's the only thing that does help."

I stared at her voluptuous body, pale white in the moonlight. "You're very beautiful."

She smiled. "No, I'm not."

But she was. Very beautiful.

We lay there for a while without speaking. Outside the cold December wind rattled the casements.

"Once this is over, I'm going to go away," Louise said. "I'm a wealthy woman now that Phil is dead, so I'm going to go away. And when I come back I'm going to marry Saul Lasker."

"Why?" I said with surprise.

"Because he's very rich, my darling. And he'll do anything I want."

"You just said you had money of your own."

"Not enough. There isn't enough of that, ever." She reached down and stroked me gently. "I won't stop seeing you, darling, even after I've married Saul. You're good at this, you know."

I stared at her for a moment, unhappily. I had no claim on her. I doubted if any man ever really had.

"What if I'd said no tonight?" I asked.

She sighed peacefully. "I knew you wouldn't."

36

Dawn broke around seven, filling Louise's bedroom with pale filtered light—the color of the lace on her windows, the pattern of the embroidery in the lace. The light woke me up—I'd scarcely been sleeping. I turned on the mattress and looked at Louise. We'd made love a second time early that morning. It was what she'd needed all along to calm her down, to chase away the ghosts, to put her to sleep. It wasn't what I'd needed.

She'd wanted someone to hold her in the dark. In the day I knew it would be different. Her need would lessen, while mine would remain. What hurt me was that she'd known that—she'd counted on it.

The thought depressed me so much that I got out of bed and started to dress. The moment she felt my weight shift off the mattress Louise opened her eyes, as if her sleep depended on the presence of a body beside her. I didn't flatter myself that it depended on me.

Her face was drawn with fatigue, her eyes puffy with it. She sat up in bed, and the blankets slipped beneath her breasts. Even across the room she smelled of sex—and sleep and the sweet, floral fragrance that she wore.

"You're going?" she said groggily.

"Yes."

Arching her back she breathed out a sigh. Her long nipples hardened in the cold air. "You don't have to go, you know."

"I have things to do," I said.

Louise glanced around the room uncertainly, as if she

didn't remember how we'd gotten there. "I was fairly . . . crazy last night, wasn't I?"

"You got upset. It happens to all of us."

"It doesn't happen to me. If I said anything stupid . . ."

"Don't worry, Louise. I won't tell."

She brushed the hair back from her forehead. "You're pissed off, aren't you?"

"No," I said.

"Yes, you are."

Pushing herself up on the pillows she leaned against the headboard and stared at me sadly. "Harry, I truly like you. You're a good man—good in bed, good for me. But don't try to change me. Okay? I can't be that person. I tried to be someone else when I married Phil. It doesn't work." Her face turned hard and remote. "Sooner or later you run up against your past. And *it* doesn't change. It doesn't want *you* to change, either."

When I didn't say anything, Louise lay back on the pillows and closed her eyes. "I'll try to find that file you wanted. What was her name?"

"Chase. Jeanne Chase."

"Chase," she said dully. "Do the police think she's involved?"

"Parker thinks the case is closed. And since it's his jurisdiction it *will* be closed, unless I can come up with something fast."

"About Phil and this woman?"

"Yes."

"You're wrong, Harry. But I'll find her file for you if I can, and call you later today. I owe you that." She rolled on her side, away from me, so I couldn't see her face.

I drove back slowly to the apartment on Ohio. I'd only had a few hours sleep and I felt very tired. And very old.

Too old to being play love-games with a pro like Louise Pearson.

I would be pushing forty-five come fall. The bachelorhood I'd half courted was already on me. I'd seen too many years to kid myself about a woman who gave me a hard-on. I wasn't what she wanted. And what she wanted wasn't enough for me.

I took a hot shower when I got home, trying to steam Louise out of my body and brain. But she stayed inside me like a dull ache. She'd stay in there for a while.

After the shower I wandered into the bedroom and sat down heavily on the bed. Through the blinds I could see the day dawning in earnest in a blaze of light. Sleepily I picked up the phone off the nightstand and called Shelley Sacks at his office. He didn't sound particularly happy to hear from me. But then he was still keeping secrets that he knew I wanted to share.

I made an appointment to see him in the afternoon. I didn't mention Jeanne Chase to him. I wanted to see him face-to-face when I did that. It wasn't only Jeanne Chase I wanted to talk to him about.

Lying down on the bed I shut my eyes, thinking I'd rest for a few minutes.

I didn't open them again until the telephone rang around noon.

I'd been dreaming about Louise—about the way she'd looked on the porch, bathed in white light. It turned out to be Louise on the phone. For a few moments I didn't know whether I was awake or asleep.

"Harry," I heard her say in a heavy voice. "The State Patrol just called. They found the kids."

I shook myself. "They found the kids?"

"They're bringing them out of the Miami River right now. They need me to make the identification."

"I'll come get you," I heard myself say.

She hung up. I sat there on the bed for another minute waiting for time to catch up to me—real time not dream time. But I was in it already. As I got dressed I couldn't shake the feeling that I was in them both.

It took me fifteen minutes to drive from Clifton to Indian Hill. Louise was waiting for me outside the door of the estate house. Lasker, her intended, was there too.

"I don't know if I can do this," Louise whispered as I came up beside her.

"Perhaps you shouldn't," Lasker said.

"I can go," I told her. "I know what Kirsty looks like. You can come to the morgue later, if necessary, for Ethan."

"Good," Lasker said, clapping me on the shoulder.

I shrugged his hand off. Hard. For the first time since I'd met him I saw his smile completely vanish. Grinning I squared around to face him.

Louise stepped between us. "I'm going with you," she said to me. To Lasker she said, "Go home."

She went over to the Pinto and got in. Lasker and I eyed each other for a moment, before he drifted over to his Porsche.

I got in the Pinto and drove off.

Louise didn't say anything as we headed up I-71 to 275. The scene with Lasker hadn't registered with her. It woke me up, though.

I gunned the motor as we tore through the rolling farm-land on the western edge of Hamilton county. The day was clear and bright and everything around us sparkled with ice, even the dark, turned earth.

I-275 deposited us on Harrison Pike, heading west past tin bait shops and loaf-shaped diners. The highway jogged southwest at Taylors Creek, and the scattered roadside businesses gave way to undeveloped lots, trashy fields dotted with scrub pine and river maples. To the east I could see the forested ridge that rose above the far bank of the Miami River. I couldn't see the river itself yet, just the ground clutter on its western bank and a few rusted pedestrian bridges—bare steel hoops—rising above the treetops.

A mile farther on the river came into view, thick with plate-ice that flashed in the sun. A mile after that I saw the cop cars—a nest of them in a gravel clearing above the Miami's western bank.

Louise saw them too. Reaching over she grabbed my hand and squeezed it tightly. I glanced at her face. She looked scared to death.

I slowed up and pulled off the highway, turning left onto a slick, gravel lane. Down we went, half sliding toward the police cars and ambulances in the clearing below us.

"Oh, Christ," I heard Louise whisper.

I pulled to a stop and parked the car on flat ground. Glancing at Louise I opened the door and got out into the brilliant sunlight. She got out, too. Together we weaved through the tangle of cars to the riverbank.

The area above the river was teeming with men. Cops and ambulance drivers and newsmen. The air was filled with the smoke of their breath, and the steamy exhalation of the river itself—like a fire in the midst of the deep, frozen cold. A cop stopped us as we started down a dirt trail to the river's edge.

"Officials only," he said, barring the way.

"This is the kids' mother," I said, gesturing to Louise. "Mrs. Pearson."

"Christ, I'm sorry," the cop said heavily. He was just a kid himself, and he looked genuinely hurt. I knew at once that whatever was waiting for us at the end of that trail had to be pretty goddamn awful.

Louise didn't understand that. She looked overwhelmed by the activity going on around us.

I caught sight of Larry Parker standing hands on his hips on an outcropping above the river. I called out to him and he turned his head. His face was grim.

"Wait here," I said to Louise.

She nodded once, quickly.

I let go of her arm and walked over to where Parker was standing.

"They shouldn't have called her here," he said angrily.

"It's bad?"

He pointed down. Immediately below us the bank fell away in a tangle of frozen vines and crusty shale to the water's edge. The Miami was frozen solid all the way across. Two men in wet suits were kneeling on the ice, about ten feet out. They were looking down at something between them. All around them the ice smoked in the sun like doused embers.

Fighting the glare I ducked and squinted to make out what the two divers were looking at. Then I saw it.

It was a human face—or what had been a human face—half submerged in the frozen river. A foot or so to its right a human hand dangled like a wilted lily above the ice. The hand was as white as snow, except for the nails, which had turned jet black with stagnant blood.

"Jesus Christ," I said, turning away. After a moment I asked him if he was sure it was the Pearson children.

Parker nodded. "It's them. We're going to have to use chain saws to cut the bodies out." He glanced over his shoulder at Louise. "They shouldn't have called her down here."

"I'll take her home."

I turned to go and Parker grabbed my arm. "This is a terrible thing, Stoner. More terrible than you know. You

can see through the ice in places around the girl's body—
see what the bastard did to her." His mouth filled with bile
and he spat it out on the dark frozen ground. "If there's
somebody left to punish for this," he said bitterly, "I want to
know."

"I thought you said this case was closed."

"Don't be cute. You've been talking to Foster. You know
how things stand. If you've got new information I want it. I
want who's responsible for that."

He pointed to the river.

But I wanted her, too. As badly as Parker did. At that
moment finding Carla Chaney was all I could think of.

37

Louise didn't say a word until we'd gotten in the car and started back to Indian Hill.

"Are they sure it's Ethan and Kirsty?" she said.

"Yes," I said bitterly. "It's them."

Louise's head sank to her breast. "Oh, God. Kirsty."

She put her hands to her ears as if the thing was a noise she could block out of her head.

"I want this to stop." Grabbing my arm she said, "I want *you* to stop."

But I wouldn't have stopped at that moment for anyone.

She knew it, too. Dropping her hand to her side, she stared miserably through the window. "You're not going to stop." She said it hollowly, like I'd passed a judgment on her —or her powers of persuasion.

Louise laughed bitterly. "What are you going to find at the end of this, Harry?"

"Carla Chaney."

"I thought you said her name was Chase."

"They're one and the same."

Louise looked surprised. "All right, say you do find her— Chase or Chaney. You think she's just going to let you cart her off to prison for the rest of her life? What are you going to do—shoot her?"

"If necessary."

"Bravo!" she said with heavy sarcasm. "You'll kill the killer and then everyone comes back to life. Phil and Stelle and Ethan and Kirsty. Our big happy family."

"There were others."

"And you're going to avenge them all." She laughed again. "You're a fool, Harry. A dangerous fool."

"Why dangerous?"

"Because you're trying to change things that can't be changed—histories that were built up like limestone over years. You blame Carla Chaney-Chase for all this trouble. But you're wrong. Each one of us Pearsons is equally to blame for what happened here. The whole damn family."

She stared at me a moment and then sighed defeatedly. "Oh, hell, go find your woman. Be a hero. Who knows—maybe she's ready to die, too."

It was almost three when I got to Shelley Sacks' office in Clifton. I pulled up in the lot, parked beside his silver Merc, walked around a hedge to the front of the duplex, then upstairs to the second-floor waiting room. There was no one else in the waiting room. Even the nurse was gone from her cubicle. I wondered if Sacks had gone out, too. But I found him in his office, sitting behind the desk.

He looked up as I came in. The desk lamp reflecting off the lenses of his glasses hid his round blue eyes, but the rest of his face looked drawn.

"Hello, Stoner," he said wearily.

"Where is everyone?"

"I closed the office today. I didn't feel up to other people's problems." Tenting his fingers in front of his face, he said, "This has been the worst week I can remember since . . ."

"Estelle died?"

He nodded.

I sat down on a chair across from him. "Why don't we start there, then. With Stelle and Phil."

Sacks shifted uncomfortably in his chair. "Stoner, I'm not going to discuss certain things. I've told you that. I promise my patients confidentiality."

"Even when they murder each other?"

"What do you mean by that?"

"I mean Phil Pearson killed your friend, Estelle—and then covered up her murder."

"That is a dreadful accusation," Sacks said, unfolding his tented fingers. "A terrible accusation. The man just died, for chrissake."

"I have proof. Records of money paid to Rita Scarne by Phil Pearson—a thousand dollars a month for over a decade, paid out to cover up the murder of his wife. A murder that Phil planned with the help of Rita and two of her friends."

Sacks leaned back in the chair and the reflections in his glasses went out like snuffed candles. I saw his eyes for the first time, troubled, rimmed with red.

"He was paying Rita a thousand dollars a month?"

"To conceal murder."

Sacks shook his head, no. "You're wrong. There was no murder. If Phil was paying the woman money it was for something else."

"Like what?" I said.

He was going to balk. I could see it in his face. I pounded the desktop with my fist, making him jump.

"I don't want to hear about your ethics again, Sacks. Those two kids are dead. The State Patrol found their bodies today in the Miami River."

"Oh, my God," Sacks said, going pale. "Kirsty?"

"Dead," I said harshly. "Ethan is dead. The Scarne woman is dead. Talmadge is dead. Because of something that was covered up thirteen years ago. Something *you've* been helping to cover up with your silence ever since Ethan told you what he saw that September day. I've read the transcript of the coroner's inquest. You didn't mention a word about Ethan, Doctor. You blamed what happened on bad luck—you're still blaming it on bad luck."

"To an extent that's what it was," the man said defensively.

"Why? Because Phil Pearson wanted it to look that way?"

"Christ, no."

Sacks took off his glasses and pitched them on the desk. Pinching the bridge of his nose he shut his eyes and rocked back against the window, crumpling up the blind. Sunlight filtered through the gap, powdering his shoulder and neck with pale, golden light. Sacks touched at his neck as if he could feel it like a chill.

"Phil didn't try to conceal anything from the police, Stoner. I was the one who told the officers to ignore Ethan's story."

"Why?"

"Why?" He laughed lamely. "What earthly good would it have served to raise suspicions of murder on the basis of a child's hysteria? *I* knew Estelle had killed herself. I even knew why. But the police might have seen the situation differently. At the very least, Phil's career would have been ruined. I saw no reason to take that chance."

"How would letting Ethan tell his story have jeopardized Pearson?"

"The police are dogmatists," Sacks said. "Once they started thinking in terms of a murder they look for motives. In this case . . . they might have concluded that Phil had a reason to get rid of Estelle."

I leaned forward eagerly in the chair. Phil Pearson's motive for murder was at the heart of the case. It was the one of two large blanks left in the story—his motive and Carla. "What reason did he have to murder Estelle?"

"You're not listening to me," Sacks said sharply. "I said he *didn't* have a motive to be rid of her. It was she who wanted to be rid of him. If things had worked out differently, Estelle would have divorced Phil that winter."

"*She* would have divorced him?" I said confusedly. "I thought Pearson intended to divorce *Stelle*. That's what Louise told me."

Sacks shook his head. "That was wishful thinking—probably fostered by Phil himself. Believe me, he would never have divorced Stelle *or* married Louise if fate hadn't taken a hand. Phil simply depended on Stelle too deeply and in too many ways. Emotionally, physically, financially."

"Financially?"

"All the money was Stelle's. Phil didn't start making a decent living until a couple of years after she died. In fact he was very poor for those years, because her estate was tied up in probate."

I didn't say it to Sacks, but that would explain why the payoffs to Rita had begun three years after Stelle's death.

"Money wasn't the real issue, anyway," Sacks went on. "Phil would never have divorced Stelle if for no other reason than he needed her forgiveness so badly."

"Forgiveness for what?"

Sacks took a deep breath. "Do you know anything at all about Phil's family history, about his father in particular?"

"Louise told me that his father was a drunk. She also said that she thought Phil might have been abused by him, sexually."

Sacks nodded. "Abuse is such a dreadful thing, and at the same time so commonplace. More often than not it goes undiscovered. And even when it is discovered, it is usually hushed up by the family or ignored. Unless the children can work through the trauma therapeutically, they invariably have serious emotional problems for the rest of their lives. They simply can't love anymore, not as adults. They can only love dependently—or cruelly. As victims or persecutors. Tragically that means that many of them end up as abusers themselves."

Suddenly I knew Phil Pearson's ugly secret. Knew why he'd been so afraid of exposure, so evasive about his past and his children's pasts, so terribly afraid of what his son and his daughter might accidentally reveal about him—and themselves.

Hearing Sacks say it aloud only underlined the horror of it.

"In the spring of 1976, Stelle discovered that Phil was . . . that he'd been sexually abusing Kirsten."

"He abused his daughter," I said, feeling it fully.

"It broke Stelle down. Broke both of them down, really. Phil just managed the break differently."

"You mean Louise?"

"And his work. Stelle didn't have his support system. She was quite fragile anyway, with long-standing emotional problems. Problems of self-worth, problems of sexual identity. This thing hit her precisely where she was most vulnerable. She worshiped Phil when they first married. But she had always feared that Phil didn't love her back—that he'd married her for money and social connections. Discovering that he'd been abusing Kirsty simply destroyed the little ego she had left."

Sacks' lips trembled violently, and he put a hand to his mouth to cover them. "I tried so hard to make her well. But as the depression waned, the manic stage began. Her anger welled up, and all she could think about was hurting Phil as he had hurt her. She wanted to expose him, to divorce him, to take his money and his name. Above all she wanted to take Kirsty and Ethan away from Phil forever."

"You don't think that's a motive for murder?"

"You're missing the point," Sacks said irritably. "He was

so racked with guilt himself he thought *he* deserved to be murdered. I think he would have welcomed it."

"I suppose that's why he threw himself into an affair."

"Phil was constantly having affairs. Louise was hardly the first. They were never particularly romantic things, anyway. He just wanted someone to talk to—to ease his loneliness, to assert his manhood. But none of his women, not even Louise, could absolve him for what he'd done to Kirsty. Only Stelle could do that. *Phil knew that, Stoner.* Stelle knew it, too. She knew Phil would do anything to make amends."

"Did that make a difference to her?"

"It might have—over time. If she'd had the chance to work it through. She never got that chance."

For a time neither one of us said anything.

"The abuse," I said. "That was what Kirsty had been repressing?"

"Yes. The affair Kirsten had with her teacher last spring, you know about that, don't you?"

I nodded.

"And you know about the lesbian roommate?"

"I know about Marnee," I said, although frankly I hadn't thought of her as part of Kirsten's psychodrama.

"Kirsten was reenacting this childhood trauma with both of them—symbolically reenacting it. An older man who used her sexually and then rejected her. A woman whose love Kirsty couldn't accept because it was tinged with jealousy and possessiveness. Even her search for this imaginary killer was part of the reenactment—a displacement of her guilt about her father and her rage against her mother onto a convenient stranger."

I thought of the girl's face, floating in the frozen river like a stone flower.

She hadn't gone on that journey with Ethan to kill an

imaginary stranger. In her own mad way she'd made an
effort to face the reality of her past. To face the violence
inflicted upon her and the violence that had been done to
her mother. She hadn't been looking for a scapegoat. She'd
been looking for the truth—and for a measure of justice
that was long overdue.

"Talmadge wasn't imaginary, Doctor," I said heavily.
"Phil used him to kill his wife and then paid Rita to cover it
up."

"Use your head, Stoner," Sacks said. "If Rita Scarne *was*
blackmailing Phil, it was over his abuse of Kirsty—not
Stelle's death. Rita was there, after all, almost every day.
Part of the family. She could easily have picked up on this.
Stelle didn't hold much back, except around the children."

But I wasn't convinced. Money, prestige, career—not to
mention his children. Those were damn good reasons for
homicide. Sacks was simply blind to the possibility that
Stelle hadn't killed herself. And I thought I understood
why. He needed Stelle's suicide the way Ethan Pearson had
needed her murder. Because he'd loved the woman and
felt he'd failed her. Clinging to the idea of her suicide was a
way of both punishing and excusing himself, by injecting an
element of fatality into a situation that he couldn't control.

There was no point in debating it with him. Besides there
was something else I wanted to know. "Blackmail or murder, two other people were involved in this thing besides
Phil and Rita. Two people who had killed once before and
disguised it as suicide. You know about Talmadge. You don't
know about a nurse named Carla Chaney. Do you remember her?"

The man stared at me blankly. "Why should I?"

"She worked for you in 1975 and '76. In the Jewish Hospital Doctors' Building."

"For me?" Sacks shook his head decisively. "I never hired anyone named Chaney in 1975 or any year."

"You're sure of that?"

"Quite sure."

"How about a woman named Chase?"

Sacks looked startled. "Chase? What would she have to do with it?"

"She and Carla are the same person."

"You're imagining this," he said nervously. "You must be imagining it."

"Why?"

"Because it's impossible, that's why. The woman you're talking about is a friend."

"She was a friend of Phil's, too, wasn't she? In fact I'd be willing to bet that they had a torrid little affair back in late '75 or early '76. Maybe he kept seeing her after he and Louise began their 'platonic' relationship. Because, believe me, Doc, Carla was not a platonic lover. She was an ice-cold bitch who had killed to get ahead—and who probably put the idea of killing in Phil's addled head.

"The woman you know as Jeanne Chase *is* Carla Chaney, Doctor. And Carla Chaney is a borderline psychotic—a woman who arranged to murder her own family and to murder the real Jeanne Chase and to murder Stelle Pearson."

"I don't believe you!" he shouted. "There was no murder!"

But he no longer looked or sounded convinced of that. Jeanne Chase had changed his mind.

38

Although I pressed him hard, Sacks refused to answer any more questions about Jeanne Chase. I had the feeling he was no longer holding back out of principle, but because he wanted to confront the woman himself. And that was a bad idea. He was angry and he was upset—so much so that his voice had begun to shake with emotion and his brow to pop sweat. He looked, for all the world, like a man betrayed by a lover. It was that kind of deep, personal hurt.

"Doc," I warned him, "don't try anything stupid. Carla is very dangerous."

Sacks stared at me for a long moment. "I have been a very great fool," he said in a voice that was just barely under control. "And I will handle this."

I started for the door.

"Stoner?" he said.

I looked back at him.

"She worked here when Stelle had her breakdown. She had access to the files." He took a deep breath and added: "To Phil's file, too."

The thought had already occurred to me. But I didn't like the way he put it. It was almost as if he was telling me what to do, if something should happen to him.

I sat in Sacks' parking lot for a full fifteen minutes before starting the car and driving back to the Riorley Building. Even then I didn't feel right about leaving him alone. He'd had a doomed look on his face when I left the office. And he was a man who believed in fate.

I phoned Al Foster as soon as I got to the office—to see if

he had a lead on Jeanne Chase or the bankbooks. But a desk sergeant told me that he was out. I couldn't just sit there, waiting for Al to get back. And I had no way to find Jeanne Chase, save through Shelley Sacks. What I did have was the bankbooks. I decided to do something about them.

There was a First National branch office right across the street from the Riorley. I walked back down to the lobby, crossed over Vine, and went into the bank. The managers' desks were at the back in a mahogany-paneled alcove set off from the barred cages of the tellers by a short mahogany fence. I sat down on a bench outside the fence until one of the assistant managers came out to collect me.

The tag on his desk said "Steven Moran." And it was clear that Steven Moran was relatively new to the bank and not yet hardened in the ways of commerce. An ordinary, unbusinesslike grin kept flirting across his face, and he kept fighting it back like a drunk playing sober. There'd come a time when he wouldn't have to work so hard at looking like a banker.

Getting Steven Moran was a break for me. He *wanted* to help—he thought that was what they'd hired him for.

I took out Ethan's bankbook and told him my story: "A customer left this damn thing in my manager's office last week. Now my manager's gone on vacation and the rest of us can't quite figure out who it belongs to. Nobody remembers an 'E. Pearson' coming in, and we don't have him on file. One of the secretaries suggested that I pop over here and see if you could help with a phone number or an address."

"I can try," Steve Moran said earnestly. "Let me take a look."

I handed him the book and he examined it. Biting his lip he turned to a computer on his desk. The screen was facing away from me so I couldn't see what he was up to. But I heard him punching the keyboard.

"That's odd," he said to himself.

"You have something?"

"Yeah, but it doesn't say E. Pearson." For just a second I could see him wondering whether I was on the level. I smiled affably, and that grin of his came back on. He should have been playing softball instead of sitting behind a desk.

"According to the computer the account is owned by a woman. Jeanne L. Chase."

"No E. Pearson?" I said, trying not to look too confused—although the fact that Phil Pearson wasn't the owner of the account did, in fact, throw me.

"The account's in the name E. Pearson," the kid said, looking a little confused himself. "But Jeanne L. Chase owns it." His grin came back on, as if he'd had a brainstorm. "Maybe she's a relative of the kid's—or a friend of the family. People do that sometimes when a kid is underage."

"Do they?" I said uneasily.

"I've got an address if you want to get in touch with her."

"That would be fine," I said.

"Eighty-nine fifty Kenwood Road. There's no phone listed."

I went from the bank to the underground garage where the car was parked. It was past five when I got onto 71-North. The rush-hour traffic was heavy, and it was close to six when I got off the expressway at the Kenwood exit.

I'd tried not to think about that damn bank account on the way out—about what it meant. Some of it was obvious. Phil Pearson hadn't been paying Rita Scarne off—at least not directly. Jeanne L. Chase had. Which meant that Jeanne L. Chase had access to a lot of money—her own or someone else's. The fact that the account had been established in Ethan's name suggested that Phil was still the likely source.

That's as far as I let myself take it. But I sure as hell didn't like the direction it was going.

The development that Jeanne L. lived in on Kenwood Road only made me more nervous. Eighty-nine fifty was a luxe little complex, a couple miles from the Kenwood shopping district, a couple more miles from Indian Hill. The condos were single units shingled in cedar shakes that had weathered to a seaside grey. They had tall smoked-glass windows and fenced grounds and built-in garages, and each one was twisted like a different letter of the alphabet—or the same letter drawn in a slightly different hand. Stylish hideaways for those who could afford them. Like Phil Pearson.

The sun was down by the time I got to the complex. I flipped on the lights and coasted down a tar drive, past those big block letters. The ground floors were fenced off in front, so all you could see were the second story windows with their dark glass panes reflecting the twilight.

Eighty-nine fifty was the last lot on the street. I knew which one it was without having to hunt for the number. Shelley Sacks' grey Merc was parked in front.

I pulled up behind the Merc and got out. The wind was blowing hard, and I ducked my head against it as I walked toward Jeanne L. Chase's condo. As I got closer to the fence I heard a creaking noise. The fence gate had been left ajar and was swinging in the wind. I looked around—at the other condos on that part of the block. The nearest one was a good thirty yards away—across the drive. There were no lights coming from it. No lights at all on that part of the street. Looking back at the fence I opened the gate fully and went in.

There was a stone walkway inside, cutting across a small

yard to the front door of the condo. I walked up to the door
and knocked. When no one answered I tried the doorknob.
It wasn't locked.

The house was completely dark. Without the twilight to
guide me I had to stand in the doorway for several moments
while my eyes dark-adapted. Eventually I found a dimmer
switch on the wall and pressed it. A row of recessed lights
came on overhead, lighting a carpeted hallway with a large
lacquered mirror on the right-hand wall and several
framed Japanese and Indian prints on the left. The place
looked just as posh as could be, until I glanced at one of the
prints. They were artily framed but what they pictured
were perverse sexual acts—some of them involving children.

I began to notice a stale smell in the hall. A smell like dirt
and old sex mixed together with something else—something fresh and terrible.

I walked quickly to the end of the hall. It forked to the
right and left—right into a large living room, decorated
with Italian leather furniture, left into a stairwell, leading to
the second floor. The living room was dark, so I couldn't see
the framed pictures on the walls. But I could guess what
their subject matter was. Something on an end table
gleamed in the hall light—a water pipe, I thought.

I looked up the dark stairway to my left. The bad smell
seemed stronger there. There was a switch on the wall. I
flipped it on and immediately flipped it off again.

It was a gut reaction—a twitch. There was blood on the
stairs. A good deal of it.

I turned the light back on and started up, stepping over
the dark, glistening spots of blood. The smell of sex and
death grew much stronger as I neared the landing. Sex and
death and flowers. Her scent.

The top floor looked to be one large room, with a tall,

A-frame ceiling. A ceiling fan dangling from the center beam had been left on. It slowly revolved above the brass bed on the floor beneath it. The bed was the only piece of furniture in the room. It gleamed in the semidarkness—the brass fittings, the stained silk sheets. A body lay on the bed —Sheldon Sacks' body. He was naked, bloody from the waist down, and very, very dead.

I didn't examine the body. I didn't want to look at what she'd done to him. He had come there to confront her— perhaps he had summoned her there on the phone after I left the office. Who knows what he had in mind. But he'd been no match for Carla.

Neither had I.

39

I drove back to Sacks' office. I didn't even bother to call the cops. There would be time for the cops later.

I'd found the key to his building in his trousers and a key to the alarm box. I used one to get in and the other to give me some time with his files. It took a few hours. I'd guessed most of it anyway. I was a damn good guesser by then.

I took her employment file with me when I left.

It was almost midnight when I got to Indian Hill—to the unmarked street in the midst of the woods. I pulled up in the driveway and sat there for a while, wondering if she'd come out again, wrapped in silk, to play in the moonlight.

But she didn't come out.

I opened the car door and walked across the lawn.

The front door was open. I went in. Down the hall to the sitting room, where she was waiting by the fire. Behind her the stale Christmas tree winked red and blue.

I sat down across from her on the leather captain's chair.

For a while she looked at the fire—her hand to her cheek, her face sleepy-looking in the firelight, her eyes heavy with sleep. She'd had a long day.

"Shelley told me you'd be coming," she said.

"I just saw him."

She laughed—her teeth red in the firelight. "Did you?"

"What do you have planned for me?"

"For you?" she said. "Oh, I see. You made a joke."

"It's no joke, Louise, Carla, Jeanne. Which do you prefer?"

"Carla is right," she said, letting her head loll against the chair. "Carla is first."

"So I've seen."

"Don't be mean, Harry," Carla Chaney said. "I've seen enough cruelty in my life. Now I want it to stop. I want it all to stop. I'm through."

She showed me her hands—both sides, as if she'd cleaned them real good, cleaned them for me. "See."

But I didn't see.

"I guess I understand about Tallwood and Talmadge. But your own son?"

"That was Talmadge," she said bitterly. "I didn't want that."

"And Jeanne Louise Chase? What did you want him to do with her?"

"She was a vindictive bitch, who would have destroyed me if she could. I didn't let her."

"Which brings us to Stelle—poor Stelle. Without her money and her house and her friends—Phil was just a weak man with no future. And she was going to take it all away from him. Either that or he was going to go back to her and beg her forgiveness. Either way you were screwed. So you got Talmadge out of the hospital, and Rita . . . well, she was already on hand. Or did you recommend her for the nursing job, too? Whisper her name in Phil's ear? Tell her to call in sick on the day you scheduled the job?"

"Something like that," Carla Chaney said.

"Why Shelley? Why the stepkids?"

She smiled sleepily. "Why not you, last night?"

I shuddered where I sat. "That's no answer."

"Shel had been fucking me off and on since I met him—whenever he could get it up, whenever he felt like it, whenever he wanted a dirty thrill. That was what the condo was for—a love nest. What Shel didn't know was that I took every guy I slept with there. He was fucking Stelle, too, before she died—the good doctor. Phil's close friend." She laughed, baring her teeth. "Tonight he wanted to fuck me one more time before he turned me in. I let him do me—in the ass. Then I gave him what he deserved."

She said it as if that was what every man who had ever laid a hand on her in violence had deserved—the long line of abusing men, from Tallwood to Sacks.

"Why Ethan and Kirsty? What did they deserve?"

"Herb was going to kill me," she said simply. "I'd set him up for Jeanne's murder. Rita and I did. I had to do something after he got out of prison. When Kirsty called Shelley on the way to town on Sunday night, I saw a chance."

"She called Sacks?"

"From a phone booth outside Indianapolis. He wanted to keep it a secret—to let Kirsty work the thing out therapeutically. That was his vanity." Carla Chaney smiled. "He couldn't keep a secret from me."

"Then it was you who made the call to the motel on Monday and told them where to find Talmadge?"

She nodded. "I didn't think Kirsty was still with Ethan. I really didn't. She told Shel on Sunday night that she was going to go back to Chicago. I guess it was just bad luck that she didn't."

I stared at her and she turned away.

"Don't look at me like that," she whispered. "I'm no monster."

"You told Talmadge they were coming, for chrissake! In Prospect Park on Monday night."

"No, I gave him drugs. So he'd be asleep when they came. But he didn't take them until later, until after . . ." Her mouth trembled. "I didn't want Kirsty to die. She was a little . . . like me."

For a split second I saw a look on her face that I'd never

seen before, save on the faces of desperate men. "I killed him *for her,* too."

"C'mon," I said heavily. "We're going to the cops."

Carla shook her head. "I'm not going anywhere. I took some pills about fifteen minutes ago. Fifteen minutes from now . . . I'll be asleep."

"For chrissake, Louise!"

She stared at me almost pityingly. "Don't do anything . . . okay? Just stay here until I fall asleep. That's all I ask. I don't like to be alone in the dark. You know that."

"Louise . . ."

"I won't try any tricks. I could have done you last night. I could do you right now. I could make it look like an accident. Believe me."

"I believe you."

"But I've given up. I tried to explain it in the car today." She got to her feet. "Just stay here until I'm asleep. Then you can call the police."

Louise unbuttoned her blouse as she walked over to the door. I saw her body again—beautiful in the firelight.

"Why are you doing this?" I asked her.

"Because I'm tired." She smiled sadly. "I've lived too many lives."

I didn't say it but, in truth, it had only been the one.

"I'm going upstairs to the bedroom," she said as she walked from the room. "In ten minutes or so, come up and . . . kiss me good night."